He cursed himself for ten kinds of fool. He might not be able to die, but she certainly could. He lengthened one of his claws and sliced her gown down the middle. After he pulled it off her, he tossed it aside and hurried to remove her wet stockings.

His hands shook as they came in contact with her skin, just as silky as he had imagined it to be. He left her chemise in place and reached for a blanket. It took every ounce of his control not to rip her thin chemise from her and drink his fill of her luscious curves.

As he began to spread the blanket over her, he spotted her fisted hand and a strip of leather hanging from her grasp. It must have been what she was after on the cliff. He frowned as he felt the pull of something. It took but a moment for him to recognize it as magic.

"Just who are you?" he murmured.

DANGEROUS
HIGHLANDER

DONNA GRANT

This is a work of fiction. All of the characters, organizations, and events portrayed in this novel are either products of the author's imagination or are used fictitiously.

For information address St. Martin's Press, 175 Fifth Avenue, New York, NY 10010.

ISBN-13: 978-1-61523-798-2

Printed in the United States of America

For Mom and Dad,
you always told me I could be anything I wanted to be.
Thank you—for everything. I love you!

For my husband whose faith in me has never faltered.
You're my real-life hero.
I wouldn't be here without you, sexy.

ACKNOWLEDGMENTS

This series wouldn't be here without thanks to many people.

Thank you to my husband for being willing to sit in the restaurant on our date nights (and any other time—especially right when he's falling asleep at night) and discuss my ideas. Thank you to my wonderful children for understanding when my music is on and I'm typing that I'm in my "zone." Huge thanks to my parents for picking up the kids from school when I needed to finish a scene.

To my brilliant editor, Monique Patterson. Thank you for all the support, encouragement, and fabulous editorial input and vision. To the best editorial assistant out there—Holly, you're awesome. Thanks also to everyone at St. Martin's working behind the scenes to get this book on the shelves.

Thank you to agent Roberta Brown for being the first to see the potential in this series and helping to get it sold.

To my extraordinary agent, Irene Goodman, for having such passion and belief in me.

To the other great Dangerous Authors for being so supportive. I'm lucky to be involved with such a wonderful group of writers.

To Lisa Renee Jones for her invaluable advice. To Georgia Tribell, Mary O'Connor, and Robin T. Popp, just for being there.

THE BEGINNING

There once was a land of legend, of lore. A land filled with magic and hope. Though the Celtic tribes warred with one another, all of that came to an end with the arrival of Rome to their shores.

The mighty kingdom of Rome, intent on ruling the world, slowly worked its way across Britain. Until it reached the highlands and encountered a foe like none other. Despite their victories, nothing the Celts did could make Rome leave their precious land.

With no other recourse, the Celts turned to their trusted advisors and allies, the Druids.

Respected and revered, the Druids were like any society. Their magic came in the purest form from the earth, but there were ones who wanted more—more power, more control . . . more of everything.

Inevitably, the Druids split into two sects. The *mie* stayed true to their magic and continued to heal the sick and offer their knowledge to clan leaders. The *drough*, however, chose human sacrifices and black magic to grow their power.

It was the *drough* who had the answers for the Celts.

The *mie* cautioned the tribal leaders against using black magic, but the Celts knew their hold against the Romans was waning. So the Celts allowed their greatest warriors to step forward and the *drough* to cast their spells and call up the gods long buried in Hell—gods that once ruled the earth with brutal tactics and violent ends.

But they were the only ones who could defeat Rome.

The gods, freed at last, eagerly answered the Druids' call and bound themselves into each clan's fiercest warrior. Those warriors, with the aid of the gods inside them, attacked every Roman they encountered. Battle after battle ensued, until, finally, Rome abandoned Britain.

Yet the gods were still thirsty for blood, still hungry for battle. With the Romans gone, the warriors turned on one another . . . and anyone who got in their way. The rivers and land ran red with the blood of the Celts as death permeated the air.

The *drough*, finding their magic useless, joined forces with the *mie*. Yet nothing the two sects did could put the gods back in their prison in Hell. The gods refused to relinquish their hold on the warriors, growing stronger with each heartbeat, each kill, until the warriors were no longer the men they had once been.

A gathering of Druids was called. It was unlike anything that had occurred since before the split. Magic pulsed over the land as they put aside their differences and struggled to find a way to help the Celts. But no amount of magic the Druids called up freed the warriors.

Unable to send the gods back, the Druids combined magic and black magic to create a spell that bound the gods, in effect freezing them inside their hosts. The warriors returned to the men they once were and resumed their lives having no memory of the atrocities they had committed.

Yet, inside each warrior, the gods waited. With every generation the gods moved from warrior to warrior, passing down and forever a part of the family's bloodline.

And so the Warriors were born.

The Druids, knowing what they had created, knowing what would happen in the future, stayed near the Warriors. Forever keeping watch. Even when the Druids' faith, the very thing they were, caused them to hide for fear of being killed, they had no choice but to watch. All of mankind was at risk.

The true story of Rome's departing from Britain was forgotten. It passed into legend and myth amongst the Celts with each retelling of the story. Only the Druids knew the truth.

Then one *drough* found hidden scrolls. More power hungry than any *drough* before her, Deirdre set out to unbind the gods and control them. Thereby giving her the army she needed to rule the world and become a goddess before whom all men would tremble.

The scrolls, however, only listed one tribe—the MacLeods.

Deirdre turned her eye to the MacLeod clan. There she would begin. . . .

CHAPTER ONE

West Highlands of Scotland

Spring 1603

"Ye've gone daft, ye have."

Cara adjusted the basket on her arm. The brisk wind from the sea pulled tendrils from her braid to fly haphazardly into her eyes. She tucked them behind her ear and smiled at Angus. He had only one tooth left in his mouth, and what little hair he had stood on end, waving about in the vicious sea wind. "I'll be fine, Angus. The best mushrooms in all of Scotland are within walking distance."

"Ye stay away from that castle, lass. 'Tis full of ghosts it be. And monsters." He shook a gnarled finger at her, his white, fluffy brows furrowed deep in his wrinkled forehead.

He needn't remind her. Everyone in clan Mac-Clure knew of MacLeod Castle. For centuries the stories of how the entire MacLeod clan had been massacred had been passed down from generation to generation. Tales of ghosts that roamed the land and castle were also told to frighten young children.

But it did more than scare the bairns. Even adults swore they saw movement in the shadows of Mac-Leod Castle.

No one dared venture near the old ruins for fear of being eaten alive. It didn't help that strange, furious sounds, almost like howls, could be heard emanating from the ancient fortress in the dead of night.

Cara inhaled deeply and turned her head to look at the castle. It stood dark and foreboding against the ominous clouds coming their way. Grass, bright green in the warming weather, surrounded the stones that protruded from the landscape while the dark blue sea set a fantastic backdrop to the castle. The castle itself had two connected towers that had at one time served as the gatehouse. The gate had burned in the slaughter, leaving nothing left.

The castle wall that was easily twelve feet thick still stood, its stones blackened by the fire, with many of the sawtoothed merlons and crenels broken and crumbling. There were six round towers that stretched to the sky, leaving only one with the ceiling intact.

Cara had wanted to look inside the bailey and castle but had never been brave enough. Her fear of the dark, and the creatures that lurked in it, kept her out of the stronghold.

"They are simply stones turned to rubble," she said to Angus. "There are no ghosts. Nor monsters."

Angus moved to stand beside her. "There are monsters, Cara. Heed me words, lass. Ye go near the ruins, we'll never see ye again."

"I promise I won't go in the castle, but I must get near it to get the mushrooms. Sister Abigail needs them for her herbs."

"Then let the good Sister go herself. She's not one of us. Ye are, Cara. Ye know the tales of the MacLeods."

"That's right, Angus. I do." She didn't bother denouncing her MacClure ties. She was a Sinclair, though no one knew it. It was just one of her secrets she kept from the clan that had taken her in when she was a small child wandering the forest.

Nay, she wasn't a MacClure, but she didn't correct Angus, one of her only friends. It felt good to belong to something, even if it was just in her mind. Not even the nuns who had raised her made her feel as if she truly belonged. They had loved her, in their own way, but it wasn't the same thing as a parent's love.

Not that she blamed any of the MacClures for not opening their homes to her. When the nuns had found her, she had gone days without food. She had been filthy, barefoot, and still so in shock at her parents' deaths that she refused to speak. She doubted anyone wanted to know that her parents had sacrificed themselves to save her, their only child.

Like most Highlanders, the MacClures were a superstitious lot and feared Cara and what had driven her from her home. It was that same superstition that kept everyone away from the ruins of the castle that stood on the cliffs. With one last look at Angus and his furrowed brow, she lifted her skirts and turned to start toward the ancient ruins, ignoring the tingle of apprehension that ran along her spine.

His words were soon drowned out by the breeze and the cries of birds. Cara kept a watchful eye on the sinister clouds moving toward her. If she was lucky, she would be back inside the nunnery before the first drop landed.

She set out, enjoying the spring wind and the call of the razorbills that made their homes in the cliffs. Ever since the spring equinox and her eighteenth year, strange things had begun to happen to her. She would feel a sort of . . . tingling . . . in her fingers. The need to touch something overwhelmed her. Yet she feared that sensation, so she kept her hands to herself and tried her best to ignore the need that called to her. Being more different than she already was would not endure her to the MacClures—or the nuns.

The village of the MacClures had been built but a short distance from the old community of MacLeod Castle. After the massacre, it hadn't taken the other clans long to divide up the lands of the MacLeods, and the MacClures were one of the first.

It was a sad story, and every time she looked at the castle she couldn't help but wonder what had actually happened. The MacLeods had been a great clan, feared and respected, and had been destroyed in a single night. Yet no one had claimed responsibility for the annihilation.

A shiver ran through her as she recalled the animalistic howls and screams she sometimes heard at night. She told the children at the nunnery it was simply the wind racing across the sea and moving between the ruins. But deep inside, she knew the truth.

There was something alive in the castle.

The closer she got to the old castle, the more the hairs on the back of her neck stood on end. She turned her back on the ruins, scolding herself for letting her fear take hold. There was nothing to worry about now. It was daylight. Only the dark of night brought out her true fear.

She briefly closed her eyes and tamped her growing fright down. A gasp escaped her lips when the necklace she always kept hidden warmed against her skin.

She pulled the necklace out of her gown and stared at the vial and the silver knot work that wound around it. The necklace had been her mother's, and the last thing she had given Cara before she died.

Cara dropped the necklace and pulled in a shaky breath. Her mother had bade her to keep it with her always, protecting the vial. Cara couldn't think about the night her parents died. It brought too much guilt, too much anger, to know that the people who had loved her, cared for her, had surrendered their lives so she might live.

She glanced down to see the mushrooms she was supposed to pick. No one knew why they grew only along the path to the castle, and few braved the ghosts to harvest them. Some claimed it was magic that brought the mushrooms, and though Cara would never admit it to anyone, she thought it very well could be magic. She had volunteered to go this time because Sister Abigail needed them for little Mary's fever.

Cara loved helping the nuns with the children. It satisfied a piece of her heart that knew she would never have a child of her own. Her decision to become a nun had been a sound one. Yet there were times she felt . . . incomplete. It always happened when she saw a couple about the village. She wondered what the touch of a man would feel like, what it would be like to bring her own child into the world and look into the loving eyes of her husband.

Stop it, Cara.

Aye, she needed to stop. Keeping her mind on that track would only bring her melancholy for what could never be and rage over her parents' deaths.

She began to pick the mushrooms and enjoyed the time alone that she rarely got at the nunnery. Her mind wandered, as it often did, while she plucked the shrooms from the ground.

It wasn't until her basket was nearly full and a large cloud blocked out the sun that she looked up, startled to find she was closer to the ruins than she had planned to go. She had been so intent on the mushrooms and her daydreaming that she hadn't paid attention to where she had walked. Or how long she had been out.

But now that she was at the castle, she was intrigued by it, forgetting the approaching storm. Even after three hundred years the scars from the battle and fire could still be seen in the stones.

Cara's heart hurt for everyone who had died. No one had ever discovered why the clan had been killed. Whoever had attacked had spared no one, not even a babe. The entire MacLeod clan had been wiped away in a single night.

She shuddered as if she could hear the screams and the sound of flames surrounding her. It was all in her mind, she knew, but that didn't stop the terror from taking hold. Her blood turned to ice, and fear clawed at her, begging her to run.

Yet she couldn't move.

Cara blinked and forced her gaze away from the castle to calm her racing heart as her necklace heated once more. It was so hot that she took it off and held the leather strap by two fingers. She had never feared the necklace before and rarely taken it off since her mother had placed it around her neck. However, there was something decidedly odd about it now, had been since the equinox. It looked the same, but she knew what she had felt.

The wind suddenly picked up and swirled around

Cara. She gasped for breath and dropped the basket in an effort to pull the hair out of her eyes.

"Nay!" she screamed when her mother's necklace was ripped from her hands.

Cara followed the precious link to her parents as it bounced over the rocky landscape to land near the edge of the cliff.

With her heart in her throat and her hands tingling with that strange sensation again, Cara hurried to the necklace as the first fat drop of rain landed on her arm. The wind suddenly dropped in temperature. Cara glanced up to see the storm had grown larger than she had anticipated. With the breeze beginning to howl, she inched closer to the necklace.

A bolt of lightning zigzagged across the sky a heartbeat before the clouds opened up and the downpour soaked her. After several days of constant rain, the ground was already soggy and unable to hold any more water.

Cara got down on her hands and knees, uncaring of the mud that soaked her skirts, and scooted closer to the necklace. Tears coursed down her face.

Please, God, please. Don't let me lose the necklace.

She should never have taken it off, never have feared the very thing that her mother had kept close to her heart. An image of Cara's parents flashed in her mind, driving home yet again how lonely she was, how alone in the world she always would be.

"I'm not leaving without the necklace!" she screamed into the wind. Her mother had entrusted the vial to Cara's care, begging her to keep watch over it. She wouldn't let her mother down. Not now, not ever.

———————

Lucan MacLeod stared out over the landscape he had loved since the first moment he had realized what it was as a lad. He leaned his forearm against the edge of the narrow window in his chamber in the castle that faced the south and gave him a view of the cliffs and the sea.

He never grew tired of the beauty of the Highlands, the rolling waves of the sea before it crashed into the cliffs. There was something amazing about the smell of the sea mixed with the heather and thistle. This land calmed the raging anger inside him as nothing else could.

It was the Highlands. His Highlands. And he loved it.

What he didn't love was being trapped, and that's essentially what had happened ever since he and his brothers had returned to their home over two hundred years ago.

That was their life now. And he hated it.

How many times had Lucan raged at the inability to leave the castle? How many times had he sat in his chamber as the fury over what had happened to him and his brothers consumed him? How many times had he begged God for a way to make it all go away, to free him from the dark torment that threatened his very soul?

But God wasn't listening. No one was.

They were fated to hide away from the world, watching as time changed everything around them. While they endured. Alone. Forever alone.

He briefly closed his eyes and remembered what it was like before their lives had been ripped apart. It was a lifetime ago that he had stood at that very window watching the clan, hearing the children's laughter over the roar of the waves. That time seemed like a dream now, a dream that faded with each day that passed, each beat of his heart.

As the son of the laird, Lucan had never wanted for anything. Whether it was food and drink or female company. Women had always sought him out, and he readily accepted them.

He had taken their touch, their smiles, and their bodies for granted. Now all he wanted was to feel a woman beneath him. He had forgotten what it was like to have the soft curves of a woman's flesh against him, to have her wet heat surround him as he thrust inside her.

There were times his need had been so great that he had thought of leaving the castle and finding a wench. All it took was one look at his brothers and he would remember why they had locked themselves away, why they didn't allow themselves to be seen.

Lucan and his brothers were dangerous. Not to themselves, but to everyone else. There was great evil out there, and it wanted to use them.

Over two hundred years of confinement in the castle. But what else was there? They couldn't be seen, not as they were, the monsters they had become. As the middle son, he had always been there to make peace for his brothers. A rock, solid and steady, to keep them all together, his mother had called him. He didn't allow himself to think what was becoming of him and his soul.

Fallon had taken the role as heir to the clan seriously. Everything he did, everything he thought about, was for their clan. He hadn't known what to do with himself when there was no clan, and with the beast constantly hammering for control and no way to reverse what had happened, he had turned to the wine.

As for Quinn, they had nearly lost him to the beast. Lucan snorted. Beast seemed such an understated name. There was no monster inside them. It was a primeval god banished to the pits of Hell. Apodatoo, the god of revenge, was housed within each of the MacLeod brothers. A god so ancient, there were no records or tellings of him. And he was far worse than any beast.

Whenever this despondent mood struck Lucan, as it often did when it rained, he took himself off to his chamber away from his brothers. They had their own worries. They didn't need to see him grappling with his inner demons. He could wallow in his self-pity the rest of the day if he allowed himself. But he wouldn't. His brothers needed him.

He took a deep breath and had started to turn away from the window when something caught his eye. Lucan's gaze narrowed as he spotted a breath-taking vision. It was a woman, a very young, shapely woman who had dared to come close enough to the castle that he could see the comeliness of her heart-shaped face. He wished he could see the color of her eyes, but it was enough that he saw her full lips that begged to be kissed and her high cheekbones that turned pink in the wind.

And the thick, dark braid that hung down her back to her waist. What he wouldn't do to see that hair unbound and falling about her shoulders. He fisted his hands and he imagined running his fingers through the tresses.

Her gown was plain and worn, but that didn't disguise her small waist and rounded breasts. She moved with the freedom of one who enjoyed being outdoors, of one who reveled in the beauty around her. The gentle curving of her lips as she looked out at the sea tugged at something inside him. As if she wanted the freedom to fly on the wind currents.

She picked the mushrooms with care, her fingers tender as she placed them in the basket. When she had stared at the castle, she had looked as if it pained her, as if she had known what had taken place.

Something inside him shifted, cried out for him to learn about the woman. The more he watched her, the more she intrigued him.

No one dared come this close to the castle, much less look at it with such curiosity. If he had known such a beauty was near, Lucan might have left the castle in search of her.

He ignored the wind that rushed past him, and squinted through the driving rain to watch as she suddenly cried out and chased something toward the edge of the cliff. Thunder boomed and lightning lit up the darkening sky. Already they had had so much rain.

"What are you doing?" his younger brother, Quinn, asked as he walked into the chamber and moved to stand beside Lucan. Quinn looked out the window. "God's blood. Is she daft?"

Lucan shook his head. "She was picking mushrooms. Then she raced toward the edge of the cliff."

Quinn snarled, his rage never far. "Stupid wench. She'll fall to her death."

Lucan jerked away from the window as his enhanced hearing heard the shift in the earth. He wasted no time in brushing past his brother and running out of the chamber and down the corridor before jumping over the rail and straight down the three stories to the bottom floor. He landed on his feet in the great hall, his knees bent and his fingers on the ground to keep his balance. His skin tingled as the god surged within him.

"Lucan?"

There was no time to explain to Fallon, the eldest of them, what Lucan planned. The girl's life was at stake. He hurried from the castle, unmindful of the rain and wind that whipped at his hair and clothes.

He ran under what was left of the gatehouse when he heard her scream as the soil moved beneath her. He leapt into the air and landed a few feet from her just as her hand closed over a necklace and the ground began to give way.

Lucan dove across the space and latched onto her wrist before she could plummet to the rocks and water below. Hanging by his hand, her feet dangling over open air, she blinked up at him, her dark eyes wide with fear.

"Hang on!" he yelled over the storm.

Her muddied hands slipped in his grasp and her feet scrambled for purchase in the rocks of the cliff. She screamed, her tears mixing with the rain.

"Please!" she cried. "Dinna drop me!"

Lucan used his strength and began to pull her up when the earth moved once more. He held on to her as he slipped over the side. At the moment when they both would have fallen, his fingers grabbed hold of a rock.

He looked from the edge of the cliff to the woman. He would have to swing her up, it was the only way to save her, but if he did . . . she would see him for what he really was.

"I'm slipping!"

He couldn't get a better grip without dropping her, but if he didn't do something soon, she would slide out of his grasp. He tightened his hold, but the more he fought against losing her, the more she slipped.

Until suddenly he held nothing.

Her scream echoed through him, wrenching his gut. Without a second thought he unleashed the god within him, the monster he kept locked away. In two leaps down the cliff, he was at the bottom amid the rocks with enough time to hold out his arms and catch her.

He waited for her to screech in terror once she saw his face, but when he looked, he found her eyes closed. She had fainted.

Lucan let out a sigh. He hadn't thought beyond saving the girl, but now that she was in his arms, he didn't regret it. It had been decades since he had held a woman, and her lush curves and soft body made him instantly hard. And wanting.

The rain continued its assault, but Lucan couldn't stop staring at her heart-shaped face and high cheekbones. The gentle curve of her neck as her head tilted toward him.

"Shite," he mumbled, and bounded back up the cliffs.

He landed as softly as he could so as not to disturb the woman and found Quinn watching him with narrowed eyes full of malice and hate. It was a look he had gotten used to over the course of three hundred years.

"Well, well, *Brother*," Quinn said between clenched teeth. "What have you been keeping from us?"

Lucan pushed past him and strode to the castle through the driving rain. There would be time for questions later.

Quinn caught up with him. "What in God's bones do you think you're doing? You can't bring her to the castle."

"I canna leave her in the weather, either," Lucan argued. "Do you want to take her to the village like this? Besides, she's fainted, and I don't know where she lives."

"It's a mistake, Lucan. Heed my words."

They might be monsters, but that didn't mean he had to act like one. For too long they had hidden in the castle, watching the world through the windows of their crumbling home. This was his one chance to do something good, and he wasn't about to pass it up.

Not when she feels this delicious in my arms.

Lucan cursed his body and tamped down any more thoughts of the woman's full breast pressed against him or her scent of heather and earth that filled his senses. The soaked material of her gown molded to her body like a second skin and gave him a glimpse of a hardened nipple.

He swallowed, wanting to close his lips over the tiny bud and suckle. His balls tightened and his blood heated until he shook with need.

With a kick, he opened the castle door and walked into the great hall. Fallon sat up from lying on the bench in the center of the room and raised a dark brow in question.

"Lucan, I'm drunk, but I'm not inebriated enough to miss the fact you have a woman in your arms. In the castle. Which isna allowed, I might add."

Lucan ignored his brother and took the stairs two at a time to his chamber. It was one of the only ones in good enough condition to put the girl in. Fallon never used his chamber, and Quinn had destroyed his in one of his many fits of rage. None of the others had ever been seen to.

There hadn't been a need.

Once Lucan laid her on the bed, he built up the fire to help warm her and tried to calm his raging body. The need, the *hunger*, he felt for her alarmed him. When he straightened, he wasn't surprised to find Fallon and Quinn standing in his doorway.

"Should we undress her?" Fallon asked, his eyes focused on the girl. "She looks soaked through."

"She is." But Lucan wasn't about to test himself with that kind of temptation. Not until he held his hunger in check. His hands fisted just thinking about pulling the material away from her body and drinking in the sight of her creamy skin. Would her nipples be as dark as her hair?

Quinn stepped forward and lengthened his claws. "I'll remove her gown."

With lightning speed Lucan moved between his brother and the bed on the opposite wall. The girl was his responsibility. If he left her to Quinn he would likely tear her in two with his wrath, and Fallon would forget her when he turned to his next bottle of wine.

"Leave her to me," Lucan said.

Quinn's lips pulled back in a snarl. "All these years you've lectured us on how I've given in to the god inside when all along, *Brother*, you've done the same."

Fallon ran a hand down his face and blinked his red-rimmed eyes. "What are you talking about, Quinn?"

"If you'd stay off the wine long enough you would have known," Quinn bit out.

Fallon's dark green gaze, so like their father's, narrowed on Quinn. "The wine is better than what you've become."

Quinn laughed, the sound mirthless and hollow. "At least I know what day it is. Tell me, Fallon, do you recall what you did yesterday? Oh, wait. It was the same thing as the day before and the day before that."

"And what have you done besides tear up everything Lucan builds?" Fallon's eyes snapped with fire, and a muscle in his jaw jumped with his anger. "You cannot control the beast long enough to take a piss."

Quinn smirked. "Let's find out."

"Enough!" Lucan bellowed when the two took a step toward each other. "Get out if you're going to fight."

Fallon chuckled, the sound empty. "You know I won't fight."

"That's right," Quinn said, resentment lacing his voice. "We wouldn't want the great Fallon MacLeod to tempt his god."

Fallon closed his eyes and turned away, but not before Lucan saw the despair in his elder brother's eyes. "We all have our curses to carry, Quinn. Leave Fallon be."

"I can take care of myself," Fallon said, and faced Lucan. Fallon glanced from the girl to Lucan. "What were you thinking, bringing her here? You know no human can enter our domain, Lucan."

The girl shifted on the bed, and all three of them stilled, watching to see if she would wake. When she didn't, Lucan blew out a breath and motioned for them to leave.

"I'll be down in a moment," he promised.

Once they were gone, he pulled off her sodden shoes. He needed to get her out of her gown lest she caught a chill, but he didn't trust his body—or his hands—to keep away from the temptation of her curves.

Her hair, a glorious chestnut, had darkened with

the rain. He moved a lock of hair that stuck to the side of her cheek and marveled at the feel of her smooth skin. Her face, fair and unblemished, captivated him with her high forehead and delicate structure.

Though his only impression of her eyes had come when they were wide with fear, he remembered they had been the deepest brown he had ever seen. Now he noticed the long, dark lashes that fanned her cheek as she slept.

Lucan hadn't dared touch a woman since that fateful day so long ago. He didn't trust himself or the god. But now a woman lay in Lucan's bed, asleep and oh, so enticing. It took but a heartbeat for him to decide to touch her.

He ran his finger down her face to her full, plump lips. The scent of heather drifted over him. Her scent. God, he had forgotten how soft a woman's skin could be, how sweet they could smell.

Unable to stop himself, he traced her mouth with his thumb. He longed to bend down and place his lips over hers, to slide his tongue into her mouth and hear her moan of pleasure, to taste her.

It might have been centuries since he had a woman in his arms, but he still recalled the feel of breasts pressed against his naked chest, of cries of pleasure as he thrust inside her. He still recalled the feel of a woman's hand as she caressed his shoulders and wound her fingers in his hair.

He remembered much too well.

Lucan's body throbbed with need as he imagined pulling away the girl's clothes and cupping her breasts and rolling her nipples between his fingers. He jerked away from her, afraid he would give in to the hunger that consumed him. That's when he noticed her lips had begun to turn blue.

He cursed himself for ten kinds of fool. He might not be able to die, but she certainly could. He lengthened one of his claws and sliced her gown down the middle. After he pulled it off her, he tossed it aside and hurried to remove her wet stockings.

His hands shook as they came in contact with her skin, just as silky as he had imagined it to be. He left her chemise in place and reached for a blanket. It took every ounce of his control not to rip her thin chemise from her and drink his fill of her luscious curves.

As he began to spread the blanket over her, he spotted her fisted hand and a strip of leather hanging from her grasp. It must have been what she was after on the cliff. He frowned as he felt the lull of something. It took but a moment for him to recognize it as magic.

"Just who are you?" he murmured.

Lucan allowed himself one look at her body. Lean legs, flared hips, a waist so small he could span it with his hands, and plump breasts with hardened nipples.

His hands and mouth longed to touch her.

He swallowed the desire that surged within him. His balls jumped in anticipation, but Lucan wouldn't give in. He couldn't. He laid the blanket atop her and turned to go. The girl had been in danger, and he had saved her.

That was all.

That's all there could be.

CHAPTER TWO

Lucan faced the hearth in the great hall. They didn't need the heat from the fire, but Fallon liked to be reminded of their life before everything had changed.

The orange and red flames devoured the wood much like the god had devoured Quinn. Lucan rubbed his hand over his jaw and sighed. He had a woman. In the castle. It went against every rule they had, but God forgive him, he didn't regret it. Despite what he was, what was inside him, he was still a man.

"Lucan."

He started at Fallon's voice. "I thought you were passed out."

"Not yet." Fallon had always been the serious one of them, but at least he used to smile. There once was a gleam of laughter and hope in his green eyes. Now there was nothing but emptiness in his gaze. How Lucan wished Fallon had found the cure he had searched for, but once he had discovered there was no way to reverse what had been done to them, Fallon had lost all hope.

"Tell him," Quinn ground out as he stormed into the hall from the kitchens.

Lucan sighed and turned to his brothers. Once the great hall of MacLeod Castle had been full of people and beautiful tapestries. Candelabras had given light, and weapons from ancestors had adorned the walls. All that was left of the hall now was a primitive table with two benches and three chairs he had built, placed now before the hearth.

After they had reclaimed the castle, he and Fallon had fixed the roof over them so the rain wouldn't get in. That was before Fallon had turned to the wine. Lucan gazed at his elder brother and wished he had the answers for all of them.

Quinn's face darkened, his skin turning black as the god yearned to be free. "Tell him."

"For God's sake, Lucan, just tell me," Fallon said wearily, and raked a hand through his tousled dark brown hair. His hair used to streak with gold when he spent time outdoors. Now it was the same dark brown as their mother's, his eyes green like their father's, but darker, like the ferns that grew in the forest.

Lucan blew out a breath. "I let my god out."

If there was anything that could clear Fallon's eyes, it was that. They had learned very early on that the god inside them would do anything to be set free and anger only made it more powerful. They couldn't control themselves when the god was loose, which was one of the reasons Fallon turned to the wine.

For Lucan, he had wanted to be the one in control. So he had spent decades learning to master his god. It had been more difficult than Lucan had imagined, and many times he had almost given up and turned to the bottle as Fallon did. But only the love of his brothers, and Lucan's need to make things right, kept him going. The day he had learned he could be in control of when he let the god out and when he didn't had been a glorious one.

But he hadn't been able to tell his brothers.

Fallon sat straighter and set aside the bottle of wine. "You did *what*?"

"The girl was about to plummet to her death. I had no choice."

Quinn punched the wall next to him, his fist going through the stones. When he pulled his hand out, his nails had lengthened into claws and his pale green eyes went black. "You had a choice. You could have let her die. We cannot let anyone know we're here. Isn't that what you tell me night after night?"

"Lucan," Fallon said with a shake of his head, his voice soft. "What have you done?"

"I'm still the man I was," Lucan said in his defense. "Before we became . . . as we are, I couldn't let another die, and I won't do it now. We've sat here, hiding in this crumbling ruin of our home, for over two hundred years as we've fought any Warriors and wyrran that dared to come near us. How much longer do you think we can continue to fight? We were lucky. We escaped, and we've managed to keep away from her ever since."

Quinn's shoulders dropped and he sighed. His eyes returned to green and the claws disappeared. "I hate to admit it, but maybe Lucan is right. I refuse to go back into that prison, Fallon."

"Nay," Fallon said, and rose to his feet. He swayed slightly and held on to the table to steady himself. "I told you both that we're in no position to fight her. You've both done it anyway."

Lucan hated talking about *her*. Deirdre had been the one who had ordered their clan murdered. Deirdre had been the one to summon them to Cairn Toul mountain. Deirdre had been the one who had unleashed the god within them. Deirdre, a woman so beautiful she could make angels sing, but with a heart as black as Satan.

"I'm a Warrior, Fallon. Deirdre turned us into this monster, and though I refuse to join her, I also refuse to sit by and let her evil take over Scotland. You know we are stronger when we all three fight together. We could do so much more damage to Deirdre if you would but join us."

Fallon shrugged. "Join you? Nay, Brother, I think not. Our fate was sealed the moment Deirdre spoke that spell."

"You've just given up then? On everything?" Quinn looked from Fallon to Lucan. "I always hated how you nagged me as a lad about doing the right thing, Fallon, and now you won't."

Fallon scratched his chin in need of a shave. "There isna much you do like, little brother. You both know, as well as I, she will take us eventually. We're just putting off the inevitable."

"I'll fight to the end. I won't go back into that mountain," Lucan said.

Fallon slashed his hand through the air. "None of that is important right now. The girl in your bed is."

The image of the girl, her head thrown back and her dark hair spread around her as she writhed naked beneath him, flashed in Lucan's mind. He bit back a groan and shifted to help ease the cockstand he'd had since she first landed in his arms.

"I'll take her to the village tonight," Quinn said.

Lucan stepped forward, the fury quick and strong within him. He didn't understand his need to protect the woman, only that he needed to. It wasn't just his hunger to touch her, but something that went much deeper. "She has magic about her," he confessed. When Quinn didn't back down, Lucan felt his god stir. "You won't touch her."

Quinn's eyes turned black—even the whites of his eyes went obsidian. Ever since the god had been unleashed, each time he came out, they turned black. Quinn peeled back his lips to show his fangs and let his claws lengthen once more.

"Stop it, Quinn," Fallon's voice filled the hall. "I forbid us to fight. We did enough of that in the early days."

It was a good thing they healed quickly, because each of them would bear untold scars after the fights they'd had when they had been unable to control the beast. While the rest of Scotland tore apart the Mac-Leod land, the brothers ripped into one another, again and again.

Fallon's gaze landed on Lucan. "Magic? Are you sure?"

"Positive. It's not strong, but it's there."

"What do you plan to do with her?"

In truth, Lucan had no idea. He knew what he wanted to do to her in his bed, but that was one chance he couldn't—and wouldn't—take. "She doesn't know anything about us."

"She'll know she's in the castle. We've done a good job of keeping people out, but I don't know how much longer that can last. Especially if the girl tells everyone there are no ghosts inside the castle."

Lucan and Quinn had cultivated the idea of ghosts and monsters to keep people away. With Quinn's howls and his claws scraping the stones it had been easy to frighten everyone.

"I can take her now," Lucan said. "I'd rather not,

though. The storm hasn't let up, and she was already chilled. Besides, I want to know where the magic is coming from."

Quinn shook his head, his mass of light brown hair moving with his head to brush his shoulders. "She needs to go. Now."

"Or what?" Lucan demanded. "You'll hurt her?"

"I won't have her jeopardize what we've spent years building, magic or not," Quinn snarled.

"Lucan," Fallon said.

Lucan ignored Fallon and laughed at Quinn. "We don't have anything but a falling-down ruin of a castle."

"It's ours, though," Quinn said through clenched teeth. "She'll destroy it all. I refuse to allow that."

"You won't touch her," Lucan stated, ready to let the god out again if he had to.

"Lucan!"

He jerked his head to Fallon to find him staring to his right. Lucan followed his elder brother's gaze and found the girl standing on the stairs, her large eyes staring at Lucan with a mixture of terror and distrust.

The gown Lucan had laid out for her had belonged to Quinn's wife. It was centuries out of date, but it fit her well enough. The girl's eyes were rounded and riveted on Lucan, as if she was afraid to shift her gaze. Her face was still pale, though her lips were no longer blue.

Lucan took a step toward her. He knew he needed to keep his distance, but she was here because of him. Despite what he and his brothers were, they wouldn't hurt her, and he needed to make sure she knew that.

"She didn't dare," Quinn said, and started toward the girl.

Before he could get past, Lucan grabbed Quinn by his tunic and brought him up short. "Leave her."

"She's wearing Elspeth's gown!"

Lucan glanced at the girl to find she had taken a step back on the stairs, her hands spread on the stones on her right. The stairs weren't well fortified. She could fall and hurt herself. She was mortal, after all.

"*I* gave her the gown," Lucan said as he turned back to his brother and growled.

With one last look at the girl, Quinn jerked out of Lucan's hands and stalked away. It was only after he glanced at Fallon to find his face pale and guarded that Lucan realized Quinn hadn't controlled the god within him. The beast had been visible.

Shite!

How did one explain the unexplainable?

Lucan swallowed and unclenched his hands, realizing too late that his nails had elongated. Had his eyes changed? His skin? She hadn't run away screaming, but her gaze had darted to the door several times.

He walked slowly to the stairs, not wanting to frighten her any more than she already was. Out of the corner of his eye he saw Fallon shift toward her.

Her knuckles were white from grasping the wall. One bare foot peeked from beneath her skirts. The stones were always cool, and in this weather exceedingly so. If she wasn't careful, she would become ill.

Lucan let his gaze roam over her, noting how the gown accentuated her large breasts and narrow waist. Her neck was slender, graceful, while tendrils of damp hair curled about her face. He wished he had thought to loosen her hair. He would love to see it fall about her shoulders and run his hands through the thick mass.

"I fell," she said all of a sudden. Her voice was soft, barely a whisper in the storm that howled around them. Her gaze flicked to Fallon before returning to Lucan.

Lucan would have to think fast. She had fainted, so she didn't realize what had happened. "I caught you. Remember?"

Her brows furrowed and she shook her head. Her dark eyes regarded him steadily, not accepting his lie. "Nay. I slipped from your grasp. I fell."

"And I caught you," Fallon said. "We saw you from the castle and hurried to help. I climbed down the cliff in case Lucan wasn't able to hold you."

Lucan could see in her gaze that she wanted to believe them, but doubt lingered in her gorgeous mahogany eyes. Especially after she had witnessed Quinn's transformation.

"I'm Lucan," he said. He used to be able to charm anyone, but it had been years since he had tried. "That is my elder brother, Fallon."

Fallon gave Lucan a shuttered look. It hadn't occurred to him that they might want to give different names. The story of what had happened to them had never died down. It had turned into a legend that was likely to stay around forever.

"Lucan?" she repeated. "Fallon?"

Lucan could see her mind working through it, realizing that not only were some people in a castle that was supposedly deserted, but they also had the same names as in the legend.

Lucan cursed inwardly. It was unlike him to be so careless. With Fallon always inebriated and Quinn unable to control his rage, it had been left up to Lucan to take care of everything. He had never failed them.

Until now.

He motioned to the chair near the fire. "Come. Warm yourself."

When she didn't move, he backed away from the stairs to give her room. "You have nothing to fear from us."

"Then who removed my clothes?"

Lucan glanced away, but not before he saw Fallon raise a brow. "You were soaked through. I dinna wish for you to catch a chill."

She shuddered at his words, and again he motioned to the fire. Thunder boomed around them, shaking the very ground. It propelled her down the stairs and in front of the roaring fire, though.

With her back to the flames, she regarded the brothers. She kept herself stiff, like a cornered animal waiting for an attack. "Am I to be kept here?"

Fallon rolled his eyes and reached for the wine as he once more took his seat at the table, murmuring something that sounded like "wenches."

Lucan shook his head. "I would have returned you to the village, but with the storm I thought it better to get you out of the weather."

"Then I can leave now?"

It took everything Lucan had not to shout nay. Instead, he clasped his hands behind his back and gave a quick jerk of his head. "If you wish to brave the weather."

"Your accent is . . . different." Her head was cocked to the side, her braid falling over her shoulder to tease the bottom of her breast.

He forgot to breathe as his rod swelled. He could imagine palming her breasts, pinching her nipples until they were hard little nubs. Then he would wrap his lips around them, suckling them until she cried out his name.

". . . isn't that right, Lucan?"

He jerked and turned to find Fallon staring at him. His mind had been so preoccupied with thoughts of the girl he hadn't heard a word his brother had said.

Fallon blew out a breath. "Food."

"Aye. Food." Lucan stalked off to the kitchens before he made a bigger idiot of himself.

Who knew a wisp of a girl with chestnut hair and mahogany eyes could turn his blood to boiling and his body hard with just a look?

CHAPTER THREE

Cara's mind reeled. *MacLeod Castle.* She racked her brain for what had happened to bring her here.

She remembered staring at the ruins, entranced with them. Almost as if they had called to her, beckoned her. Then she had taken off her necklace because it had burned her.

The wind had snatched it from her hand, but she had managed to grab it. She remembered feeling the soft ground shift beneath her, then give way before she could move to safety.

Then she'd stopped. When she had looked up it was to find . . . Lucan. He had held her by one arm, struggling to keep her from falling while his sea green eyes begged her to hold on. She had slipped from his grasp; of that she was certain.

The horror of falling, knowing she would hit the rocks below and die, still made her heart pound in her chest. But she didn't remember anything after seeing his eyes grow large as her hand slipped out of his.

Could his brother, Fallon was his name, have been

below to catch her as he claimed? It was the only explanation, but a part of her continued to be wary.

The men were keeping something from her. It was an odd feeling of certainty, the same type of feeling she'd had over the past few weeks as if someone watched her.

There was a roar that was immediately drowned out by thunder, but there was no mistaking the sound. She jumped and scooted closer to the fire.

The image of the other man who had become angry at seeing her in the gown flashed in her mind. Had it been a trick of the candles, or had his teeth elongated?

She glanced at the door, wondering if she could make it. They had told her she wasn't a prisoner, but she wasn't sure how much to believe.

"We won't stop you."

She looked to find Fallon with his elbows on the table and a bottle of wine in his grip. His hair was the color of freshly tilled earth, dark and thick. He was handsome enough with his strong jaw and wide, firm lips, but it was his dark green eyes that bespoke pain silent and profound.

He gestured to the door, his gaze not moving from the bottle. "Leave."

"I'm not safe here, then?"

He chuckled and lifted the bottle to his lips. He drank deeply and shrugged. "Lucan won't let anything happen to you. He's the best of us. I don't know what's worse, though, the storm or staying here."

Despite the fact that Fallon was inebriated, she saw the truth of his words in his eyes when he glanced at her. Fear snaked down her spine. Her necklace, which she'd found in her hand, vibrated beneath her gown between her breasts. It had never done that before, but it made her distinctly aware of her surroundings.

Who were these men? Was it mere coincidence they had two of the same names as the brothers of the MacLeod legend? Was the third named Quinn?

Did she really want to know?

Angus had told her monsters resided in the castle. It could be the old man had known far more than he had been willing to say.

Cara squeezed her toes together. Her feet were like ice on the bare stones, but she hadn't been able to find her shoes or stockings when she raced from the chamber. The storm was fierce, but she should be able to make it back to the village.

In the dark? Alone?

She inwardly cringed at the fear that always took hold of her when night fell. She took a step to the door, the light from the fire and the candelabras making her hesitate. When Fallon did nothing but look at her, she took another step. Her hand was upon the latch to open the door when Lucan walked into the hall, a platter of food in his hand.

His gaze locked with hers as he froze. She licked her lips and realized her chances of getting free were slim. And it was the longing and loneliness she saw in his green eyes that gave her pause.

Lucan was tall and broad shouldered, a wall of solid muscle and rippling with sex appeal. He was gorgeous and dangerously powerful. His tunic did nothing to hide his muscular chest, which tapered to a narrow waist, then to long legs that bulged with muscles encased in brown breeches. His ebony locks fell past his shoulders in waves, and he wore a single small braid on either side of his temples like the warriors of old.

At the collar of his dark green tunic she saw the thick gold torc around his neck. He didn't wear a kilt or any tartan that would tell which clan they belonged to, which was odd. Any Highlander, and these men were most certainly Highlanders, always wore his tartan.

Her heart skipped a beat when she let herself really look into Lucan's face. He had dark brows that slashed over eyes thickly fringed with black lashes. His nose was slightly bent from a break, but it paled in comparison to his mouth. Lips full and wide parted, then tilted down in a frown. A tremor shivered through her as she wondered what it would feel like kissing those lips.

As soon as the thought crossed her mind, she grimaced. She was to be a nun. A nun shouldn't have those kinds of thoughts, even if they were her deepest desires.

"Don't leave," Lucan said.

Cara saw Fallon's gaze narrow out of the corner of her eye, but she didn't move. She couldn't. Lucan's gaze wouldn't release her, and she was caught in his hypnotic eyes as they pulled her toward him.

Lucan set the platter on the table. "No one should be out in such weather."

As if on cue, lightning lit the sky before hitting its mark with an earth-shattering crash. The boom resounded around them a heartbeat before thunder rumbled threateningly.

"You're not a prisoner here. I give you my word," Lucan continued. "You'll be safer here until the storm blows over."

Cara glanced at Fallon to see him watching her, his face unreadable. What should she do? From the conversation she had heard coming down the stairs, they wanted her gone.

Not everyone. Lucan wants you to stay.

Every fiber of her being told her if she stayed, her life would be forever changed. But how could she leave in this weather? In the dark?

She could hear the wind, knew the gusts could push her off the cliff if she wasn't careful. She had managed to survive death once that day. Did she want to test it again so soon?

With a sigh, Cara dropped her hand from the latch and walked to the table. "Until the storm stops then." She was ravenous. She'd had little in the way of food for her noon meal because she had wanted to get to the mushrooms.

She sat and reached for the platter. The meat was cold but delicious. She quickly ate it and the few bites of cheese and bread. When she looked up, Lucan had taken the seat across from her and next to Fallon.

It was disconcerting to have both men staring. Now that she was closer to them she could see that while Fallon's hair was dark, it wasn't black like Lucan's. Fallon's eyes were a dark green while Lucan's were a vibrant green, making his black lashes more prominent.

She looked at Lucan's lips again. They were so . . . sensual. She blinked, surprised at her thoughts. Her stomach fluttered and the vial warmed against her skin. She jerked her gaze to his eyes to find him watching her, his stare intense, hot. Her blood heated. No longer did she have the chill that she hadn't been able to shake since waking in the strange chamber.

"I never thanked you," she blurted out, needing to fill the silence.

Lucan shrugged away her words.

Fallon drummed his fingers on the table. "Might we have the name of the woman we saved?"

Cara closed her eyes in embarrassment. When she opened her gaze, she focused on Fallon. He didn't make her feel . . . off balance as his brother did. "My apologies. I'm Cara."

"Cara."

She shivered at the sound of her name on Lucan's lips. Despite her internal warning, she found herself staring into his eyes. "Aye."

"Do you live in the village, Cara?" Fallon asked.

Without taking her gaze from Lucan, she answered, "Aye."

"Are you married?" Lucan asked.

Cara clasped her hands in her lap beneath the table. "Nay."

Fallon pushed the bottle between one hand and the other. "Parents?"

She frowned, unsure why they needed to know about her parents. She understood that as the eldest, Fallon wanted to discover all he could about her, but why? She didn't talk about her parents. To anyone, not even the nuns. Why then? It wasn't like she could harm the brothers.

Then she realized that she could. No one was supposed to be in the castle.

"Does it matter?" she asked.

Fallon snorted. "It does to me."

"Enough," Lucan said in a voice as hard as steel.

Cara licked her lips, unused to having someone take up for her. She lifted her gaze from the table and looked around the hall. There had been work done to it that wasn't visible from the outside. It wasn't as extravagant as she assumed the hall was in its prime, but it was enough to shelter them from the elements.

"You three live here?" she asked.

Fallon threw Lucan a glance. "When the need arises."

Another crash sounded behind her. She jumped and glanced at the door behind her. Something was certainly going on in MacLeod Castle, but what? Her curiosity had always gotten her into trouble. And though a part of her told her to run and never look back, another part—a dangerous part—told her to find out.

Lightning lit the hall, and when it faded, Cara found black eyes staring at her from behind Lucan and Fallon. She opened her mouth to scream, for she had never seen eyes completely black, without a trace of color.

"Quinn," Lucan barked as he jumped to his feet.

"It was you, wasn't it?" Cara demanded as fear laced through her. She had been mistaken to think she was safe. She stood and backed away from the table. "You were the one who watched me from the window."

All three men jerked their gazes to her, their brows furrowed.

Quinn snorted. "I've never seen you before today."

"I know." She took another step back, suddenly terrified. "It was once I was here. You were in the window, your eyes glowing yellow as you watched me."

Instead of the refusal, or even an explanation, as she had expected, Fallon's face paled and Lucan placed his hands on the table as he leaned toward her and searched her face.

"What happened?" Lucan asked. "I need every detail, Cara."

She was unable to stop the wave of alarm and anger she felt from the three men. She took another step back and looked at Lucan. His gaze was steady, strong, and nonthreatening. It dampened some of her fear. "I . . . I opened my eyes to see," she said with a shrug, ". . . something in the window. Its eyes were yellow in the darkness."

"Shite," Quinn grumbled, and turned away.

Fallon stood and tossed the bottle of wine in the fire, causing the flames to hiss as the liquid fell on them. "Quinn."

"I'm on it," Quinn said as he bounded up the stairs.

Cara's heart raced, her breathing difficult. What were they doing? Surely what she had seen had been her imagination. Right?

Then why did you say something?

Because, deep down, she knew what she saw was real.

No one's eyes can glow yellow.

And no one's eyes can turn black, either.

She turned toward the castle door to find Lucan standing before her. Her hands fisted in her skirts as she tried to control the panic that ate at her every night. The dark. The monsters. They never went away.

"Come with me." He held out his hand. His sea green eyes promised safety, but they couldn't mask the desire she saw there as well. "I will protect you, Cara. I give you my word."

There was anther boom. Thunder again? Or something else? She couldn't go out in the storm and the darkness. There was only one choice. She swallowed past the lump of dread in her throat and placed her hand in Lucan's big, warm one.

He pulled her after him as he raced from the great hall through a doorway and down a set of stairs. Her feet, numb from the stones, faltered on the steps. His arm wrapped around her, steadying her.

Her heart slammed into her chest at the feel of his hard muscles against her. She inhaled the smell of sandalwood, lightning, and power. A heady mix that left her breathless and all too aware of the big male who held her against his hard body.

Even when she had her balance, he didn't remove his arm, and God help her, Cara found she liked having his warmth, his strength.

She should be wary of him, but the current that ran through the castle was one of battle. Battle from something that was evil and . . . wrong, and she wanted no part of it.

"Where are we going?" she asked as they traveled deeper under the castle.

"Somewhere safe."

There was no light, and she stumbled in the darkness again. This time, Lucan lifted her in his arms. She gripped his thick shoulders, the muscles beneath her hands moving and bunching as he carried her.

"I canna see," she whispered.

"Don't worry. I can."

"How?" she wanted to ask, but instead held on tighter as he increased his speed. The stairs ended and he ran on what sounded like dirt. She thought she heard the squeal of a rat, but it could have come from her.

She had never liked being frightened. Late at night when the wind would move over the land, she would huddle in her blankets, squeezing her eyes shut for fear of what she might see if she opened them.

Suddenly Lucan slowed, then stopped. He set her down beside him and rattled a chain. His fingers closed around her wrist as a door squeaked open.

"Stay here," Lucan murmured.

Cara wrapped her arms around herself. She was used to the Highland weather, but the damp down here was seeping into her bones. It didn't help that she didn't have her shoes or stockings to help warm her legs.

Light flared and she glanced inside the room to see Lucan setting a torch in its holder on the wall. He motioned her forward.

Her gaze fell on the door and the lock he had opened. "Am I to be locked away now?"

Lucan shook his head. "I've no time for explanations, only time to get you safe."

"From what? The storm?"

"The creature you saw."

She stilled. The hairs on her arms stood on end as a fear raked down her back. "Creature?"

"I don't know why it's here. But we will find out."

He pulled her inside the room and turned to leave. The thought of staying by herself made her blood turn to ice even as sweat covered her skin.

"Where are you going?" She tried to hide the panic in her voice but failed.

Lucan cupped her face with one hand, his green gaze startling in its fierce intensity. It was the look of a Highlander, a warrior willing to fight to the end.

"I'm going to protect you. And find my answers." He said the last in a voice laced with steel.

Cara watched as he closed the door behind him before she touched her cheek where his hand had been. No man had willingly made contact with her as Lucan had. Her skin was still warm from his touch, and the smell of sandalwood lingered in the small chamber. She didn't know Lucan, but for some unexplained reason she trusted him. Her life was in his hands against . . . creatures.

When she had seen the yellow eyes, she'd promptly shut her own, afraid she hadn't been dreaming. It left her body shaking to know she had been awake.

She pulled her mother's necklace from beneath her gown and wrapped her fingers around the vial. It was warm to the touch and pulsed with energy. Normally, she held the vial when she needed comfort, but this time it did nothing to calm her.

Cara's legs gave out and she slid down the wall to the dirt floor. She drew her knees to her chest, wrapped her arms around her legs, and lowered her forehead to her knees.

She should have listened to old Angus and stayed away from the castle. He'd known there were monsters.

Cara's head snapped up, realization dawning. Angus had known.

CHAPTER FOUR

Lucan raced back to the great hall, his blood pumping in his veins. It had been a few months since he had fought, and he found himself looking forward to it. Apodatoo, the god within him, clawed to be free, to mete out his vengeance on those who would dare to attack the castle.

And Lucan freed him.

Lucan's teeth elongated, and his nails grew to sharp, black claws that could behead a man with one swipe. His skin tingled as it changed to ebony. He had learned after being turned in Deirdre's mountain that each god had distinct powers and when a Warrior let his god out the Warrior changed to the color of the god.

Lucan, Fallon, and Quinn changed to black.

By the time Lucan reached the great hall, Quinn and Fallon had their hands full. The brothers had witnessed for themselves the varied monsters men turned into when a god was inside them.

A small pale yellow creature launched itself at Lucan. He jerked his hand up to impale the thing on his claws and cut off its head with his other hand.

With a jerk, he flung off the dead monster and readied for the next attack. He grimaced. A wyrran. Creatures made by Deirdre's black magic.

Again and again the wyrran came at them, smaller than Lucan remembered. They were completely hairless, their mouths so full of teeth that their thin lips couldn't close over them. The wyrran hissed and screeched and yelled, but they didn't roar as Quinn did, as a Warrior did.

"You. Will. Die!" Fallon bellowed as the blade of his sword severed a wyrran's head from its body.

Lucan glanced at his brother, amazed that even now Fallon hadn't given in to the god and changed. He didn't have long to think about it, though, as four wyrran jumped from the walls onto him.

They clawed and bit at his flesh. Lucan threw one off him after it gnawed on his shoulder. Another he beheaded with a slash of his hand. The one on his leg he kicked toward Quinn, who ripped it in two.

Lucan reached behind him to the wyrran that hung on his back. Its claws dug into his waist and shoulders. He could feel his blood dripping from him, the pain dulled by the fury inside him.

He grabbed the creature by the back of the neck and flung it over his head. The wyrran landed on its back with a howl, its teeth bared. Lucan knelt beside it and plunged his claws into the creature's abdomen and ripped out its heart.

"I hate these damned things," Fallon said as he made his way toward Lucan.

Lucan tossed aside the heart. He rose and noticed the blood on his brother. "Me as well."

"It seems Deirdre wants a battle."

Lucan blew out a breath as he looked at all the dead bodies of the wyrran. They were Deirdre's pets, used by her to track whomever she wanted. "Are they all dead?"

"I think," Fallon answered. "Where is Quinn?"

Lucan shrugged. "He was just here."

Then they heard the howl, Quinn's howl of rage. Lucan pointed to Fallon with his claw. "Stay here in case more come."

Fallon nodded, and Lucan leapt onto the stairs and raced to find Quinn. Lucan followed the growls and bellows to the top of a tower where Quinn battled a tall, slim monster. Lucan climbed closer to them, the wind and rain making it difficult to see. Until lightning streaked across the sky and he saw the royal blue skin of the Warrior.

"Shite," Lucan murmured as he recognized that Quinn battled one like them.

Quinn was strong, but his adversary moved so quickly Quinn couldn't keep up. In a heartbeat, the beast had Quinn on his back, his head hanging over the side of the tower. One long royal blue arm lifted, its claws aimed at Quinn's throat.

They might be immortal, but they could be killed if their heads were removed. Lucan had failed his brothers once already by bringing Cara into the castle. He wouldn't let them down again.

He jumped and landed beside the Warrior. Lucan backhanded him and followed the Warrior as he fell over the side of the tower. He heard Quinn bellow his name, but Lucan couldn't stop. Not now.

The Warrior landed on his feet next to the cliff moments before Lucan dropped down beside him.

"You just won't die, will you?" Lucan taunted the Warrior.

Blue lips peeled back in a laugh. "My mistress is

tired of your games. She wants you back at her mountain."

Lucan's blood went cold. "Deirdre can want all she wants, but we're not going anywhere."

The Warrior shrugged. "Though she wants you, MacLeod, do you think you three are the only ones she's after?"

They circled each other, waiting for a time to strike. "Isn't that why *you* came?" Lucan couldn't imagine another reason why Deirdre had sent part of her army to the castle.

The Warrior threw back his head and laughed. "You have no idea, do you?"

"Tell me."

"Ah, Lucan," he said. "We are all just men who are fortunate enough to have powers unlike any other. Why deny what is in your blood? Give the god inside you what he wants."

"Become like you, you mean? Bowing to Deirdre and her need to dominate? Despite the evil inside me, I fight on the side of good."

"Do you really think you have a choice? The Druids set in motion things that cannot be undone. Hide in your castle for as long as you can, but be forewarned. This isn't the last you've seen of us."

Lucan lunged at him, but the Warrior disappeared into the night. Lucan started after him, but Quinn's shout from the battlements brought him up short.

"Hurry," Quinn said before he jumped to the ground and rushed to the castle.

Lucan ran under the gatehouse, through the bailey, and into the castle. To find the great hall empty except for Quinn. Where was Fallon?

"What is it?"

Quinn's chest rose and fell rapidly, the rain dripping from his black skin. "I heard Fallon."

Lucan opened his hearing. It took him a moment, but he finally heard Fallon's voice. "Shite. He's below the castle. Where I hid Cara."

Cara covered her ears with her hands, but nothing drowned out the sounds coming from above. The inhuman screeches, the eerie screams. It reminded her too much of the night her parents died, a night she fought every day to forget.

She tried to hum, anything to mask the sounds. At least there was light from the torch. She wouldn't be so calm if it were dark. How she loathed the dark.

Her fingers began to tingle, and this time she gave in to the urge to touch something. She placed her hands on the dirt floor as another boom shook the castle.

As suddenly as the battle in the castle began, it ended. She leaned her head against the wall behind her and fixed her gaze on the door, silently waiting for Lucan to come for her.

There was a light scratch on the door that sounded like claws. She rose to her feet, assuming it was Lucan or his brothers. Until the door rattled on its hinges.

She took a step back and ran to the wall, her gaze darting to the door and the dust and dirt that flew every time it was jerked.

"I know you're in there. I can smell you and your magic," a deep, raspy voice called from the other side of the door.

She glanced around the small chamber. Magic? What was he talking about? She had no magic. There was also nowhere to escape, no place to hide. The only thing separating her from whatever was on the other side was a wooden door that was centuries old. How long could it last?

As soon as the thought flitted through her mind, the wood cracked. An evil laugh filled the chamber as the man doubled his efforts in pulling apart the door.

The wood splintered with a loud crack. Cara flattened herself against the stone wall, her heart in her throat. She screamed when an ash-colored hand pushed through the hole in the door.

The monster's claws scraped on the wood, gouging the door with five long streaks. Cara squeezed herself into a corner, icy prickles of terror racing over her skin. With one yank, the door was wrenched in two. She screamed again when a face, the same ash color, came into her line of sight.

Thick horns rose through the man's blond hair atop his head. He laughed, peeling back his lips to show his fangs. His eyes were the same color as his skin and scanned her up and down as he chuckled.

"What a reward I will get for being the one to find you." He pulled the rest of the door off its hinges and made to step into the chamber.

He got no more than one foot inside before the tip of a sword pushed through his stomach. Cara's heart stopped as the creature looked down at the blade protruding from his abdomen. A heartbeat later the beast was jerked out of the chamber, his claws raking down the sides of the stones.

Cara caught a glimpse of Fallon, his tunic covered in blood.

"Are you all right?" Fallon asked.

She nodded.

"I'll keep him occupied. Get out and find Lucan."

Fallon moved into the darkness of the corridor. Grunts and growls filled the space as Fallon and the monster fought. Cara started toward the doorway and stopped when she saw seedlings had sprouted where her hands had been. With no time to think about it, she reached for the torch. No matter how much she strained, it wouldn't loosen from the holder.

Cara blinked back the tears that threatened. Her fear had made her too frightened to move the night her parents were killed. If she didn't do something now, she would receive the same fate as they had.

Yet she couldn't see. How could she get past the monster if she didn't know where he was?

"Cara!" Fallon shouted. "Run. Now!"

She lifted her skirts and shouldered her way through the broken door, all the while praying she didn't crash into anything. She could hear Fallon and the other man—monster—in their skirmish. Fallon grunted and something heavy hit the wall.

Cara tried to dart past them, but something bumped into her, knocking her off her feet. She pitched forward, her skirts forgotten as she put her hands out to catch herself. She landed with a hard thud and hit her chin on the ground, biting her tongue.

Tears welled in her eyes as pain swam through her and the metallic taste of blood filled her mouth. She tried to get to her feet, but something grabbed her ankle. The laugh that echoed around her sent a chill of foreboding through her.

"Just where do you think you're going?" The monster jerked back on her ankle, pulling her toward him.

Cara clawed at the ground, dirt clumping under her fingernails. She kicked back with her other foot and missed. The second time she tried, she connected with something. There was a grunt, and then the beast cursed and gave her leg a vicious yank.

With her breath coming in ragged gasps, she began to pray, mumbling the prayers the nuns had taught her to help ease her fears.

"You belong to us," the monster said. "You and the Demon's Kiss." The beast's hands gripped her waist, hauling her next to him.

Cara knew if the creature left with her Lucan would never find her. No one would ever find her. That was enough for her to put aside her terror and strike out with her hands and feet. She hit the monster multiple times, but he never eased his hold.

When he gained his feet and started walking, Cara knew she had one last chance in Fallon, if he wasn't dead. "Fallon. Fallon, please!"

One moment she was being held above the ground, and the next she was on her stomach with a heavy weight atop her. She tried to move, but the creature was too heavy. He pinned her to the ground and laughed in her ear.

Then she heard Lucan's voice yell her name in the dark. She tried to wiggle from underneath the weight only to have a large hand wrap around her arm, his claws digging into her skin.

"If you want them to live, don't move," the beast murmured.

Cara blinked and tried to see in the darkness. Everything had gotten quiet. The only sound she heard was her own harsh breathing.

"Cara!" Lucan called. "Are you hurt?"

The beast squeezed her arm. "Dinna answer him."

"He can see," she whispered, not knowing whether the beast could or not.

There was movement near her, coming closer with each heartbeat. Cara clenched her teeth to keep them from chattering in fear and cold.

She was jerked to her feet, the creature behind her with one of his claws at her neck.

"Back off, MacLeod. If you don't want her throat slit, you'll let me pass."

"Why are you here?" Fallon asked from her left.

She sent up a silent prayer of thanks that he was still alive.

The beast laughed, the sound unnatural. And evil. "I've come for the Demon's Kiss. And the woman."

The silence that met his statement told Cara the MacLeods had no idea what the Demon's Kiss was either.

"You have two choices. You can let her go and fight me, or you can die where you stand." Lucan's voice had grown closer with each word.

The creature growled. "I'm not leaving without the woman."

"Then you die."

The monster let out a loud bellow of pain, but he didn't release her. Cara squeezed her eyes shut, thankful it was too dark for her to see anything. The sounds of blades sinking into flesh were terrifying enough.

By the beast's yells, all three brothers were attacking him with their fists and weapons. Finally, his hold on her relaxed enough for her to get free.

Cara stumbled in the dark, one hand on the stone wall to catch her balance. She didn't know which way she was headed, and it didn't matter anymore. She had to get out of the dark and into the light.

Strong arms grabbed her shoulders, firm enough to halt her but light enough that she could break if she so desired.

"Cara. It's Lucan."

She sagged against him as all her emotions fell away. She had just gone through her greatest fear. But she was safe now. Safe with Lucan.

When he lifted her in his arms and walked away from the screams behind her, she was all too willing to wrap her arms around his neck, lay her head on his shoulder, and allow him to carry her burdens for a bit.

"What was that thing?" she asked after several moments.

"Later."

His heat surrounded her, brandishing the cold and fear that had held her in its grip for what seemed like an eternity. She took a deep, steadying breath. "I thought I was going to die."

"I told you I would protect you." His voice held a note of displeasure, as if she should have known better.

Cara sank into his warmth, amazed that he could chase away the chill so easily. She was all too aware of the hard, lean man pressed against her, and his scent that put her senses into a whirl. Her breasts tingled from the contact, and she had the overwhelming desire to run her fingers through his ebony locks.

Lucan began to ascend the stairs that would take them to the great hall. Each step brought her farther into the light. When she could stand the awareness no more, she lifted her gaze and found him watching her.

Their eyes locked. Cara might be naïve about the ways of men, but there was no denying the hunger that darkened his eyes. She tried to swallow past the lump of excitement in her throat. Her chest felt constricted, her gown too tight against her skin. She wanted to be free of her clothing, to feel his skin against hers.

When his gaze shifted to her lips, Cara thought he was going to kiss her. It was there in his eyes, in the set of his jaw. He wanted her. And she wanted him.

Confusion filled her. She had pledged to become a nun, to fill her life with God and helping others. There was no place in her life for Lucan or the passion he stirred within her. Right?

She didn't know. The longer she was around Lucan the more the idea of her taking the vows of a nun was preposterous. She had wanted a home, a family. She had found that at the nunnery with the Sisters and the children. She might not truly belong, but they welcomed her.

It took her a moment to realize Lucan no longer climbed the stairs. They were once more in the great hall, the storm still raging outside, much like her emotions.

Lucan released her legs, her lower body sliding down his until her feet touched the floor. Not even the cold stones could chase away the heat that engulfed her, though.

"Cara."

A shudder went through her when he whispered her name with desire, with need . . . with hunger.

She forced her gaze away from him before she forgot the nunnery and gave in to the pleasure Lucan promised. That's when she saw the blood and dead bodies that littered the great hall. She wasn't sure what the diminutive pale yellow things were, but they were all dead.

"Cara." His fingers tightened around her waist as if he wanted to hold her against him. His voice was edged with worry, and a hint of dread.

Thunder boomed, making her jump. She looked at Lucan to find his expression closed off and waiting. Something jabbed into her waist. It wasn't Lucan's hand that frightened her but the claws from his fingers.

Cara jerked out of his grasp and stepped backward. She stumbled over something, and when Lucan made a move to help her she hurried to twist away.

"Nay!" she shouted, her heart pumping wildly in her chest when she saw the dried blood on his chest through what was left of his tunic. "Stay away from me. I don't know what you are, what any of this is, but I want to return to the village. Immediately."

"Don't let her, Lucan," Quinn said from behind her.

She whirled around to find Quinn by the castle door and Fallon righting the table and benches. She hadn't heard the two come into the great hall, but then again she had been preoccupied with Lucan and the delicious feelings he invoked.

The blood staining the brothers' tunics along with the rips and tears of what was left of their clothes made her realize they were injured. She wanted to help, but how could she when she wasn't sure what they were, much less what was going on?

She fought back the panic and tears when she realized Quinn had said she couldn't go to the village. "Why? Why can't I return to the village?"

Quinn met her gaze. "There's nothing of it left to return to."

CHAPTER FIVE

Lucan sat before the fire, his legs stretched out before him and his ankles crossed. After he had changed and cleaned the blood off him, he had grabbed a bottle of Fallon's wine, but it sat untouched on the floor next to him.

It had taken all of his control—and he had plenty of it—not to go after Cara when she had run up the stairs, tears glistening on her cheeks.

He had seen the fire in her eyes, knew she was attracted to him. If he would have taken her anywhere else but the great hall, things would have turned out differently. But he hadn't been thinking. He had wanted to get her out of the dungeon and into the light so he could see if she had any injuries.

She had taken one look at the hall, and he had known she would be sickened. The god inside him had roared, demanding Lucan make Cara his. He had restrained the beast, but just barely. That's when she had felt—and seen—Lucan's claws. Whatever feelings she had for him had vanished when she realized he wasn't human.

He wasn't a god, either. How did he explain what he was when he didn't really know?

"The storm is waning," Fallon said as he took the seat next to Lucan.

Lucan shrugged.

Fallon blew out a breath and looked down at his torn tunic. "How did you expect her to react, Lucan? She was terrified. The Warrior had her and fully intended to leave with her."

"I know." And he did. He hadn't expected anything from Cara, but the hot jolt of desire had been intense, the hunger devastating.

Quinn knelt before the hearth and stoked the logs. "What did you and the blue-skinned Warrior you shoved off the tower talk about?"

Lucan sat up and rested his elbows on the arms of the chair. He had forgotten about the Warrior after seeing Cara in danger. "He said we weren't the only things Deirdre was hunting."

"That doesna bode well," Fallon said, his brow creased. "I assumed Deirdre had finally come for us."

Lucan shook his head slowly. "She hasn't come for us because I think she's waiting on something, but what I don't know. He made it sound as though taking us back with them would be an added benefit."

"What did your Warrior have to say?" Quinn asked Fallon.

Fallon ran a hand down his face. "He knocked me senseless, and I think I blacked out for a moment. When I came to, he had Cara and he was telling her how they had come for her."

"I heard him say something about a Demon's Kiss," Lucan added.

Fallon leaned back in the chair. "I heard that as well."

"Well? What is it?" Quinn asked.

"I wish I knew," Fallon answered.

Lucan rose and began to pace. There was too much going on that they didn't have answers to. "I think Deirdre sent her wyrran after Cara."

Quinn crossed his arms over his chest. "It's a possibility. By the looks of it, they attacked the village first."

"Looking for Cara, I assume. So then they came here?"

"Aye," Fallon said. "I heard the Warrior tell Cara he smelled her. Her and her magic."

"Shite," Lucan murmured again. Magic, wyrran and Warriors. Deirdre definitely wanted Cara.

Fallon snorted. "If Deirdre only sent the wyrran and two Warriors, they weren't expecting to find her here."

"Then the Warrior I spoke to didn't lie," Lucan said. "They really were hunting something else."

"Cara," Quinn said.

For a long moment the brothers sat in silence. As much as Lucan hated to admit it, Cara was involved whether she wanted to be or not. Deirdre wanted Cara, but was it only because of her magic? If he were a betting man he would place a wager on the Demon's Kiss, whatever that was.

"You'll have to talk to her," Fallon said into the silence.

Lucan sighed. "I know."

"They'll come again," Quinn said. "They won't stop until they get Cara."

Lucan rubbed his eyes with his thumb and forefinger. "Aye. I know that as well. And we need to know what the Demon's Kiss is as well as what kind of magic she holds."

Quinn moved to Lucan's vacated seat. "Next time, Fallon, you'll be more of a benefit to us if you let the god out."

Fallon glared at Quinn for several heartbeats. "Never," Fallon growled before he stood and walked away.

Lucan waited until Fallon was gone before he looked at Quinn. "That could have been handled better."

"It's the truth, whether either of you want to believe it or not. The Warrior nearly killed Fallon. If he lets the god out, he'll have more strength as well as being able to control his power."

Lucan knew it all to be true, but he understood why his brother refused to give in. "I'll talk to him. Until then, leave him be."

Quinn shrugged, but Lucan saw his hand clench into a fist.

"Tell me about the village," Lucan urged. He needed to know what he could and couldn't tell Cara.

"There's nothing left. The wyrran destroyed it all. They started at the nunnery, as far as I can tell. They didn't spare the children."

Lucan knew all too well how the wyrran killed. It had been them that had massacred the MacLeod clan. "Were none left alive?"

"Just one."

By Quinn's guarded expression Lucan guessed it was the old man who supplied them with food. "Angus?"

"Aye. He didna have long to live. He asked about Cara, told us to keep her safe."

Lucan wished the old man had made it. He had

information they could have used. Lucan glanced at the stairs, his thoughts on the woman who had stirred his desires and awoken a hunger he hadn't known he had. It had been a couple of hours since Cara had run away from him. Was it enough time for her to realize he wouldn't harm her?

"Putting it off won't help," Quinn said. "With Elspeth, it was always better to face something head-on. I cannot imagine it would be any different with another woman."

Lucan stared at his brother. Quinn hadn't spoken of Elspeth since the day she and their son had been murdered.

Quinn threw Lucan a wry smile. "Contrary to what you might think, I haven't forgotten what it was to be human, to be a husband and father."

"I never doubted it." Lucan placed a hand on Quinn's shoulder before he walked to the stairs.

"Be patient with her," Quinn called.

Lucan just hoped she would listen to him. Seeing the fear in her gaze had been like a dagger in his chest. She had trusted him, and he had scared her.

He walked silently up two flights of stairs and down the corridor to his chamber. The glow of a fire flickered in the hallway, and he let out a breath he hadn't known he was holding. There weren't many places Cara could have hidden in the ruins, but she could have tried.

Lucan hesitated at her doorway before he leaned his head around to peer inside the chamber. He found her curled on her side, her arm beneath her head. Every candle had been lit and placed around the chamber. With the candles in addition to the fire, the room was ablaze in light.

He leaned against the door frame and watched Cara sleep. In her hand she clutched something against her, as if she was afraid to let it go. She shivered when the wind howled through the window.

Lucan walked to the bed and covered her with another blanket. He wasn't sure if it was fear or the wind that made her shake. It could be a little of both, especially after what she had seen that night.

Unable to stop himself, he ran a finger down the side of her face to her jawline. Petal-soft skin met his touch and made him burn. Though he knew he should keep his distance, he found himself sitting on the bed, her body curved around him. His blood heated, his heart pounded. God's bones, how he wanted to taste her, to run his tongue over her plump lips and mold soft curves against him.

His hand moved to the end of her braid. With a flick of his fingers, he unbound her hair. He lifted a strand to his face and inhaled her fragrance of heather.

He closed his eyes, letting her scent move through him. His body throbbed with need, with a longing that only grew the longer Cara was near.

When he opened his eyes, he found her watching him. Her mahogany gaze held a hint of caution, but he also saw courage that warmed his heart. He waited for her to speak. She had questions, and he would answer them.

"Is the village really gone?"

He nodded. "Aye. The attack was on the village first."

"Is anyone alive? There could be those who need care."

Lucan glanced away from her face. "None were left alive."

"Oh, God." She put her hand over her mouth and squeezed her eyes shut.

He understood her pain. He had experienced much the same emotions upon seeing his clan gone.

She wiped the tears from her face and opened her eyes. "The children?"

He shook his head, unable to find the words.

Her tears came faster, her lips trembling. "What happened here tonight? What were those things?"

Lucan took a deep breath. "I wish it were easy to explain, but it isna. Those beings, those creatures you saw dead in the great hall, were made from evil and Druid magic. They are called wyrran."

She sat up and leaned her back against the headboard, her knees to her chest. "Magic? There is no such thing as magic."

Lucan didn't know whether to believe her or not. Her dark gaze was open and honest, and he couldn't deny that his gut told him she believed she spoke the truth. How could she have magic and not know it?

"Magic is real. Look at what you saw tonight. Those were very real," he said.

"There are those who say the Druids were good people."

"Just like with anything, there is a good side and an evil side."

She licked her lips and wiped away the last of her tears. Lucan clenched his jaw to stop a moan when he imagined tasting her mouth with his own, sweeping his tongue between her lips, and drinking the intoxicating flavor of her.

Lucan forced his breathing to remain calm, to remember Cara was frightened and in need of protecting, not ravishing. Yet he knew she would fit him perfectly, that their lovemaking would be earth-shattering.

No woman had ever inspired such need, such yearning. Such *hunger*. He couldn't turn away from Cara any more than he could turn out the god inside him.

"I need to know what is going on, Lucan." Her voice was stronger, the determined glint of her eyes telling him she wouldn't give up until she knew the truth.

If Deirdre was after her, Cara deserved to know the reality. All of it. No matter how painful it was for him to tell it.

"Long ago, in another age, the Romans tried to take control of Britain."

She nodded. "Britain, but never the Highlands."

"The Romans wanted the Highlands, but the Celts never gave up fighting. Many generations saw the Romans grow in numbers, their territory increasing with each year. The Celtic tribes fought the Romans as best they could."

"But they weren't able to beat them back because they didn't align together," she said.

Lucan grinned, impressed by her knowledge. "The clans turned to the Druids for aid. The good Druids, or *mie*, were the ones the tribes sought for counsel and healing. They knew what the Celts needed was beyond their abilities. The *mie* looked to nature for their magic.

"It was the other Druids the Celts needed. Those Druids, the *drough*, were ones who used human sacrifices and dark magic and forgot their true Druid ways. The *drough* knew to defeat the Romans the Celts were going to need special assistance."

Cara leaned her chin on her knees. "What kind of help?"

Lucan shrugged. "At the time, I'm sure the Celts, desperate to have their land returned, would have done anything to get the Romans out of Britain."

"So," Cara urged. "What happened?"

"The *drough* used their black magic and forbidden spells to call up ancient gods long buried in Hell. These gods took the strongest warrior from each clan, possessing him."

Cara swallowed. "How many gods were called up?"

"No one knows."

"And the gods? How ancient?"

Lucan glanced at the fire. "So ancient that their names were lost over time."

"I see. Go on."

"With the gods now inside the warriors, they easily defeated the Romans, beating them back again and again until Rome finally left Britain, never to return."

"Then it worked," she said, the corners of her mouth tilting up.

"It worked, but when the Druids tried to call the gods back to Hell, they refused to leave the warriors. With no one else to fight, the warriors turned on each other."

She scooted closer to him. Her brow was furrowed, her concentration steady. "I cannot imagine that's what anyone thought would happen."

"Nay. It took both sets of Druids to find a spell that would bind the gods inside the Warriors, since the gods wouldn't release them. As long as a god is free in his Warrior, the man is immortal, with immeasurable strength and other abilities. With the gods bound, the Warriors returned to their mortal selves.

"The Celts continued life as if nothing had happened. The possessed Warriors and what they had done was lost to legend over time. Forgotten except for the families of those Warriors. Others said the tale to be nothing more than something to frighten people."

"But it wasn't," Cara whispered.

"Many, many years later it is said that a Druid priestess of the old, dark ways came upon a scroll with the story. Somehow, she discovered how to unbind the gods within the Warriors."

Cara frowned. "Why would she want to do that?"

"She wanted—wants—to control the Warriors, to lead an army unlike any other over Britain. She wants control of Britain, and the world."

"You're one of those Warriors, aren't you?"

Lucan blew out a breath and rose to walk to the hearth. He leaned his hands upon the stones and let his gaze drown in the red-orange flames.

"Three hundred years ago, I was the middle son of the laird of the MacLeods. Quinn was already married, with a young son of his own. Fallon's bride had been chosen and was on her way to the castle. The three of us, with twenty MacLeod men, set out to meet her and her guards."

Lucan swallowed. He had never spoken of that day to anyone, not even his brothers. By unspoken agreement, they had kept their thoughts to themselves.

"Everything went according to plan," he continued. "We got Fallon's bride and started toward home. We were leagues away when we saw the smoke. We left the girl with our men, and Fallon, Quinn, and I rode toward the castle."

He paused, reliving the scene in his mind. The stench of death, the eerie silence, and the crows that feasted on the dead. Yet none of it compared to seeing the once lively and bustling castle in flames or the ground littered with their clan. So many bodies, men and women, young and old. Bile rose in his throat when he recalled seeing an infant still in its mother's arms lying dead with her.

"Lucan, you don't have to," Cara said.

He held up his hand to silence her. He needed to speak of it. He hadn't realized it until then, but once he had begun, he couldn't stop.

"When we saw the castle on fire, we knew something awful had happened. Yet we heard no shouts from our father or other men, as there should have been if they tried to put the fire out. It wasn't until we reached the castle that we saw what had happened."

He straightened and turned to face Cara. Her dark gaze was steady and held so much sorrow that it nearly broke him.

"They must have attacked as soon as we left, because the crows were already there, feasting. They killed every man, woman, and child. Not a horse, sheep, or chicken was left alive. Everything was dead. And burning."

He closed his eyes and swallowed past the nausea that overcame him each time he thought of the reek of the deceased. "Death hung in the air, infusing everything. We had no idea who had attacked or why. All too soon, Fallon's bride and the other men reached the castle.

"The woman took one look at what had happened and had her men return her to her family. It was for the best. With our father's death, Fallon became laird to a clan that didn't exist. He didn't know what to do. None of us did."

"Did you try to discover who had done it?" Cara asked.

He nodded. "There were too many to bury, so we burned the bodies and turned our attention to vengeance. The twenty men we had with us we sent off in different directions to spread the word about what had happened to see if we could gather any information. Fallon wanted me and Quinn to stay at the castle with him until the others returned. He said a laird had to remain in case some of the clan got free and tried to return."

"None returned, did they?"

Lucan walked to the bed and lowered himself on it. "Nay. No one returned. Months went by with no news from our men. It wasn't until years later that we learned they had been killed by Deirdre's wyrran."

Cara cocked her head to the side. "Who is this Deirdre?"

"An evil woman who I hope you never meet. She is the start of all of this, the Druid priestess who found the template to unbind the gods."

"By the saints," Cara murmured, and crossed herself.

Lucan snorted. "If we had known the day we received her missive what would happen to us, we would never have gone."

Cara's eyes widened in disbelief. "You went to see Deirdre?"

"We had no idea who she was. She told us she had information on the massacre of our clan. Even Fallon refused to stay behind for that. We made the trek deep into the mountains to see her. Once we were there, she told us of her plan to rule Britain and how she needed our help.

"Too late we realized she had been the one to murder our clan, but she shackled us before we could escape. Her magic is strong, but then most black magic is."

"The talk of magic is hard for me to believe."

"After everything you saw tonight, you think I'm lying?"

She shook her head and looked at her hands. "I never said that. I simply said it's difficult to believe."

Lucan wished he had that problem. "We saw first-hand what Deirdre's magic had brought forth. The pale, small beings were the first she called to her, fash-ioned from black magic, anger, and power. Next, she set about finding the clans who had the gods inside them."

"What did she do to you?"

"She unbound the god."

Cara shrugged. "I don't understand."

"When the Druids bound the gods, they passed from generation to generation, always possessing the strongest warriors. Sometimes the god would only pass into one warrior, with others like me and my brothers, the god would separate. Alone, Quinn is a force to be reckoned with, but when the three of us fight together, we are nigh unstoppable."

"What happened next?" Cara asked when he paused.

Lucan scratched his chin, wondering if he should continue. Then he realized he might as well. "Once our god was released, it gave us the power to break out of her shackles, magic or not. We left the mountain, but we raged at what she had done. The angrier we became, the stronger the god grew. We dinna know how to control the powers we suddenly had. Decades passed as we hid in the mountains learning what we had become. We fought each other constantly, each blaming the others for what had happened."

"None of you were to blame," Cara said.

"Maybe. Fallon tried again and again to bind our god, to no avail. He learned first that if he drowned himself in wine, it dulled the god. Once he discovered that, there was always a bottle in his hand. For Quinn, it was much worse. He lost his wife and his son in the slaughter. He held himself responsible for their deaths, since it was his job to protect them. In his eyes he failed, since he lived and they did not."

"And you?"

"With Quinn unable, and unwilling, to control his rage, and Fallon drunk, someone had to take care of them."

"So it fell to you."

He shrugged. "That duty led me to learn how to control the god inside me, to learn how to use the powers to my advantage without letting the god free."

"So you turn into the thing that attacked me tonight?"

"Not exactly," Lucan answered. "As I said, each clan had a different god. Each god had certain powers, or abilities."

She reached out and touched his hand, her fingers moving over his nails. "And the god inside you?"

"Apodatoo, the god of revenge. I have enhanced hearing and quick speed added to my strength. I can also control darkness and shadows."

"Control them?"

"Aye. I can move the shadows to my will, and the darkness I can use to my advantage."

"At any time?"

"Nay. Only when I release the god do I have full control of that power. The rest I have all the time."

She bit her lip. "The man that tried to take me was ash colored."

"I fought one that was royal blue. When the god is released and in control, the man transforms and becomes what the god was."

She glanced at his hands again.

Lucan curled his hands into fists. "Aye, Cara. I also turn. You saw Quinn partially turn, though I don't think you realize it."

"His eyes turned black."

"Aye. Our skin, our eyes, and our claws turn black. Each god has a color that gets transformed to us when we release him."

Lucan stilled as she moved closer and touched his face. "Do you forget who you are when the god takes over?"

"Nay, though I can hear him. I always hear him whether he is unleashed or not. But I don't forget who I am, or who I am protecting."

"If I hadn't seen it with my own eyes, I would find your story impossible to believe. You were the one who caught me when I fell, weren't you?"

"Aye." Lucan licked his lips. It was time to ask her. "Do you have magic?"

Her brow furrowed and her eyes became distant for a moment. "I . . . I don't think so."

"Do you know why the Warriors were after you?"

"Nay," she said with a shake of her head.

He'd expected that. "Do you know what a Demon's Kiss is?"

After a moment's hesitation, she pulled something free from her gown and held out the necklace with a vial at the end of it. "I think this is what they want."

Lucan looked at the small elongated silver vial with Celtic knot work surrounding it. It was held about her neck by a thin strip of leather. Could something so small be what Deirdre was after? "What is it?"

"My mother's blood."

CHAPTER SIX

Cara waited while Lucan stared at the vial. He leaned close, but he never touched it. She wasn't sure if what the ash-colored Warrior had called the Demon's Kiss was the vial around her neck, but a nagging memory she couldn't bring into focus told her it was.

She swallowed and tried to think past his question of whether she had magic. She didn't know what magic was, so how could she know if she had it?

What about when the vial warms?

There was the possibility the vial was magic. She had been so young when her parents were murdered, but she never heard her parents speak of magic. She would have remembered that.

Yet . . . there was something about Lucan's question that made her remember the tingling in her fingers and the sprouts in the cell that hadn't been there before she'd placed her hands on the dirt.

It was enough to give her pause.

"What is so important about your mother's blood?" Lucan asked.

She shrugged, jerking her attention back to Lucan. "I wish I knew."

His gaze narrowed as he leaned back and crossed his arms over his chest. "Tell me of your parents, Cara. Where are they?"

"Dead." She dropped the vial, the weight of it landing against her chest with a soft thud.

"Were they MacClures?"

She hesitated. She had never told anyone she recalled her surname, but Lucan had been honest with her. "Nay. My parents were Sinclairs. The nuns found me wandering the forest and brought me back with them to the nunnery where they raised me."

Lucan shifted and turned toward her on the bed. He tucked a strand of her hair behind her ear, then laid his hands on her shoulders. "I'm going to keep you safe, Cara. I vow it to you. But I need to know about your parents and the vial. The more I know, the better I can protect you."

"I understand." And she did, but the thought of opening up the memories of her parents' deaths left her shaking with dread. She wrapped her arms around herself to try to remain calm.

"They're just memories, Cara. They can't hurt you."

She swallowed and looked into Lucan's sea green eyes. There was such warmth and compassion in them. He had shared his story with her. The least she could do was share hers. "I was only five summers. I remember always being happy, my mother always laughing. I can't recall her or my da's face anymore, but I do remember the laughter. And her smile."

Lucan gave Cara an encouraging nod.

"Da was late for supper one night. Mum paced

our cottage, wringing her hands in between telling me to eat. I knew something was wrong."

"Do you remember what clan you belonged to?" Lucan's hands began to rub up and down her arms, giving her warmth.

She shook her head.

"It doesna matter. Go on."

"When Da finally returned, he was sweaty and breathing hard. He held his sword and it dripped with blood." She remembered watching the blood drop from the blade to a puddle on the floor. It had been so bright, so thick. "Da was scared. Mum began to cry, her tears silent as they turned to look at me."

Cara didn't pull away when Lucan drew her against him. She inhaled his scent and his heat, letting it relax her. Her arms wrapped around him, her hands gripping his tunic as if he were her lifeline.

"What happened?"

She laid her forehead on his shoulder and drew in a shaky breath. "Mum put me in a hole we'd dug beneath the floor of our cottage. It was large enough for all of us, but they wouldn't come with me. I started to cry, begging them not to leave me.

"Mum kissed me and put her necklace around my neck. She told me to stay safe, to stay quiet no matter what I heard. She then whispered words I couldn't understand, but she told me it didn't matter."

Cara couldn't stop trembling. Lucan's hands were firm and gentle, soothing and encouraging.

"They were protecting you," he said. "Did you hear what they thought was coming for them?"

"Nay. Da faced the door, his sword ready. He winked at me over his shoulder and told me everything would be all right. He had never lied to me, so I let Mum shut me in the hole. She pulled the rug over the small door and whispered that she loved me."

Lucan's hands had moved to her hair, stroking the long, thick strands and massaging her scalp. His touch helped control the horror that filled her with every memory that surfaced. Shivers of delight ran from her head down to her fingers and toes. She liked Lucan's touch. She liked it too much.

"I'm here," he whispered. "I didn't let the Warrior get you before, and I won't let the memories harm you now." He turned her so that she lay across his legs, his arms supporting her.

With her head resting on his chest, his heart beating beneath her ear, she found the strength to continue. "I heard the eerie screeches and screams long before they attacked the house. I tried to see through the slats of the floor, but the rug hid everything.

"I heard Mum and Da whisper that they loved each other a heartbeat before the door burst open. I screamed, but they never heard me. My parents fought them, but it was over so quickly. Then there was silence."

"Did you leave then?"

She shook her head. "There was silence, but I knew whatever had killed my parents was still there. It wasn't long before I could hear cloth ripping and the beds being overturned. I sat huddled in the hole with the screams of my parents echoing in my ears."

Lucan's hand held her head against him, his thumb rubbing slow circles behind her ear. Her skin prickled and warmed with his touch. "How long did you stay?"

"I don't remember. I was too afraid to leave at first, but hunger drove me out. When I stepped out of the hole and saw what they had done to my home and my parents, I knew I had to get as far away as I could."

Cara swallowed and squeezed her eyes closed as she recalled seeing her mother on her stomach, blood dripping from her mouth as her empty eyes stared into nothing.

"That's when the nuns found you?" Lucan asked.

"Aye. I don't know how long I walked," she said, guessing what he would ask next. Tears clogged her throat. Her eyes grew heavy with each stroke of Lucan's large fingers through her hair.

No one had ever touched her with such tenderness before. The nuns had been kind, but they could never replace her parents. And because she planned to take her vows, the men of clan MacClure gave her a wide berth.

"The screams I heard tonight. They remind me of what killed my parents."

Lucan stiffened. His warm breath fanned her cheek. "Thank you," he whispered.

Cara tried to open her eyes. There was so much she needed to know, so many questions she had, but her eyes refused to obey. Her body was exhausted. For the first time in years, she found she wasn't afraid of the dark. Not when Lucan held her.

Just as she drifted off to sleep she thought she felt Lucan's lips on her forehead.

Lucan stared at the beauty in his arms. Cara had endured a terrible blow with the loss of her parents. Any number of things could have happened to her while she wandered the Highlands. Thankfully, the nuns had found her.

It was the wyrran that had killed her parents. But

why? And he was relatively sure her mother had used some Druid magic to hide Cara, and maybe even the necklace, from the wyrran.

Lucan didn't know much about Druids. In fact, he knew hardly anything other than that there were good ones and evil ones, which didn't help Cara. As far as he knew, only Druids could use magic like Cara had explained. But if her parents were Druids, why did Deirdre want them killed?

He threaded his fingers in Cara's chestnut tresses again, letting the cool, silky mass glide over his hands. He couldn't remember the last time he had touched a woman's hair, or even cared to.

The past three hundred years had made him think of many things he had taken for granted. Like touching someone. Lucan hadn't trusted himself near a woman since Deirdre had unleashed the god within him.

No matter how great his need became, he always took care of it himself. He couldn't take the chance of exposing what he was to anyone. Yet in his arms was a woman who not only had seen what he could become but also still trusted him enough to let him hold her while she relived painful memories.

She had heard his story, knew the truth, and still looked at him with trust in her dark, fathomless eyes. He had never seen someone so beautiful, so breathtaking. If he had seen her before Deirdre, he would have claimed Cara for his wife. There was something special about her, something innately pure that called to him on a level he couldn't—and wouldn't—ignore.

In all his three hundred and some odd years, no one had affected him like Cara did. He shifted and groaned as his cock rubbed against her hip. Desire, white-hot and violent, shot through him, making his rod ache.

Cara murmured and nestled against him. Her lips were parted, her breathing even as she slept. He knew he should set her aside and let her sleep, but he couldn't let go. Her curves were too soft, her scent too sweet.

His hunger too great.

Nay. He wouldn't let go of Cara. Not now. Mayhap not ever.

Fallon watched Lucan from the shadows of the corridor. The way he stroked Cara's hair and held her gently against him made Fallon realize their existence couldn't continue as it was any longer—at least not for Lucan.

Fallon watched his brother's face, the longing and desire and need mixed together as he stared at Cara. Fallon had never seen Lucan look at a woman so, and whether Fallon wanted it or not, Cara was now a part of them.

Only time would tell for how long, though.

There was no way Fallon would allow himself to care for any woman, not with the god inside him. For one thing, he was immortal and would outlive everyone. For another, he was a monster. No woman would be able to tolerate what he became when he wasn't drunk from the wine.

And no woman wanted an intoxicated fool.

Fallon turned away from the scene with Lucan and Cara. It hurt too much to see how desperately his brother wanted the woman. If it were in Fallon's power to give her to Lucan, he would.

At one time Fallon had thought himself invincible. He would be the next laird of the feared and respected MacLeods. How quickly everything had changed, in a matter of hours.

He was laird now, but laird to no clan or lands. He was nothing.

Nay. You're a monster, unable to control your own feelings.

Rage and hopelessness ripped through Fallon. He felt the god stir within him, longing to be free, to use the powers that were his. Fallon hurried to the hall and reached for the half-empty bottle of wine. He drank deeply until he could no longer feel the god.

Only then did the anger inside Fallon ease. He rested his head on his arms and realized he had failed his brothers. As the eldest, he should have been the one to learn to control the god as Lucan had. As eldest, Fallon should have been able to help Quinn with his rage and grief. As eldest, Fallon should be the one shouldering the problems of their family instead of turning to the wine.

But he couldn't.

The torment of what he had become after Deirdre unbound the god had left a deep scar on Fallon's soul. He no longer trusted his own judgment. He was unfit to use the title of laird or attempt to lead his small family.

His father would be ashamed of him, but then again his father hadn't seen what Fallon had done with the god raging inside him. Fallon had slaughtered animals, destroyed anything in his path. God's blood, he had attacked his own brothers!

Thank God they were also immortal, or he would have their deaths on his conscience as well.

CHAPTER SEVEN

Cara rolled over and stretched. She had slept deeply, never waking, as she usually did, from nightmares involving creatures with eerie shrieks and her parents' screams.

She opened her eyes to see the first rays of dawn pouring through the window to fill her chamber. It surprised her to find all the candles blown out and the embers of the fire barely visible. Yet she was warm.

Lucan.

In a blink, the events of the previous day played in her mind, from her near fatal fall, to the attack, to the shared memories between her and Lucan. He had held her, reassured her, when she would have fallen apart. His sleek, hard body had cradled her, awakening a desire, a craving, to touch and caress him. To learn the man beneath the clothes. She ducked her head, embarrassed by her thoughts, but despite the shame, the thoughts didn't go away. Instead, her mind grew bolder.

His mouth had been close to hers. Had she but

tilted her head, she could have brushed her lips against his. Warmth spread through her as she imagined what it would be like to kiss Lucan MacLeod. He was a warrior, a Highlander with raw sexuality that would have made even Sister Abigail have such impure thoughts.

Cara sat up and saw an indentation on the bed. She leaned forward and smoothed her hand over the blankets. There was still a bit of warmth there and a hint of sandalwood, which meant Lucan had stayed with her all night.

Just knowing what he was—what was inside him—should have frightened her. But he had saved her, protected her from the very things that tried to take her from him. She shouldn't trust him, but she found that she did.

She threw off the covers and spotted her shoes and stockings near the hearth. With a smile, she hurried to dress. It wasn't until she was descending the stairs to the hall that she wondered if the dead bodies were still there.

With her hand on the stone wall beside her, she slowed her steps and glanced around the great hall. There wasn't a dead body or spot of blood to be found. Everything was just as it had been before the attack. Even Fallon lying on the bench at the table, an arm draped over his eyes. After Lucan's tale, she understood why Fallon drank as he did.

Quinn strode into the hall and to the table, his light brown hair ruffled from the wind. Her heart broke for Quinn. After three hundred years he still hadn't gotten over the loss of his wife and son.

Cara took the final steps down the stairs and

looked toward the hearth. Somehow she had known Lucan would be there. He stood with his back to the fire, his gaze on her.

Just looking at him sent a little thrill running through her, making her impossibly aware of him. She found herself walking toward the hearth and didn't stop until she stood in front of him.

"Good morn." His voice was deep and rich, sliding over her as his gaze did.

"Good morn. I found my shoes," she said, and lifted the hem of her gown to show him.

One side of his mouth lifted in a grin. "I thought you might need them. And your stockings."

Cara glanced at the fire as she felt her body heat under his gaze. "You stayed with me all night."

He nodded.

"Thank you. I haven't slept that well in a very long time."

"My pleasure." He motioned to the table. "Are you hungry? We don't have much."

She followed him to the table. Fallon had sat up, his eyes bleary as he ran his hands through his hair. Quinn slid onto the bench beside Fallon while Lucan sat next to her.

Though she tried to ignore the stares of the three brothers, it was impossible to do so. Finally, she put her hands in her lap and said, "Thank you, all of you, for saving me last night."

Fallon lowered his gaze from hers. "The Warrior nearly got away with you."

"But he didn't," she said.

Beneath the table, Lucan's hand closed over hers. She looked at him, amazed at how her heart sped up with just a touch from him.

"Lucan told us of your tale," Quinn said between

bites. "You don't remember what clan you belonged to?"

She shook her head. "I wish I did, but I don't know if that makes a difference."

"It does," Lucan said. "Remember how I told you there were a number of clans who had the god inside them? Your clan might be one."

"I thought you said you dinna know what clans were involved, and I cannot see how my mother's blood can help."

Fallon coughed into his hand. "The Warrior said he had come for you and the Demon's Kiss."

"I think the Demon's Kiss is my mother's necklace," she said, and pulled the vial from beneath her gown. She refused to take it off, so she leaned forward so that Fallon and Quinn could look at it.

When they were done, she sat back and ran her fingers over the cool metal of the vial. The memory that had nagged at her while she told her tale to Lucan had come to her in her dreams. "I heard my mother call it Demon's Kiss only once, late at night when she thought I was asleep. Da had told her then there was something coming for her. I hadn't remembered that until last night."

Lucan's thumb moved back and forth over her knuckles. "Did your father say what was coming?"

"Nay."

"And you never heard them talk of magic or Druids?" Fallon asked.

Cara shook her head.

Quinn pushed his empty trencher away and drummed his fingers on the table. "Why does Deirdre want Cara and the necklace?"

"Deirdre?" Cara repeated. "Surely it cannot be the same Deirdre who awakened the god."

"Believe me, it is," Fallon said, hate dripping from every word. "She may not have a god inside her, but she is immortal thanks to her knowledge of black magic."

Cara found what little appetite she had, had vanished. She hoped to never meet this Deirdre who had destroyed the MacLeod clan, the brothers, and now Cara's people. Too late she remembered the village. "I want to see the village."

Lucan's stroking of her hand paused. "I don't know if that's a good idea. We haven't had a chance to bury the dead."

"I need to see it." She looked into his green eyes and saw worry there. "Please, Lucan."

The brothers exchanged a glance. Lucan let out a sigh and gave a quick jerk of his head. "Only if you promise not to wander off. We stay together."

"Are you expecting those . . . things . . . to attack again so soon?"

Quinn snorted. "There's no doubt the wyrran will attack again. They want you and that vial, not to mention Deirdre will do anything to get us back under her control. She'll most certainly send her pets back for another attack."

"With more Warriors," Fallon added.

Cara turned her gaze to Lucan. His jaw was clenched, a muscle working in his cheek.

After a moment of silence, Quinn rose and leaned a foot on the bench. "If Cara is going to stay, and it looks like she is, she needs to know how to defend herself."

"She doesna stand a chance against a Warrior." Fallon sent a glance at Quinn that said he didn't think Quinn was thinking straight.

Lucan, still holding her hand, leaned his other

elbow on the table. "Quinn has a point. I don't want Cara in another situation like she was in last night. Deirdre's wyrrans aren't immortal, and they're small enough Cara should be able to hold her own against them."

Fallon sighed heavily and rose from the table. "I suppose I'll see if I can find her a weapon."

Cara didn't know whether to be glad they were going to show her how to protect herself or worried that they were going to show her how to protect herself.

When Fallon and Quinn moved away from the table Cara grasped Lucan's arm. "Can't I just hide like before?" she whispered.

His smile was tender as he looked at her. "If I thought that would keep you safe, aye. The Warriors were able to find you despite me putting you deep in the dungeons. That Warrior said he smelled you, which means he smelled the magic. Hiding will do you no good."

"Wonderful," she said, and briefly closed her eyes.

Lucan rose and held out his hand for her. "Everything will be all right. Trust me, Cara."

"I do," she said before she even realized the words passed her lips. She put her hand in his and let him pull her from the bench.

His eyes darkened when her body brushed his. She found it difficult to take a breath being so close to him, and even though she knew she should put some distance between them, she couldn't.

Cara forgot to breathe when his hand cupped her face, his fingers sliding in her hair and teasing the skin at her neck. Tremors of delight, of anticipation, raced over her skin.

She tried to remind herself she was going to take

the vows of a nun, but never feeling Lucan's touch again seemed a sin in itself.

"I'm supposed to protect you," Lucan murmured.

Cara rested her hands on his muscular chest and nodded. "You do."

"Then who protects you from me?"

Before she could begin to understand what he meant, his mouth covered hers. His lips were firm, insistent, as they moved over hers seeking, devouring. She was powerless to pull away as she sank under his spell, her desire flaring to life like dry wood on a fire.

She clung to him, her hands fisting in his tunic as he pulled her against him. A moan tore from her throat at the feel of his hard body and his arousal that pushed against her stomach.

He slanted his mouth over hers, while he held her head with one hand and gripped her hip with the other. He groaned when his tongue slipped through her parted lips to mate with hers. He kissed with a skill that left her breathless. And wanting more.

A delicious heat spread from between her legs and settled in her stomach. Her breasts felt heavy, her nipples aching and hard.

When he ended the kiss, Cara opened her eyes to find her arms wrapped around his neck, her fingers in his thick locks. She hadn't even realized she had risen up on her toes.

"My God," Lucan murmured.

Cara couldn't agree more. Her gaze rose to find his eyes hooded, the desire there for her to see, to feel. She tried to swallow, but her body wasn't her own. Her gown was confining, her skin too tight. The emotions inside her left her feeling confused . . . and wanting. Needy.

Somehow she managed to step away from Lucan,

to loosen her hold on his tunic. It was with much re-
luctance that she let her hands fall from his chest.
The absence of his heat was instant, the loss of his
hard body against hers immediate.

What would the nuns think of her if they knew
she longed to rub her body against his, to feel the
rigid length of his arousal, to have him lie atop her
with nothing but their skin touching?

Cara turned to face the door, anything to bring
her heated emotions back under control. To her mor-
tification, Fallon held open the door, watching them.

"Stay with us," Lucan said as he guided her toward the door.

Lucan, his hand on her elbow, helped her down
the slick steps of the castle to the bailey where Quinn
awaited them.

"Fallon?" Quinn called.

Cara paused beside Lucan and turned to see the
eldest MacLeod brother standing in the doorway of
the castle.

Lucan's brow furrowed and he took a step toward
his brother. "What is it, Fallon?"

"I've not left the castle. In over two hundred years
I've not left the castle." When he raised his gaze to
them, Cara saw the panic and desperation.

Lucan bounded up the steps and pulled Fallon out
of the castle. "There's no one left. It will be fine."

"I need my wine."

Fallon tried to return to the castle, but Lucan
stopped him. "Nay, you don't."

A moment later Quinn was on the other side of
Fallon. "Come, Brother. I've ventured out plenty of
times, and no one saw me. Well, no one besides Angus," he said with a grin.

Before Cara realized just how much Angus had

known of the brothers, she was halted by Quinn's smile. It transformed him. Gone was any trace of the god, and in his place was a handsome man with teasing green eyes and brown hair streaked with gold.

She watched the three brothers, wondering how many hearts they broke before their clan had been killed and they were turned immortal. All three were incredibly good-looking, but it was Lucan with his sea green eyes and secret smile that made her heart miss a beat.

Lucan and Quinn got Fallon down the steps and out of the bailey. He stopped after they walked under the gatehouse and turned to look at the castle.

"God's bones. I'm amazed it's still standing," Fallon said.

Lucan chuckled. "Our ancestors built it. Of course it's still standing. Not even Deirdre's army could topple it."

His comment brought a smile to Fallon's lips. With a nod, the eldest brother turned toward the village. Cara hadn't missed the sparkle in his eyes. She couldn't imagine staying confined to one place for days, much less centuries.

She liked watching the brothers interact. Even Quinn had softened, his rage almost forgotten. Cara smiled as Quinn punched Lucan in the shoulder over some comment, their laughter blowing on the breeze as they walked to the village.

Lucan looked over his shoulder at her, his smile gone. She frowned, wondering if he was upset because she had lagged behind. All she had wanted to do was give the brothers some time alone.

Then she saw the smoke.

The three men stopped and waited for her. Lucan threaded his fingers with her. "Are you sure?"

Nay. "Aye."

"There isn't much to see," Quinn said.

Cara didn't pull away when Lucan tugged her beside him. At the sight of the first dead body she knew she was going to need his strength.

Fallon glanced at her. "Why do you need to see this death?"

"I want to make sure they didn't leave someone alive, or someone that needs help."

"They didn't." Fallon stalked away.

Cara looked at Lucan. "How does he know?"

"Quinn came last night to check."

Words eluded Cara as her gaze fell on person after person lying dead. It was like a bad dream she waited to wake from. People she had talked with, laughed with, were forever gone.

She couldn't stop the tears when they came to the nunnery and she saw the nuns lying dead atop the children. The poor Sisters had done their best to shield the children, but not even the nuns' prayers helped them.

Cara's gaze caught sight of bright red hair. She hurried toward it, ignoring Lucan's call. The sight of little Mary's pale face brought another rush of tears. Cara didn't glance up when Lucan knelt beside her.

"I was collecting the mushrooms for Mary. She had a fever and Sister Abigail was mixing some herbs for her."

Lucan didn't say anything. He stayed beside her, giving her the time she needed to say farewell. When she started to rise, he was there to help her.

"Do we bury them?" she asked.

"Nay," Quinn said from the doorway, his emotions guarded. "There's too many."

Fallon walked into the nunnery and shook his head. "If this hasn't already gotten back to the MacClure laird, it will soon. We need to leave everything as it is."

"I agree," Lucan said. "The fewer people that know of us the better."

Cara didn't want to leave her people lying out to rot, but the brothers were right. They couldn't be found out. If anyone learned what the brothers were, they would be hunted mercilessly.

"Let's gather what we can," Fallon said. "Any food or weapons you find bring to the castle."

Lucan stopped her when she would have followed Quinn and Fallon. "Is there another gown you would like to get?"

She glanced down at herself. She was sure Quinn wanted her out of his wife's gown. "I doona have another."

"We'll find you one."

Cara nodded and walked behind him, numb and grieving, as he piled weapons and gowns in her outstretched arms. She blinked through more tears. The trek back through the village was worse than when she first saw it. The rain had washed most of the blood away, but her stomach turned when she saw a puddle filled with red.

"Don't look," Lucan warned.

"First my parents. Now the village," she said through her tears. Anger and guilt consumed her and settled like a stone in her stomach. She had done this to the village. Had the wyrran found her, the village might have been left unharmed. "How many more people have to die for me? You? Your brothers?"

Lucan turned to her, his eyes warm and steady. "We're immortal, Cara."

"But you can be hurt," she argued. "You might not die, but you feel pain, aye?"

"Aye," he answered with a small nod. "But our wounds heal quickly."

"So much death. Maybe it would be better if I went to Deirdre." She didn't want the burden of more deaths on her shoulders. Already her parents' murders were too much to bear. Now Cara had the entire village on her conscience.

Lucan grabbed her shoulders and gave her a little shake. "Don't say that. Don't *ever* say that."

"You don't know what plans Deirdre has for me."

Fallon snorted as he walked past them. "Nay, Cara, but they cannot be good, whatever they are. Deirdre is pure evil. And if she's hunting something, she wants it dead in the end."

Lucan glanced at his brother. "Fallon is right. If Deirdre gets ahold of you, it's over, Cara. Our best course is to find out what your mother's blood means to her, and why she would want it so desperately."

"More important, why wait until now to find Cara?" Fallon called over his shoulder as he walked out of the village.

Cara's head spun as she thought of the times she had felt someone watching her but could never see anyone. How the Demon's Kiss would warm and vibrate on certain occasions. All of which had begun at the equinox. Was it a coincidence?

She looked away from Lucan's penetrating gaze and gasped when she spotted Angus. She rushed to him. He sat on the ground, leaning against his cottage with his head lolling to the side as if he were asleep.

"He warned me about getting near the castle," she said to Lucan as he moved to stand behind her. "He knew about you, didn't he?"

"He did."

Emotion welled in her throat. Angus blurred in her vision as the tears filled her eyes. He had cautioned her to stay away, not because he feared the brothers but because he had wanted to keep them safe, keep them from discovery.

"He was a good man," Quinn said from beside her.

Cara jerked her head to him, startled. Quinn had been at the castle not a moment ago, but then she remembered Lucan had told her one of their powers was speed.

She glanced at Lucan behind her. "Angus was a good man. He was always ready with a smile, always willing to help. He was one of the few who weren't afraid to talk to me when I was brought to the nunnery."

Quinn nodded, his brown hair blowing in the wind. "The first time I saw Angus he was a small lad of five or six. It was night and I was prowling as I'm wont to do. He never screamed or ran away in fear, not even when he saw what I really was. Instead, he started leaving food at the gatehouse. It dinna take him long after that to approach me. He helped get us anything we needed, and he guarded our secret well."

Cara stared at Angus, his white fluff of hair lying over his eyes. Lucan laid his hand on her shoulder, his strength and comfort pouring into her with such a simple gesture.

With one last look at the people she had come to call her own, she turned toward the castle. It was time to face the future.

CHAPTER EIGHT

Deirdre ran her hands along the cool rocks of her home deep inside Cairn Toul mountain. Most Druids could hear the call of the plants and trees, but for her, she heard the stones. It was the beautiful, wild call of Cairn Toul that had brought her to the mountain.

The cave had been hidden, but the stones had told her how to gain entry. And once she had, she had seen the wondrous glory of the mountain. Her mountain.

She had spent the first six months exploring the deep, endless caves and tunnels, marking them to memory. The upper part of the mountain she took as her domain, transforming it into a palace worthy of a queen. The middle part was used as her great hall where the mountain opened up into a stunning cavern. The lower part with all its caves and tunnels was perfect for her dungeon, which she had put to use almost immediately with the MacLeod brothers.

It was too bad she no longer held them. With all her power in black magic and her Warriors, somehow the MacLeods managed to keep from being taken again. The brothers were to have been the most powerful, most persuasive, weapon in her army. And she would have them again. It was only a matter of time.

She left the stones and walked to the middle of her chamber where a bench waited for her before a small table with a mirror hung in the stones. The bench was a favorite of hers with its scrolled arms and lovely Celtic knot work carved into the wood.

Deirdre pulled her long white hair over one shoulder and sat. Only then did she release her hair to fall down her back and puddle on the floor. Her hair was her crowing glory. It had once been a marvelous golden color, but each time she dabbled in the black magic her color had faded, until all that was left was hair as white as snow.

She had gotten used to it. Her eyes, however, were a different matter. Men at one time had commented on the vivid blue of her eyes, but just as with her hair, there was only a hint of the blue that had once been. Her eyes startled everyone, and she found she quite liked it.

Her head cocked to the side and looked into the mirror as a wyrran came up behind her and used its claws to delicately comb her hair.

"Aye, my lovely," Deirdre said. "Just what I wanted."

She had made the wyrran out of necessity, but once she learned how devoted they were to her, she used it to her advantage. They were her children. At least until she had all the Warriors under her control.

Which brought her back to the MacLeods. If they ever suspected the truth, her tenuous hold would disappear. It was only fear of what she could do that held the MacLeods in check.

She was a powerful *drough*. She had been the one to unbind the gods, hadn't she? But there was more power to be had. Always there was more power.

The innocent girl from the MacClures would help to bring about that power, and once Deirdre had it the MacLeods wouldn't be able to withstand her call. They, and the other Warriors, would be hers to control. Forever.

The wyrran peered over her shoulder, its round yellow eyes blinking up at her. It snarled, letting her know someone was coming.

"I heard him, my lovely," she whispered to the wyrran. "Leave us."

There was a hard knock on her door, followed by a muffled, "Mistress?"

"Enter," she called.

She looked through the large oval mirror to find a Warrior, his royal blue skin signaling him as the holder of Ameren, the god of haunting.

"William," she said, and rose to face her Warrior. She glanced behind him but didn't see Caladh with his ash-colored skin, nor the form of a girl. Annoyance spiked through Deirdre, but she controlled it. "You are empty-handed?"

William bowed his head for a moment. "I am, mistress."

"How could a slip of a girl get away from a dozen wyrran and two Warriors?" She kept her voice even as she used her magic to call on her weapon.

The ends of her hair that scraped her ankles when she stood lifted and flew at William to wrap around his balls.

"She had help." William's voice shook, his hands clutching Deirdre's hair to try to stop the stranglehold.

Deirdre raised a brow. "Help? Who would dare to step in and help her?"

"The MacLeods."

Surprise and excitement coursed through her. She eased her grip on William's balls and used her hair to stroke his cock. Just as she expected, he hardened and lengthened through his breeches.

"The MacLeods?" she repeated. "Are you sure?"

He nodded and licked his lips, his hands now caressing her hair. "Aye. I fought Quinn, then Lucan. I saw Fallon as well. There's no mistake, mistress. It was the brothers."

"At the village?"

"In their castle."

Deirdre laughed. Of all the places. When they had first escaped her mountain, she had sent wyrran to MacLeod Castle to intercept the brothers, because where else would a Highlander go than back to his clan?

Yet the brothers hadn't returned to their castle straightaway and had managed to continue to thwart her. And they fought against her. It didn't bode well if the MacLeods had her little female. Deirdre needed Cara—more than she wanted to admit.

William's stroking of her hair grew bolder. She eyed him as she looked at the bulge between his legs. It had been a while since she had taken a Warrior to her bed, though there was only one Warrior she really wanted, one Warrior who would give her the children she needed to carry on her kingdom. Until she had him back in her control again, she would take her pleasure where she could.

"Take off your clothes, William."

He obeyed without question. Deirdre released him until he stood before her in all his royal blue glory. Her hair encircled his cock and she heard him moan.

"Were the MacLeods defending Cara?"

William's eyes were closed, his breathing ragged. "Aye, mistress. Caladh smelled her magic in the dungeons and went after her."

"You left him?"

"He's a Warrior. Unlike the MacLeods he welcomed his god and the powers that came with him. Caladh is stronger than they are."

Not if the three brothers fought as one, but she didn't tell William that. She would wait a day for Caladh to return with Cara, if he escaped the MacLeods.

"I need my army, William," she said as she walked to him and ran her hands over his thickly muscled chest.

He opened his eyes and nodded. "I know."

"Will you lead them for me? Will you bring me Cara and the MacLeods?"

"Aye."

She smiled and cupped his balls, rolling them in her hands. She brushed his rod with the back of her hand. "You are very hard."

"I want you, mistress."

"Do you?"

"Aye."

She stepped back with her arms out to her sides and her hair hanging to the floor. "Then take me."

William grabbed the neck of her black gown with his hands and with one yank ripped it from her body. She smiled when he gathered her up in his arms and strode to her bed across the room.

Desire made her breasts swell and her nipples harden while her sex grew damp. It had been years

since William had shared her bed. She had forgotten
how rough he could be, but she was looking forward
to it.

He tossed her onto the bed. Deirdre laughed and
opened her arms as he fell on top of her.

"No foreplay, William. I need you. Now."

He guided the tip of his cock to her entrance and
plunged inside her. She moaned and closed her eyes
as she pictured her Warrior thrusting inside her instead of William.

It wouldn't be long now. She would have him
back where he belonged.

The return to the castle was in silence. Lucan had
known bringing Cara to the village was a mistake,
but she had said she needed to see it. He had seen the
look of guilt in her gaze as she stared at the dead.
Nay, she would have been better not seeing the village.

Fallon sorted the weapons, looking for several to
arm Cara with. Lucan had already found her a sword,
which he sharpened before the fire.

He glanced at Cara, who sat next to him altering
a gown. She hadn't said a word since arriving from
the village. He was acutely—and painfully—aware
of her nearness. Even being the few feet apart that
they were, he felt every breath, heard every beat of
her heart.

Lucan wanted to pull her into his arms, to taste
her lips again. His body throbbed from the all-too-
brief kiss. He closed his eyes as he remembered the
way her body had swayed against his, how her nails
had scraped his scalp as she threaded her fingers in
his hair.

But most of all, he recalled her little sigh of pleasure.

He should never have kissed her, never have given in to the temptation to touch her, but it had been too much. Now that he had a taste of her, he wanted more. Needed more. It was all he could think about.

In the middle of a village with the dead lying around him, all he wanted to do was have Cara's soft body against his again, her slender arms wrapped around his neck while his fingers learned every contour of her skin.

Lucan drew in a ragged breath and shifted in the chair to ease the ache of his cock. His balls tightened when Cara licked her lips and glanced at him. He barely held back his moan.

He had thought having a god inside him was torture. It was nothing compared to the hunger for the stunning woman beside him. With her in his life, in his home, he was in a different kind of hell. A hell that was altogether worse than anything he could ever have imagined.

Because you've never wanted anything so desperately before.

That was the truth. There had been women in his clan who had caught his eye. Once he had set out to have a woman, he charmed her until she was his.

Cara, however, was different. She wasn't some simple lass. She was embroiled in the middle of a magical war, pitting Warriors against Warriors, with the most evil of beings trying to capture her.

Instead of hiding in the corner with her hands over her ears while she screamed in denial, she sat beside him sewing as if her world hadn't been turned upside down.

The problem was Lucan could see her in his life.

He could imagine pulling her close at night and waking with her in the morning. He could imagine sitting before the hearth after supper and talking of the future.

And he would pursue Cara diligently. If he weren't a monster. As it was, he had nothing to offer her.

Lucan moved the sharpening stone over the sword's blade several times in quick succession. He put all his focus on the weapon, ignoring the cravings of his body and Cara's soft flesh. Over and over he moved the stone along the sword. He tested the blade against his skin. The barest touch of the weapon caused blood to well on the tip of his finger.

"Immortal or not, be careful."

He looked at Cara to find her watching him, the needle paused in her fingers. "I willna die from a wound."

She lowered her hands to her lap, the altering forgotten. "Are you saying you cannot die at all?"

"Nay. We can die."

"How?"

"Beheading."

Her eyes widened. "How do you know this?"

Lucan lifted the sword's blade straight up in the air. He inspected the weapon for a moment before he reached for a cloth and cleaned the sword. "I know because Deirdre told us. We were daft with anger and fear, but I heard that part of her speech."

"Did she say more?"

"Aye."

"And you didn't listen?" Cara's voice had risen with every word, her face incredulous.

Lucan bit back a grin. He didn't think she would appreciate him laughing at her outrage. "I tried. I heard that part of it at least."

"There may have been something else of importance."

"Maybe. Maybe not. Regardless, it doesn't matter."

Her brow furrowed and her lips flattened as she turned her head to the flames.

"What is it?" he asked.

Cara's dark gaze met his. "How did Deirdre know where I was?"

"I wish I knew. Could someone in the village have told her?"

"It's a possibility, but I don't think so. I've told no one how my parents died, and no one knows where I came from. How would any of them have known I was the one Deirdre wanted?"

"Good question," Quinn said as he strode up. "One I've been mulling over."

Lucan raised his brows. "Did you find the answer?"

"Nay, but it got me thinking. How did Deirdre know about us? How did she know we were the ones with the god inside us?"

Lucan squeezed his eyes shut and cursed. "We've kept ourselves separate from the world, but in doing so I believe we let opportunities for knowledge pass us by."

Fallon snorted as he moved unsteadily from the table to the hearth, a bottle of wine in his hand. "That's horse shite, and you know it. Deirdre knows all of this because of her use of black magic."

"If that was the case," Lucan said, "she would have imprisoned us again."

Quinn shifted from one foot to the other. "I doona think it's her magic that led Deirdre to Cara, though I do believe magic was involved."

"That makes no sense," Cara said, and returned to her sewing.

Lucan had to agree with her. "Explain, Quinn."

"We all know that Deirdre is powerful, but how powerful? What if her magic has limits? As Fallon said, if Deirdre was that powerful, she could have captured us again."

Fallon's eyes narrowed. "Meaning she isn't all-powerful as she led us to believe?"

"Exactly."

Lucan shook his head. "I saw for myself the power Deirdre had. Even with the gods inside us, we cannot defeat her. Neither of you could have forgotten her show of power when she took us."

There was a pause, and Lucan knew his brothers were reliving the moment Deirdre had called up the black magic and the sheer force that had surrounded her. Her power had only grown in the three hundred years.

"What if she wasn't able to find Cara until now because something changed?" Quinn asked.

Lucan set aside the sword and crossed his arms over his chest. Once Quinn had spoken, he couldn't help but wonder if his little brother was right. "Cara, did anything dramatic happen lately?"

She lifted a dark brow but didn't raise her gaze from her sewing. "Not unless you consider me pledging myself to God and the nuns significant."

Lucan could only gape at her. "You were going to become a nun?"

"Aye," she replied, and bent her head closer to the fabric in her hands.

No other explanation, no reason. She was a beautiful woman who, he had no doubt, had men lusting after her. "Why?"

She blew out a breath and raised her gaze to him. "Because of what killed my parents. Because the only place I felt safe at night was in the nunnery. I wasn't a MacClure. I wasn't part of their clan. I *needed* to belong somewhere."

Her voice broke at the end and Lucan found he wanted to go to her, to draw her into his arms and shoulder her worries for her.

Lucan found it hard to breathe. Her mahogany gaze held such a wealth of regret and trepidation and resolve that he wanted to be the man who could change her life. He wanted her to turn to him when she was in need. He wanted her to want him with the same primal passion that burned his veins.

He forced his gaze away before he did something foolish like taking her in his arms again. His hunger for her was so fierce, so intoxicating, that he had to grip the arms of his chair to keep from reaching out to her.

When he found Fallon staring at him with a knowing look, Lucan knew he hadn't kept his desire a secret. He was relatively sure Fallon had witnessed the kiss that morning.

Lucan could only imagine what his elder brother would say to him. Fallon would argue that there was no place for Cara in their lives. And he would be correct.

Fallon would argue that Cara was mortal and they were immortal. Again he would be correct.

Fallon would argue that if Lucan ever lost control of the god, he could very well kill Cara. Correct, again.

But for all the arguments, Lucan couldn't stop the hunger inside him. He was like a starved man around Cara, and she the feast.

"We all need to belong somewhere," Fallon said to break the growing silence. "We're all just surprised that a woman of your beauty would choose to be a nun."

Lucan bit his tongue to keep from lashing out at his brother for calling Cara beautiful. She was beauty personified, but the fact that Fallon had noticed—and commented—told Lucan Fallon might be as affected by the same hunger that ate at him.

And there was no way Lucan was going to share Cara with anyone—even his brother.

Fallon rolled his eyes, as if he could read Lucan's mind. *Easy, Brother*, he mouthed.

Lucan glanced at Cara, but she was once more staring at her sewing. Quinn stood with his shoulder propped against the hearth, his face twisting in anger with each heartbeat.

"There has to be something!" Quinn bellowed to Cara. "Don't just sit there as if you don't care that a woman more evil than Satan himself is after you."

Lucan rose and put himself between Quinn and Cara. His nails extended into claws and he let his eyes turn black. It had been a long time since they had fought, but Lucan wasn't going to let Quinn take his anger out on Cara.

A soft hand touched his shoulder. "It's all right," Cara said. "Quinn is right."

Lucan glared at Quinn, daring him to make a move toward her.

"Did last night make you recall what it was like to let the god out?" Quinn taunted Lucan. "If you're looking for a fight, look no farther."

Fallon slammed the palm of his hand against the stones. "Enough!" he bellowed. "Quinn, control your anger. Lucan, get ahold of your . . . self."

Lucan knew he had been about to say "feelings." Grateful that Fallon hadn't let Cara know how much she affected Lucan, he gave a small nod.

When Lucan turned around, Cara stood in front of him. "Has anything happened recently?" he asked her.

"It is my eighteenth year." She paused and licked her lips. "But I think it might be the spring equinox."

Lucan jerked. He looked at Fallon first, then Quinn, to find his brothers were as shaken as he. Had hiding away in the castle, refusing to live in the world, thereby forgetting everything about it, helped them to erase the fact that their clan was destroyed on the spring equinox?

"What is it?" Cara asked. "Why do all three of you go pale?"

Lucan sank back into his chair. "Because the spring equinox was the day our clan was killed."

"Butchered," Quinn corrected.

Fallon ran a hand down his face. "How could we have forgotten?"

"I don't think it's mere coincidence," Lucan said. "Deirdre must be using the equinox to strengthen her black magic. Somehow, it's directing her to the people she seeks."

Quinn pushed away from the hearth to pace. "Shite. This isna good."

"How many of there are you now?" Cara asked. "You said there were two Warriors here last night. Does she have more?"

Lucan shrugged. "I do remember her telling us we were the first."

"She's had over three hundred years," Fallon said. "I can only guess at the number she has gathered."

Quinn snorted derisively. "And they'll be attacking us."

Cara shook out the gown she had been altering. "Surely some of them refused as you three did."

"Possibly," Lucan admitted. "I couldn't begin to know where to look to find them, though."

"Do you know any of the families of the original Warriors?"

"Nay," Fallon answered. "Neither did Deirdre. It was something she searched for. She had hoped we would be able to tell her a few names, but of course we couldn't. We didn't know anything."

Quinn stalked out of the great hall. "I'm going to check around the castle," he called over his shoulder.

"I don't believe they'll attack tonight," Lucan said. "I suspect Deirdre will spend a day or two gathering her forces to descend upon us. She wants Cara, but she'll also try to take us three as well."

Cara's dark eyes fastened on him. "What do we do until then?"

He reached for the sword he had found for her. "Until then, you learn how to wield a blade."

"In a day?" she asked with a startled laugh. "I'll be lucky to be able to point it at anything."

Lucan grinned. "I'll make sure you do more than point it. Ready to begin your training?"

"Let me change first. Quinn will be relieved to see me out of his wife's gown."

Lucan watched her race up the stairs, her skirts lifted high enough that he caught a glimpse of her ankle. He swallowed back a moan when his gaze landed on her hips as they swayed gently with each step she took.

"Be careful," Fallon said.

Lucan looked at his brother. "About what?"

Fallon gave him a bored look. "Don't play dense with me, Lucan. I saw you kiss her this morning."

"It was just a kiss." Lucan hoped saying the words out loud would make them true.

"It was more than a kiss. I saw the way you've looked at her since the moment you brought her into the castle. Just remember what we are. We aren't meant for women like her. We aren't meant for anyone."

Lucan didn't want to believe, but he knew Fallon spoke the truth. "She trusts me. Do you know how long it's been since a woman has looked at me? Since I've held a woman in my arms, felt her hair in my fingers? Can you even recall the sweet smell of a woman, the soft skin of her neck behind her ear, or the way a woman moans when she peaks?"

"Nay," Fallon bit out. "I don't remember any of those things, and it's better that way. It doesn't do anyone any good to want something they cannot have."

"We all want something we cannot have, Fallon. The object is different for everyone, whether they are Warriors or mortals."

Fallon's face was lined with weariness and fatigue. "She's a good woman, Lucan. A mortal who will die while we live on. Don't promise her something you canna give her."

And that was the crux of the matter. Lucan wanted to promise her anything and everything. Just so long as she stayed with him always.

CHAPTER NINE

Lucan waited in the bailey for Cara. The sun was high in the cloudless sky, the wind brisk from the sea. It had been days like this that he had ridden his favorite steed from the castle and raced over the land, the ground flying beneath his mount's hooves.

How innocent Lucan had been then, thinking of the next girl he would tup and wondering what ruse he would play on Quinn. The days had seemed endless, Lucan's future stretched before him like the stars in the night sky.

He caught a whiff of heather and swung around to find Cara watching him, her gaze pensive, as if she had known his thoughts. She smiled shyly and walked down the castle steps to stand before him.

"You were deep in thought."

Lucan shrugged. "Just remembering my life before, when things had been simpler."

"Did you have a good life?"

"Oh, aye. I did."

"I can imagine your mother had her hands full with three boys."

He looked to the battlements near the gatehouse where his mother used to stand, waiting for her husband and sons to return. "She was an amazing woman."

Lucan blinked and held out the sword hilt first. "Ready to begin your lessons?"

"I'm not sure," she said as she slowly grasped the pommel of the sword.

The weapon was small, the blade several inches shorter than a man's sword, but it was balanced and handled well. It was most likely made for a young lad, which would serve Cara flawlessly. She wouldn't be able to swing a man's sword, but she had a good chance with the one Lucan had found.

"You want to grip your weapon tight, but not too tight," he said, and demonstrated. Once she held the sword properly he said, "Now swing it around you; learn the weight of it, how it moves through the air. You need to trust your sword, let it become an extension of your arm."

She was a quick learner and readily did as he instructed. He saw her hesitation, though, as she was uncertain of her own abilities.

"Good," he said with a nod. "Can you feel the difference in the sword at different angles?"

She nodded, gazing at the blade. "Aye, I do. The force of the sword when I swing down is immense."

"Exactly. If you have the advantage over your opponent, a swing down will leave him cleaved in two. The only problem is that you can leave yourself vulnerable when you raise your sword over your head."

"I understand wanting to arm me against mortal men, but I believe it's pointless against other Warriors like you and Deirdre's wyrann."

"It isn't," Lucan said. "Deirdre's pets can be killed. They are small like a child and they are quick, but they can easily be outsmarted."

"I can do that."

He grinned at her words. "You willna be fighting Highlanders with swords. You'll be fighting nasty wee creatures that have foul breath and a scream that can make your ears bleed. Keep them at a distance with your sword. Here, let me show you."

Lucan moved behind her and grabbed each of her arms in his hands. His chest fit against her back, his throbbing rod into her soft backside. He wanted to caress down her arms and cup her breasts as he leaned against her, her soft sighs filling the air.

He battled against the hunger that roared to life at the contact of her body against his and tried to focus on the task at hand. Anything other than tossing her onto the ground and throwing up her skirts so he could see her body. Desire surged through him, centering in his cock that hardened to painful degrees. When she shifted her feet and rubbed against his arousal, he couldn't stop the groan of need.

"I'm sorry," she said. "I don't know what I'm doing."

"You're fine," he said between clenched teeth. All he wanted to do was turn her around and pull her into his arms, to feel her breasts against him, to hear her soft moans of pleasure as he slid his tongue inside her mouth and sampled her once again. He could take an eternity learning her body and giving her the pleasure he could only dream about, only to do it all over again.

"Lucan?"

Her voice pulled him out of his daydream. He shook his head to clear it, but the lust refused to diminish. "You're fine, Cara."

She looked over her shoulder to him, her mouth breaths from his. Her eyes widened a fraction, her lips parting. It would be so easy, so simple, to lean down and run his mouth over hers.

"They will come at you from behind," Fallon's voice rang out in the bailey.

Lucan jerked his gaze to the castle steps to find his brother watching him. Fallon's gaze held no censure, but Lucan knew what his brother thought of his uncontrollable hunger for Cara. He didn't know whether to hit Fallon for interrupting or thank him.

Fallon walked down the steps toward them. "Deirdre's pets like to sneak up on their prey."

Cara licked her lips and looked from Lucan to Fallon. "So what do I do?"

Fallon raised his hands and curled his fingers. "The wyrran use their claws. Their arms are long but not long enough to reach you if you hold them at bay with your sword."

"Their toenails are as long as their claws," Lucan added. "They like to jump on their prey, using their feet to anchor them, then biting and clawing their victims to death."

"Oh," Cara mumbled.

"The trick is to put your back to a corner so they cannot sneak up behind you."

Fallon nodded. "But be careful; they can climb walls."

Cara wasn't sure why the brothers were adamant about her learning to use a sword. By the sounds of it, she didn't stand a chance against Deirdre's "pets."

"Relax against me," Lucan said in her ear.

A shiver raced down her spine at his warm breath against her skin. She found it impossible to think with his hard, hot body against her. It made her recall his kiss, the way his hands had caressed her, and the delightful sensations that swam through her anytime he was near.

"Relax," Fallon said. "Let Lucan teach you the movements."

She gave her arms up to Lucan, watching as he moved them in deft circles, always keeping the blade of the sword in front of her.

When he nudged her legs wider with his knee, she blindly obeyed, too caught up in the emotions swirling within her, and the heat of her blood that centered between her legs.

She jerked when something was placed in her left hand. Fallon gave a nod of his head. That's when she saw the dagger.

"You'll need that as well," he said. "Don't ever lose your blades, Cara. Ever."

For the first time since she had met Fallon, his dark green eyes seemed almost clear of the wine. Almost.

"Remember how I told you to hold the sword?" Lucan asked. "Treat any other weapon the same way. Firm, but loose."

It made no sense to her, but these were men who grew up by the sword. If anyone knew what they spoke about, it was the MacLeod brothers.

She sucked in a breath when Lucan lifted her leg with his knee and lunged forward. At the same time, he thrust the sword out, the tip touching Fallon's chest, just over his heart.

Lucan nodded, his chin scraping the side of her face. "Good. Let me show you more."

Again and again Lucan would lunge her one way or the other, bringing her arms up to shield her from make-believe attacks from Fallon. Lucan pivoted her, he turned her, he backed her away, but always he had her weapons in front of her.

"Try it by yourself," Lucan said as he moved to step in front of her.

Cara instantly missed his heat. The wind from the sea buffeted her, dragging into her eyes strands of her hair that had pulled free from her braid.

She widened her stance and bent her knees. The sword was lifted, waiting, as was the dagger. It was Lucan who came at her this time. She tried to lunge away from him, but he was quick and she ended up spinning away instead.

"A good first try," Fallon said as he sat on the steps and lifted the wine to his lips. "Watch his eyes, not his arms."

"How will I know how he'll attack if I don't watch his arms?" she asked.

Lucan grinned. "Watch my eyes."

She thought the brothers were enjoying themselves entirely too much at her expense. She was a woman who had never held a weapon in her life. With skirts that hampered her movement. But she was determined to succeed. They were taking the time to teach her, and she would learn.

"Ready?" Lucan asked.

Cara stared into his eyes and nodded. For the longest time he simply stood there, watching her. There was the slightest movement of his gaze just before he stepped toward her. She spun away from him and lunged, the point of her dagger landing at his side between his ribs.

"I'm impressed."

The compliment gave her the encouragement she needed. Lucan and Fallon took turns attacking her. The faster she became, the quicker they moved.

They helped her find her weak spots and correct them.

"Your advantage is your quickness," Lucan said. "Use it to your benefit. If you find yourself fighting a Warrior, he will try to overpower you. Keep out of his reach and attack as often as you can."

"Bloody him," Fallon added. "Continue to bloody him for as long as you can."

Cara nodded. "What of your powers?"

Lucan shrugged. "I could prepare you for what we have, but each Warrior is different. Still, I suppose it could help you learn what to expect."

Her arms had begun to ache from keeping them lifted and moving in ways she never had before. But it felt good to be included in something, to have people take an interest in her.

"Aren't you going to . . . change?" she asked.

Lucan shook his head, his wavy obsidian locks lifting from his neck in the breeze. "Not yet."

"You think it'll frighten me."

"I know it will."

She was scared of what he would become, but she also knew he wouldn't hurt her. All three of the brothers had had ample time to harm her. Yet they were teaching her to protect herself against their kind.

Nay, Lucan wouldn't hurt her.

"I need to learn," she argued.

"You are."

Before she could react, he charged her. Cara tried to pivot away, but he grabbed her around the waist. The contact of his body against hers made her forget about defending herself. Then she looked into his sea green eyes and became lost.

Her breath locked in her lungs, her heart raced in

her chest. The desire that drowned out everything was too much. She tried to step away and only succeeded in pushing the point of her dagger into his arm.

"By the saints," she gasped.

Lucan's strong arms held her immobile, her skirts tangling in his legs. "It's all right, Cara."

She shook her head and dropped her weapons, but it didn't stop the blood from welling up and rolling down his arm. "I've hurt you."

"I'll be all right."

"Nay." She tripped over his feet as she made to move away, sending both of them to the ground.

Cara screeched, but before she could land on the ground Lucan had turned her so that he braced her fall. As soon as they landed, he rolled her onto her back.

"Are you hurt?" His beautiful eyes searched her face, concern furrowing his brow.

Cara saw his lips move, knew he was talking to her, but she couldn't hear anything other than the blood rushing in her ears at having him atop her. She had never known the weight of a man could be so . . . thrilling. Her hands had gripped his shoulders as she began to fall. Unable to help herself, she threaded her fingers in the silky thickness of his hair.

Her desire must have been written on her face, because his eyes darkened and his gaze fastened on her lips.

Aye. Kiss me again. Give me the promise of paradise I tasted earlier.

His head lowered, his lips grazing her chin. Just as he was about to claim her lips, a voice interrupted them.

"Lucan, is she all right?" Fallon asked.

Cara met Lucan's gaze.

"Are you hurt?" Lucan asked.

She shook her head, unable to form a coherent thought, much less speak. Her body wasn't her own whenever Lucan touched her. She wanted things, desired things she couldn't put a name to. She knew Lucan could ease the building torment inside her. His kisses, his touch . . . his heat.

"She's fine," Lucan said, his gaze never leaving hers. After another heartbeat he rose to his feet and helped her to stand.

Her fingers went to the wound she had given him. The blood was still there, but through the hole in his tunic she saw the skin had already mended.

"I told you we heal fast," he said with a lopsided smile.

Her stomach flipped when she saw the desire in his eyes. He had been about to kiss her. What would have happened if they weren't interrupted?

More important, was she brave enough to find out?

She knew she was. The feelings she had for Lucan were intense and overwhelming. For most of her life she had hidden herself away from everyone and everything, but with Lucan she wanted to experience it all. And God help her, she was ever so grateful she hadn't taken the vows of a nun yet. The idea of being a nun was laughable now that she had experienced such passion.

"It's past noon," Fallon said. "Let's go inside and eat. I'm sure Cara could use the rest."

She didn't think she could eat, not when her body throbbed with such alluring torment. And all because Lucan had lain atop her.

"Cara?" Lucan whispered as they made their way into the castle. "Did I hurt you?"

She smiled into his eyes. "Not in the least."

His hand rested on her lower back, guiding her into the great hall. His touch was comforting, and growing more so by the hour. In such a short time he had filled her senses so completely that all she could think about was Lucan.

He glanced at her, his expression unreadable. She preferred it when his desire was evident. Did he regret it now? He was immortal after all. His life could go on forever while her life would be gone in a blink. It would have been enough a week ago to send her running to hide, but not now. Mayhap not ever again.

Once more when they sat to eat, Lucan took the place beside her. She didn't miss the exchange of looks between Fallon and Lucan or the undercurrent of hostility from Quinn.

Despite the charged atmosphere, she was content beside Lucan. Without him, she wouldn't have dared to eat with Quinn and Fallon. She had hoped changing out of Elspeth's gown would help Quinn, but it only seemed to make him more livid.

As for Fallon, she wasn't sure why he kept staring at Lucan, his eyes narrowed and his jaw clenched. And the angrier he became, the more he drank.

"Cold roasted fowl again?" Fallon grimaced.

Quinn shrugged and plopped into his seat. "You should have eaten it all yesterday if you wanted something else today."

"It wasna that great yesterday."

"Then you should cook instead of holding on to the damned bottle of wine," Quinn snapped before he sank his teeth into the meat.

Cara watched the exchange with interest. "Who hunts?" she asked.

"Quinn," Lucan answered.

It seemed each of the brothers had a chore to do, though she wasn't quite sure what Fallon's was. "I can cook. I'm only passing fair, though," she offered.

Lucan grinned at her while Quinn gave a jerk of his head. "Fine with me," Quinn answered.

"You don't have to," Lucan said.

She shrugged and pulled a bite of meat apart. "I need to do something."

Fallon set his bottle on the table after a long drink. "Anything is better than Quinn's cooking."

"At least I don't see two of everything," Quinn snarled.

Cara focused on her meal. Only moments later Quinn rose from the table and strode from the great hall without a word to anyone.

She chanced to raise her eyes and found Fallon staring at her. Anger no longer creased his eyes and hardened his lips. Before the killing of his clan, Fallon had been about to be married. He had lost his home, his family, his clan, and his future wife all in one day.

"Did you love her?" Cara asked before she could think better of it.

Fallon shrugged, as if he had known what she would ask. "I barely knew my intended bride. We had met only once before she journeyed here. It was an advantageous marriage between two powerful clans."

"So your happiness meant nothing?"

Lucan pushed his trencher away and leaned his forearms on the table. "As eldest, Fallon was expected to make the clan stronger."

"I realize that," she said. "Did you even like her?" she asked Fallon.

Fallon gave a halfhearted grin. "She was pretty enough with her fair hair, but she was shy and quiet. I don't know how she would have fared in the MacLeod clan."

Cara looked at her hands as he spoke. "Quinn married for love?"

"Aye," Lucan agreed. "They were both very young when they wed. They had been inseparable as children, and when they got older, it was obvious they would marry."

Cara turned her head to Lucan. "And you? Did you have someone you loved?"

"Besides my family? Nay. There was no woman for me."

"Not for lack of them trying," Fallon said with a chuckle. "I've never seen women fall over themselves as they did for Lucan."

Lucan raised his brows and smiled. "Now wait a moment, Brother. I seem to recall you had your fair share of women as well."

Fallon laughed a full, robust laugh that caught even him off guard. "At least we never had to fight over a woman."

"Thank the saints for that," Lucan replied with a wide smile.

His eyes danced with merriment, and Cara had to wonder when was the last time the brothers had laughed.

Fallon's smile died. "I miss having a woman warm my bed." His gaze became distant, as if he lost himself in a memory.

Cara winced as she saw the stark loneliness in

Fallon's eyes. She had seen the same in Quinn's. But Lucan, his had only shown desire and concern.

"Your god was bound once. Maybe he can be bound again," she said to Lucan.

He shrugged. "We tried. For years we tried to find a way."

"But it was hopeless," Fallon said.

Lucan glanced at his brother. "The only person who knows how is Deirdre, and she's not about to tell us."

"Not when she wants to use us in her army," Fallon added.

Cara wasn't ready to give up. "There has to be a way. Just as I'm sure there are other Warriors like you, hiding from Deirdre, there has to be someone who can bind the gods."

Lucan scratched his jaw as he considered her words. "You may be right, but if there was someone who knew how, I can guarantee Deirdre has found them and killed them."

"The Druids were a large part of the Celtic life. Just as the Celts have never gone away," she said, and glanced at his torc, "the Druids haven't, either."

"They won't show their faces," Fallon said. "The Druids would be persecuted as soon as it was discovered who they were."

Cara stopped short of rolling her eyes. For such brawny warriors, they didn't think half the time. "Have you, or have you not, been hiding in this ruin of a castle for over two hundred years next to a village that never knew you were here?"

Fallon sighed. "Point taken."

She looked at Lucan. "A Druid could be a practicing Christian but still believe in the old ways."

"Say you're right," Lucan said. "How would we begin to look for them? It's not as if we have the time to travel over Scotland stopping at every village or cottage we come across."

"I haven't thought that far ahead."

"It's not a bad idea," Fallon said after a moment. "I just don't see how we could carry through with any of it."

"We could leave the castle," Cara said.

"To go where?" Lucan asked. "We have nowhere else to go."

"Why stay here?" she argued. "You said yourself Deirdre would attack again. We could leave and seek out other Warriors and see what we can discover about the Druids."

Fallon rose to his feet and reached for his bottle of wine. "It is a good plan, Cara, but I'm not leaving my home. This castle is all I have left. If I leave it, I'm afraid I'll come back to find the MacClures or some other clan has decided they want it. I couldna stop them from taking our lands, but I refuse to give up the castle."

She watched Fallon walk from the hall and out the castle doors.

"He's been outside more today than he has the last hundred years," Lucan murmured.

Cara sighed. "Only because I'm sitting in the place he usually occupies."

"Our lives got disrupted, and I think that's a good thing. For too long we've huddled in the castle, pretending we didn't exist. We fought Warriors and wyrran, but we should have been living. Learning the world that has changed so much."

"We all know the attack is coming. To stay here and wait to be outnumbered seems folly to me."

Lucan lifted one side of his mouth in a grin. "There is no place any of us could go. They know your scent now. The Warriors will hunt you unto the ends of the earth if they have to."

Cara shuddered at the thought.

CHAPTER TEN

Cara rose from the wooden tub and reached for the drying cloth. It had been a surprise to find the tub in her chamber filled with steaming hot water. She knew without a doubt Lucan had brought the tub and lugged the water up the stairs.

She hadn't realized how tired her body would be after the training she'd had that morning, but the bath had done wonders for her sore muscles.

After luncheon, the rest of the day had flown by with Lucan showing her places to hide and various ways to get out of the castle. She doubted if she would remember them all, but he had said it was important.

She was so weary she couldn't remember eating supper, but she did recall it was another quiet affair. The only comment from Fallon was about the fish Quinn had caught being better than the fowl. She had gone into the kitchen to cook, but Quinn already had everything done. Since her body ached so, she didn't complain. At least at the meal Quinn spoke, though he had nothing to say other than the castle was secure.

Cara shook her head at that. There was no way

three brothers, even immortal and powerful, could defend a ruined castle this size alone.

She touched the silver vial that hung between her breasts. She had taken it off only once since her mother had put it around her neck. What was so important about her mother's blood that Deirdre wanted it?

Cara tried to remember the night her parents were killed, tried to recall if her mother had said anything else to her. Cara had been crying and unwilling to be put in the hole under the cottage. Her mother had been speaking the entire time, but Cara couldn't remember a word she had said.

Cara dropped the drying cloth and reached for the nightgown she had taken from the village. She had just slipped it over her head and let the hem fall to the floor when she heard Lucan call out her name.

Part of her wondered what she would have done had he walked in when she was naked. The other part of her was glad he hadn't because she would have made a fool out of herself, she was sure.

"Aye," she answered. "I'm here."

He moved from the shadows, his shoulders filling the doorway. "Do you feel better?" His voice was lower than normal, gruff, and filled with emotion. And God help her, it excited her.

"I do."

He shifted to put his face in shadow, hiding his eyes from her. Cara took a step toward him and moved closer to the hearth at the same time.

"We're taking turns throughout the night keeping watch," he said.

"Even though you don't believe they'll attack tonight."

"Anything is possible, and it's better to be safe."

She licked her lips and pleated her skirt with her fingers. The longer the silence stretched between them, the more aware of him she was. He stood still as stone, and even in the darkness she knew he watched her.

"Say something," she begged.

"What?"

"Anything."

In two strides he was before her, desire blazing in his eyes. Cara took a step back, startled at the intensity. He followed her. Her heart skidded in her chest; excitement and a little bit of fear swam through her. She took another step back, and just as she expected, he tracked her.

Her breath came quick, her chest rising and falling rapidly as she waited. A heartbeat later, his arms snaked around her, yanking her against his rock-hard chest.

"Are you a witch, Cara?" He nuzzled her neck, the vibrations of his voice making her shiver.

"N . . . nay."

"You've bewitched me. I can think of nothing but you."

His gaze met hers before he lowered his head and took her mouth. He nibbled and licked her lips, molding her body against his as he did. Her arms wound around his neck. She loved the feel of his hard muscles moving beneath her hands.

She rose up on her toes and parted her lips when he sought entry. He moaned, a primitive male sound, when their tongues touched.

Cara melted against him, all her fears and worries gone, replaced by passion and pleasure. He pushed her against the wall, his body never breaking contact with hers. The kiss deepened, grew until her skin felt as if it were on fire.

Lucan clutched Cara against him, reveling in the feel of her soft curves. All day he had longed to kiss her again, to see if he could feel another jolt as he had at their first kiss. He hadn't been wrong. The jolt was there, and stronger.

But he hadn't intended to kiss her again. He had come to tell her he was taking first watch, but when he glanced inside the chamber and saw her naked beside the tub, he had lost all control.

In the darkness of the corridor he had gathered the shadows around him and watched her dry off, and had nearly cried out when she covered her spectacular curves with the plain white gown. Until she stood before the fire and he saw through the material.

He had grown so hard that it was painful. Walking away hadn't been a consideration. Having her, however, was.

Lucan groaned when her plump breasts pressed against his chest. His hunger consumed him, urged him to take more of her, taste more of her. He ground his cock against her and heard her soft moan of pleasure.

He cupped her breasts, loving the delicious weight of the orbs and how they filled his hands. He ran his thumb over her nipple, circling it until the tiny nub was hard and straining.

Cara whimpered into his mouth, her kiss turning desperate as her body writhed against him. He kissed down the slender column of her throat and continued to tease her nipple. Her hands plunged into his hair, holding his head.

"Lucan," she murmured.

The sound of his name on her lips burned him. It had been an eternity since a woman had said his name with passion and longing.

His hands moved to her hips, holding her as he rubbed his aching rod into the soft swell of her stomach. He clutched her buttocks and brought her against him, fitting her sex against his. Her startled gasp turned into a low moan.

The need to bury himself inside her hot, slick sex consumed him, drove him. He brought her leg up, holding it just behind her knee, and continued to thrust against her. Her soft moans had turned to mewling sounds, her hot breath on his neck as he lifted her higher.

He bent and closed his mouth around one pert nipple, licking it through the material of her gown. She whispered his name, her body shaking with a need she didn't understand. But Lucan did. He knew the seductive pleasure that awaited them, and he couldn't wait to have her bared before him, her body open to him in all her glory.

His orgasm was so close, and he had gone without for so long, that he would spill his seed if he didn't enter her now or leave. Cara was untouched. Of that he was sure. He couldn't make her first time wild and painful, and that's exactly what it would be, since he couldn't get ahold of himself.

"Don't stop," she whispered. "Don't ever stop."

Lucan groaned and moved his mouth to her other nipple, biting down on the little peak. She cried out, her body jerking against his.

His control was about to snap. The god inside him grew unruly, demanding release from the lust that pounded through Lucan. He could feel his skin changing, his claws and teeth lengthening. Out of the corner of his eye he saw the shadows moving toward him, the darkness closing around him as his powers surged.

He jerked away from Cara and stumbled backward. She grabbed hold of the wall to keep standing and looked at him with confused, passion-filled mahogany eyes.

"Lucan? Did I do something wrong?"

God's blood! "Nay, Cara. Never."

"Then why did you stop?"

"Because if I didna, I was going to take you."

She licked her kiss-swollen lips, making his balls tighten. "I . . . I want you to take me."

He clenched his hands into fists. "Not like this. It's been too long for me. I can't control the hunger I have for you, and I would hurt you."

"Nay, you wouldn't."

Her faith in him humbled him. But he knew he would hurt her in his craze to fill her. He was grateful to see the shadows and darkness had receded. Fallon had been right. Cara deserved a good man, a mortal man. Not one filled with Apodatoo—a primeval god of revenge.

"Get some sleep," Lucan said, and backed into the shadows of the corridor. "I will protect you."

When he was concealed in the shadows, he watched her as he had done earlier. The anguish in her eyes made him feel like the monster he was. When she locked her arms around herself and rocked back and forth, it nearly brought Lucan to his knees.

He had been the one to bring out her passion. And he had left her in a state of agony, her body unused to the feelings bubbling within her.

Lucan knew he should go back in and bring her to climax, but he didn't trust himself. He was still too close to the edge himself. Instead, he watched until she calmed enough to light every candle in the chamber and crawl into bed.

His bed.

He dropped his head back against the stones and silently cursed. He wanted her in his bed, to feel her legs wrap around him as he buried himself so deep inside her that he touched her womb. He wanted to hear her scream his name as she peaked, to feel her body clench around him and drain him dry as he spilled his seed inside her.

When he was in control enough to look at her without ripping the gown from her, he opened his eyes to find her breathing had evened into sleep.

Only then did he leave her.

Quinn stood in the bailey and flexed his shoulders, his body tensing as he held himself in check. Night had descended over the land, the moon just a sliver among the twinkling stars. He needed to prowl, to run the Highlands as he normally did on nights when he couldn't face himself.

He would run, the wind stinging his eyes, as he gave in to his primal urges and forgot the man he was.

The man I used to be.

He cursed Deirdre and her wyrran who had taken away his life and his family. Elspeth had been pure and sweet, shy to everyone except him. With him, she had opened up and let him see how much love she had to give. With him, she had shown him a simple life of happiness and harmony.

She had loved him deeply. In her own way. How many nights had he drifted off to sleep with her in his arms only to hear her whisper that she loved him, that he was her everything?

Quinn had never told her he loved her. Elspeth hadn't seemed to expect it or want it. Now he wondered if she had been hoping and waiting for him to say the words or if he had just thought she didn't need them.

The idea that she had suffered, that he hadn't made it before she died, only made the ache inside him burn deeper. After all these years, he still felt the loss of her and his son, a son he would never teach to shoot a bow and arrow, never teach to ride a horse, never teach how to wield a sword.

Resentment blazed through him. He would make Deirdre pay. She would die slowly by his hands for all the heartache she had caused in her thirst for dominance. He would see the life drain from her face, see her blood pool on the ground just as Elspeth's had.

Lucan had taken first watch, and Fallon was inside the castle with his wine. Quinn couldn't stay in the castle as Lucan and Fallon did. There were too many memories around every corner that drove his rage higher each day.

It wouldn't be much longer before the god inside Quinn took over completely. He would be gone. And maybe that wasn't such a bad thing. He had suffered too much, endured too much, to want to go on. Knowing he was immortal only made the days more unbearable.

It was one of the reasons he took such risks. Neither of his brothers said anything because they understood. But they didn't feel the pain as he did. They hadn't lost a wife and a son. They hadn't lost their entire life.

Quinn's head jerked as his ears picked up a sound.

Deer. He reached for his bow and arrow that he kept near the castle door and moved into the shadows.

The brothers didn't hunt often for fear of being seen, but with Angus no longer around to bring them food, hunting was a necessity now.

Quinn smiled. He wouldn't be running the Highlands, but he would be hunting a worthy prey.

———————————

Lucan sat atop a crumbling tower on the left front of the castle. It wasn't the highest tower, but it afforded a good view of the MacClure village. Not to mention, it gave Lucan a vantage point if any more Warriors decided to attack.

They wouldn't, not tonight. But soon.

Lucan shifted on the rocks and spotted a buck near the cliffs. He tensed, wondering if he should get his bow. They were going to need food, and killing a buck with his claws was too messy. Even Quinn, when he hunted, chose to use his bow. It allowed them to keep their bodies active, which was why they continued to train with their swords.

Just as he was about to retrieve his bow, Lucan saw movement in a shadow outside the castle wall. A moment later, Quinn drew back his bow and let an arrow fly, finding the mark in the buck's neck. Quinn was next to the deer before it had collapsed.

Lucan watched his younger brother. He missed the days of laughter and teasing with his brothers. If there was any way to help Quinn with the pain he carried, Lucan would gladly do it. But Quinn never spoke of Elspeth. He never even said his son's name.

Lucan ached for Quinn, just as he ached for Fallon. There was only so much Lucan could do for both, and it wasn't enough. He was losing his brothers, had been losing them for some time now, and he was powerless to stop it. Nothing he did, nothing he said, helped them.

He rubbed his jaw and jerked when he saw a flicker of a flame in the village. A glance toward Quinn told Lucan his brother had also seen something. Quinn jumped over the side of the cliff to the rocks below, the buck flung over his shoulders.

Lucan shifted to his feet, his knees bent and his hands on the stones. Quinn would get safely back in the castle to alert Fallon.

With his ears straining over the roar of the sea, Lucan listened for sounds from the village. He heard the stamp of a horse's hoof, the cough of a man, but how many he didn't know.

Lucan glanced around the castle to make sure there was nothing that would cause the men to come there. When Lucan saw the light from Cara's window he froze. It was far enough back that it would be difficult to see from the village, but not impossible. It was a risk they couldn't take.

Lucan jumped from the edge of the tower to the stairs below. He had always hated the narrow, curving staircase, and now most of the top of the tower crumbling on the stairs made them even more difficult to tread.

He kept his hand on the walls as he raced down the stairs to the corridor. When he stopped at the doorway to his chamber, he prayed Cara was asleep. Her fear of the dark would never let her allow him to extinguish the candles and the fire.

Candle by candle, he snuffed out the flames with his thumb and forefinger until there was only one left. He couldn't help but look at Cara then. She was on her side facing away from him, her curves outlined by the blanket that hugged her body. Her braid fell across the pillow with tendrils of hair curling around her ears and neck.

With the last candle doused, he turned to the fire. Thankfully, all the wood had already burned and only the embers were left. He quickly covered them and strode to the door.

Only to halt midstride when Cara turned over.

CHAPTER ELEVEN

Cara sighed and snuggled beneath the blanket. She had been having a delicious dream where Lucan was in her chamber watching her sleep, his sea green eyes filled with heat, with need . . . with hunger.

She wasn't sure what woke her, but as she turned onto her back and saw the chamber was cloaked in darkness, she flung off the covers. Panic wrapped its iron manacles around her, turning her blood to ice and causing her heart to pound in her chest.

A startled cry passed from her lips when she saw that not even an ember burned in the hearth. For a moment she could only stare at the candles, her eyes filling with tears. The candles didn't burn out and neither had a gust of wind blown them out. Nay, someone had extinguished them.

It was too dark, too still. Anything could be in the chamber. One of the Warriors or even a wyrran. The prospect sent a shiver down her spine. Either she could sit in the bed and wonder or she could light the candles again.

She started to rise from the bed when something heavy and solid landed on top of her, trapping her against the straw mattress. She fought whatever it was, raking her fingernails down his arm, hitting him, and even trying to bite him.

She could hear a voice but couldn't make out the words. And she didn't want to. There was no way the monster on top of her was going to kill her without a fight. She kicked and opened her mouth to scream for Lucan.

Suddenly a hand captured her wrists, jerking them over her head while another hand clamped over her mouth. She stilled, fear clawing at her belly. He leaned close, his breath against her neck. She turned her face away and closed her eyes.

"It's me, Cara. It's Lucan."

She sagged into the bed, relief flooding her. He removed his hand, his fingers brushing her lips in a soft caress. Cara became aware of his body between her legs, his hard arousal against her sex.

"It's too dark," she whispered. "I need the light."

He shook his head, his hair brushing her cheek as it fell on either side of his head. "There is someone at the village. We cannot chance them seeing a light and coming here."

She understood what he said and why he had snuffed out her candles, but she was in the grip of terror and had to have the candles burning. "Please, Lucan. Let me up. I'll light only one candle. I need it."

"Cara—"

"Please," she begged when she heard his firm voice.

"Nay."

"I have to have it." She pulled her arms to try to break out of his grip. He held her firmly without hurting her, but it only infuriated her. "Lucan."

He moved his other hand with the first to hold

her. "Cara. I'm with you. Nothing is going to hurt you."

But she knew firsthand what kind of things lingered in the dark. They were there, she knew it. Only the light would prove that she was safe.

Lucan gritted his teeth when he saw Cara was beyond listening. She wouldn't stay still long enough for him to gather her in his arms and take her from the chamber. She would fight him every step of the way, and he didn't want her hurt. So he did the only thing he could think of to calm her.

He kissed her.

The moment his lips touched hers, his hunger rushed back with a vengeance. It had never gone away, but touching her again, kissing her again, had only doubled his need.

He ran his tongue over her lips seeking entry. Her body was rigid, but she wasn't fighting him any longer. She issued a breathy moan that made his rod throb with need. Her body relaxed, her back arching as she leaned up to deepen the kiss.

Lucan slid his tongue past her lips and groaned when she touched her tongue to his. He was only going to kiss her to quiet her, but he should have known it for the folly that it was.

He deepened the kiss, losing himself in her soft, willing body. Her legs shifted, her feet running along the backs of his legs and bringing his raging cock against her. He could feel her heat, the molten desire that called to him.

His hands loosened their hold on her wrists and intertwined his fingers with hers. The kiss turned frantic, heated. The hunger consumed him, demanding he take her and sink into her moist heat to claim her as his own.

He ground his hips against her, the friction causing him to moan and repeat the movement. Her nails dug into the backs of his hands as she arched her back.

Lucan caressed his hands down her arms to her sides, his fingers grazing the undersides of her breasts. Her hands slid into his hair. He sucked her bottom lip between his teeth and ran his tongue over it. She groaned and set his blood afire.

He pinched her nipple and heard her gasp turn into a moan. He longed to pull the taut bud between his lips and suckle until she writhed against him with a hunger that matched his own.

With his other hand, he caressed down her side to the indent of her waist and over the swell of her hip. When his hand met warm skin, he smiled and slanted his mouth over hers.

In her struggle to be free, her gown had gathered at her hips, exposing her legs and sex to him. Just knowing it was only his clothes that separated them made sweat break out over his skin.

He skimmed his hand over her leg and under her plain white nightgown. The touch of his skin on her hip made his blood, already heated, boil. His thumb grazed the smooth skin between her thigh and the curls that hid her sex.

"Lucan," she murmured between kisses.

He could take her. She wanted him, possibly felt the same hunger as he did. He pushed the hem of her gown higher, rocking his swollen rod against the silky flesh of her sex.

The distinctive whistle he and his brothers had been taught by their father reached him. He knew it was Quinn, and he didn't care. He had Cara in his arms. That's all that mattered.

The whistle sounded again.

Lucan was fast losing control. If he didn't leave Cara now, he wouldn't. He would take her innocence. She might enjoy it now, but once she saw him, really saw him, she would regret her gift and hate him for it. He would rather have a cockstand for eternity than have her disdain.

He jumped off the bed and stepped away from her. His gut twisted when she sat up, watching him with wide eyes.

"What is it?" she asked.

He shook his head. "I don't trust myself with you. I lose all control with just a touch. Besides, Quinn is calling for me."

"But I want you to touch me."

Lucan squeezed his eyes closed. "Don't. Don't say that."

There was a rustle on the bed. He knew without looking she had risen and stood before him.

"Why can't I say what I mean?" Her voice was close, too close.

Lucan opened his eyes and retreated another step. "You don't know me, Cara."

"I do," she said with a sensual smile that made his balls tighten. "You're the man who saved me, the man who protects me, the man who teaches me to fight. And the man who awakens desires I didn't know I had."

"You wouldna be saying those things if you saw the monster that I am."

She hesitated. "I would."

In that instant he knew she never could, no matter how much they both might want it. "Nay."

"You don't know that," she argued.

"Neither do you."

She lifted her chin. "Have some faith in me. You've proven what kind of man you are. I know of the god inside you, and I still want you."

Lucan knew unless she saw the god unleashed, truly saw him for what he was, she would believe they could be together. There was only one thing for him to do, though he was loath to do it, for it would mean she would no longer turn her mahogany eyes to him with trust or desire. There would only be revulsion and hatred.

But it was for the best.

"Are you so sure?" he asked.

"Positive."

Lucan inhaled and released the god. He ran his tongue over his lengthening teeth, flexed his fingers as his claws extended. He didn't need to look down at his arms to know his skin, as well as his eyes, had gone black—he could feel it, the subtle tingle in his skin.

Cara's eyes widened in shock. Her lips parted as if she would speak, but no words came.

"As I thought," Lucan said, and tried to smile. He knew it came off more as a grimace but didn't care. "Stay in your chamber until one of us comes back for you."

It wouldn't be him, but there was no reason to tell her that. He turned and stalked from the chamber, hating himself with every step. He called the darkness around him, welcomed the shadows. She had been a bright speck in his future, and he had just seen it diminish into nothing. But it was for the best.

Wasn't it?

Lucan pushed Cara from his mind—or at least he tried—and hurried out of the castle. When he reached the bailey he found Fallon and Quinn.

"Where have you been?" Quinn asked.

Fallon's knowing gaze found Lucan's. "He was seeing to Cara."

Quinn swore under his breath. "We have people at the village and you want to make sure she's all right?"

The moonlight hit him as a cloud moved in the sky showing he had released the god. Quinn's eyes widened, but Fallon didn't seem surprised.

"That wasn't a good idea," Fallon said.

Lucan didn't care what Fallon thought. "It was for the best."

"What in the name of all that is holy is going on?" Quinn ground out.

"Nothing," Lucan hurried to say when Fallon started to speak. "Who is at the village?"

"The MacClure clan," Quinn answered. "They're going through the cottages now."

"Did you see how many?"

"Of course." Quinn rolled his eyes at the question.

"Well?" Lucan prompted.

"Only ten, but two left as soon as they saw what had happened."

"More will be on the way," Fallon said. "They're going to want answers."

Lucan nodded. "Just as we did. Part of me wants to give them answers."

"They wouldn't believe us."

"I know."

Quinn crossed his arms over his chest. "Right now they're more concerned with burying their dead."

"A good thing, too." Fallon sniffed the air. "The bodies would begin to smell soon."

"I'll go to the village," Lucan said as he started to walk past his brothers.

Quinn stopped Lucan with a hand on his shoulder. "Stay near Cara. You're the one who swore to protect her. I'll go to the village and make sure none of the MacClures try and venture this way."

Lucan watched Quinn leave.

"In three hundred years his anger hasn't faded," Fallon said. "Will it ever?"

"A more important question is how much longer does he have until he cannot control the god at all?"

Fallon shook his head. "You don't seem to have a problem controlling Apodatoo."

The urge to strike out at Fallon, to slam his fist into his brother's face for revenge, overwhelmed Lucan. "Someone had to look after you two. Did I want to be the one who was forced to control it and my rage? Did I want to be the one who shouldered all the responsibility seeing to each of you through the years? Nay. I didn't ask for any of it, but you certainly didn't want the role."

"Lucan," Fallon started.

"You don't get to make these decisions now. You gave up the right to lead us when you turned to the wine. Go back inside. Quinn and I will see to everything."

Lucan turned on his heel and leapt onto the battlements with a single jump. From there, it was easy to leap and climb his way back to the tower where he would keep watch until dawn. There was nothing else for him to do, and he didn't trust himself to go inside the castle.

That's where Cara was.

CHAPTER TWELVE

Cara stared at the space where Lucan had been. Her eyes had adjusted to the darkness, and with the moonlight from the window she had seen all of him. She hadn't been prepared to see him with the god set free, however. It had been frightening and a little . . . exciting.

To see him change like that, right before her eyes, had been startling. His skin had gone from the dark golden tan to black in the space of a blink. She had witnessed his claws before, but when his eyes had gone obsidian and his teeth lengthened, it had proven to her just how dangerous he was.

Dangerous, aye, but she also knew he wouldn't harm her. He had proven it to her in so many different ways.

It also infuriated her because she knew he desired her, but his fear of how she would react to him held him back. Cara had always thought herself pious and innocent, but one kiss from Lucan MacLeod and she was a wanton who thought only of his hands and mouth on her body.

Becoming a nun now was no longer something

she wanted or could do. There was no way she could think of that life, not after sampling the desire that hummed through her blood even now.

That was twice in one night Lucan had brought her body to such a state of need only to leave her. She trembled with it but had no idea how to ease herself. Knowing Lucan was in as much pain did not calm her, though. In fact, it exasperated her even more.

She paced the chamber, her hands clenched into fists as she tried to slow her breathing and cool her heated body. It took longer than she would have liked because she kept thinking of Lucan, of his soul-stirring kisses and caresses that left her breathless.

It was only then that she realized she had been standing in the dark. Alone. Cara jerked to a stop and looked around the chamber.

She sank onto the bed and smiled. It had been a long time since she had faced the dark with such bravery. She wasn't sure if she could do it again, or how much longer she could stay in the chamber without light, but she was amazed that she was there at all.

And she had Lucan to thank for that. He was the one who had tried to tell her it would be all right, that he was there to protect her. She hadn't listened to him, but when he had kissed her all her attention had focused on him, with everything else forgotten.

Warriors could have stormed the castle and she wouldn't have cared. Nothing mattered as long as she was in Lucan's arms. It seemed cruel that she had found some measure of peace and security in the one man who didn't think he was worthy to give it to her.

If anyone could protect her, it was Lucan.

She scooted back against the headboard and pulled the blankets around her. Lucan had told her to stay in the chamber until one of them came back for her. She hoped it was Lucan who came, because she was going to prove to him that she still wanted him—god and all.

The chance never came, however. She stood and readied for the day after she watched the sun break over the horizon. Her eyes were scratchy from lack of sleep and her head ached from thinking about Lucan and what could be lurking in the dark.

She feared for him. She feared for all three brothers, because despite the powerful god inside them, they weren't ready for the coming battle. Oh, Quinn wanted a fight. That much was obvious. But his rage would get the best of him.

Fallon would readily draw his sword and stand by his brothers, but that wasn't what they needed. They needed Fallon to release the god, to become a Warrior.

And Lucan. She sighed. Lucan would try to be all things for everyone because it was what he did. He would want to stand beside Quinn and watch his back as he ran headlong into the battle. Lucan would want to stay by Fallon because he understood why Fallon wouldn't give in to the god. And Lucan would want to stay next to her to protect her.

Any way she looked at it, Lucan would die. He would be unfocused, his mind on too many people to protect himself and battle the Warriors.

Cara might not know a lot, but she understood that these Warriors had accepted the god inside them and knew just how powerful they were.

For over three hundred years the MacLeod brothers had denied what was inside them. Denied it and refused to learn what their limits were. That had to change if they were going to beat Deirdre.

Cara blew out a breath and straightened the bed. Once that chore was completed, there was no reason for her to stay in the chamber. She glanced out the window but saw little of the village.

Cara left the chamber and headed to the kitchen to prepare something to break their fast. She didn't know where the brothers were, but she had to do something. She couldn't sit any longer.

When she reached the kitchen she was surprised to find it clean and neat. There were three fireplaces where meat could be stewed in one of the large cauldrons or spitted. Off to the side she spotted a large buck tethered and awaiting slaughter. Thanks to hunting and the sea that teemed with fish, the MacLeods had plenty of meat.

Cara walked to one of the windows and glanced outside. She could still see where the garden had once been. Weeds had overtaken it. The few pots that stood next to the castle were broken, smashed in the attack on the castle so many years ago.

Her fingers began to tingle and something told her to go to the garden. Cara frowned at the pile of earth. It would take months to clean the garden, and she had other things to do first. She fisted her hands and turned away from the window.

She saw something wrapped on a nearby table and walked to it. She knew before she opened it that it was bread.

Angus had been supplying the brothers with bread and, she suspected, whatever else he could get to them. She thought of the candles she had burned, uncaring of where they had come from. There was no one at the castle to make candles. They had come from the village, she was sure. Now there was no one there to make more once hers were burned out.

Cara winced at her decadence. Sister Abigail had told Cara she needed to think of others more, that she put herself in the forefront too often. When it came to the dark, she didn't have a choice over her fear.

Yet she had sat in the dark for hours. She had been terrified, but Lucan had been with her. He had promised her nothing lurked in the shadows waiting to attack.

It had been the most difficult thing she had done, to sit in the dark, her mind racing with possibilities. But she couldn't put the brothers in jeopardy, either. Lucan would never have blown out her candles had there not been danger. She understood that, and for him she had faced her demons.

She blinked and focused on the kitchen. After a bit of scrounging, she found trenchers and gathered some oatcakes and the last bit of cheese she discovered and set it in the great hall. It wasn't until she returned from the kitchen with a pitcher of water that she saw Fallon standing by the table staring at the food.

"What is it?" she asked. "Were you saving the cheese?"

Fallon shook his head. "It's been a very long time since a woman has served me."

"Sit," she said. "I would bake some bread or make soup for supper, but there are few supplies in the kitchen."

"We got most everything from Angus. He and Quinn had a special relationship."

She glanced at the door hoping to see Lucan. One heartbeat, two, and still no Lucan.

"Cara," Fallon said.

She looked at him and forced a smile. "Will it be just us this morn?"

He stared at her a moment, his dark green eyes taking everything in. "For the moment. Quinn is at the village to see if he can learn anything."

She refused to ask about Lucan, but the question burned inside her. Instead, she handed Fallon an oatcake and filled his goblet with water.

"We used to want for nothing," he said after he took a bite of cheese. "Sheep dotted the hillsides and we fished the sea. My mother cultivated a rich garden full of herbs and flowers. A steady supply of milk, water, and wine was always available for whoever wanted it. I havena had milk in so long I've forgotten the taste."

"You and your brothers have survived when others would have returned to Deirdre."

He shrugged. "Maybe. Lucan is the one who kept us together. Had it been just Quinn and I, we would have gone our separate ways years ago."

"You don't know that. Quinn loves you. You're his only link to his past, and though he may hold much anger, he won't forget that."

Fallon tilted his head to the side. "And what of me, Cara? How do you see me?"

She sat and took a bite of an oatcake and chewed, giving herself time to think. The last thing she wanted to do was anger Fallon, but he had asked. She shrugged as she swallowed the food. "I think you're afraid of the god, afraid of what you might do. I think you want to do the right thing, you want to be there for your brothers as you always have, but you've forgotten how."

Fallon smiled. "How is it you can be here for just a few days and see things so clearly?"

"I don't know." Cara lowered her gaze and turned the oatcake in her fingers.

"What do you see of Lucan?"

She had been afraid Fallon would ask. "Nothing."

"I think you're lying. You see Quinn and me for what we are. I think you see Lucan for what he is as well."

"Lucan is a good man," she said.

"Without a doubt, he's the best."

She raised her gaze to Fallon. "He . . . he fears disappointing or failing either of you. He keeps much hidden in order to keep the three of you together."

Fallon's brow furrowed. "What does he keep hidden?"

"His feelings, his wishes, his desires."

Fallon sighed and reached to the floor where he had set his wine bottle. He lifted it to his lips and drank deeply. "We've made a muck of things, haven't we?"

"You've done the best you could with what you had." Cara rose. She had thought she wanted company, but Fallon dug too deep into her own feelings. "I'm going to walk around."

"Be careful. There are places in the castle that aren't safe."

She nodded. "I will."

Lucan dropped his head back against the stones after Cara left the great hall. He had taken a spot near the ceiling, deep in the shadows where another stairway used to be leading to a different part of the castle that was now rubble.

He hadn't realized Cara had seen all of them for

exactly what they were. Her words had put things into perspective. However, he still didn't trust himself to be alone with her.

Alone? You wouldn't even eat with her and Fallon.

God help him it was true. He would want to sit near her, smell the heather on her skin, but if he did, he would want to touch her. And that he couldn't do. Not ever again.

He glanced down at Fallon to find him watching him.

"You might as well come and eat now," Fallon said.

Lucan shook his head. "I'm going to check on Quinn. Keep an eye on her."

He didn't wait for Fallon to answer; Lucan trusted his brother to keep Cara safe. Lucan jumped to the floor and strode from the great hall. Quinn had been gone too long.

Quinn hid behind one of the cottages and listened to the men talking. Twenty more MacClures had arrived and set about gathering the bodies. They were discussing burying them or burning them. Since there were about fifty bodies, the vote was leaning toward burning.

He heard movement behind him and glanced over his shoulder to see Lucan moving slowly over the grass toward him.

"What are they doing?" Lucan asked.

Quinn shrugged. "Mostly muttering about wanting to find the bastards that did this," he whispered. "I wonder if we looked as they do when we found our clan."

"You mean appalled, angry, shocked, and bitter? Aye, Brother, I'm sure we looked just as they do."

"Deirdre got perverse pleasure out of it."

Lucan snorted. "How something so beautiful could be so evil I'll never understand."

"I've never seen anyone with hair like hers," Quinn said, remembering. "It hung to the floor and was as white as snow."

"Aye. I remember. I also remember her choking me with it."

Quinn grimaced. "I'd forgotten that. It's like her magic can control her hair."

"I know."

Quinn almost grinned at Lucan's dry tone. He hadn't been himself since he'd brought Cara into the castle. Quinn had caught his brother watching Cara, his gaze steady, as if he was trying to memorize every detail. He should tell Lucan not to bother, that it didn't work, but decided to hold his tongue.

"Who is that?" Lucan asked.

Quinn leaned to the side to see who Lucan meant. When Quinn saw the petite woman with hair as black as pitch he shrugged. "She hasna said a word. She arrived with them, yet no one speaks to her and few look in her direction."

"She doesn't look scared."

"She doesn't look comfortable, either," Quinn said. "I'm not sure what her role is."

Lucan gave his chin a jerk. "Is the tall, barrel-chested man the MacClure laird?"

"Aye."

"Maybe she's his wife."

Quinn watched them for a moment. "He makes sure she stays close to him, but he won't touch her.

It's almost as if he's afraid of her. An odd way for a man to treat a wife."

Lucan only grunted in response.

Quinn was used to Lucan's quiet ways. He'd always been the thinker of them, the one who waited and watched and formulated a plan, the one with a steady head, a cool temper. It stood to reason that he would be the one to keep them together as well as master the god inside him.

Quinn had always envied Lucan's control over his emotions. But not even Quinn's calm brother could hide the fact that something disturbed him, and Quinn knew that something had chestnut hair, dark eyes, and waited in the castle.

"What?" Lucan growled when he caught Quinn staring at him.

Quinn shook his head. "Nothing. Who's watching Cara?"

"Fallon."

But Quinn had seen Lucan jerk at the mention of her name. Aye, Cara distressed Lucan, and Quinn found he enjoyed it. It was about time Lucan felt something. For far too long he had kept himself locked inside.

"Fallon will watch her," Lucan said after a moment. "I trust him with that."

"What about when the Warriors come? Deirdre may well come herself."

Lucan sighed and ran a hand down his face. "Fallon won't let the god out."

"We'll be stronger with all three of us. Even you know that."

"I know," Lucan agreed. "But you must understand Fallon's fear."

Quinn pulled his gaze away, his anger rising to

the surface. He felt his claws lengthen, his teeth sharpen. It was always the same fury every time he thought of Fallon refusing to do what could help them most.

As much as Quinn wanted to smash his fist into something, they had to stay quiet as they watched. So he turned his attention, and thoughts, back to the MacClures. "They're going to burn the bodies."

"Aye."

They sat and listened as the MacClure laird drew his men around him. The laird's voice was deep and forceful. Lucan and Quinn didn't have to move from their spot behind the cottages to hear that MacClure was sending his men to question other clans about the death of the village.

"This land is cursed," one man said. "The Mac-Leods were massacred on it. Right there at the castle."

Every eye turned to look at the castle. Even Quinn found his gaze pulled to the ruins of his home. There was no movement in the remains, nothing that would draw the MacClures' interest.

"Calm yourself, Allan," the laird growled. "The land isn't cursed. Don't be spreading lies."

Allan shook his head and took a step back. "It is, laird. Why else would a village on the land that used to be the great MacLeods' die the same way as the MacLeods?"

"We don't know if it's the same. The MacLeod massacre is a legend."

"A legend that begins in truth," the woman said.

Her straight black hair, unbraided and unadorned, lifted in the constant breeze from the sea. She let her gaze travel the circle of men.

"What are you saying, Isla?" the laird demanded.

Quinn nudged Lucan with his hand. "I've seen her before."

"In the village?" Lucan asked.

"Nay. Before, Lucan."

It didn't take long for him to realize Quinn spoke of a time before the god had been unbound.

Lucan's lips thinned. "Where?"

"I cannot remember."

"Are you sure you're not recalling a woman that looked like her? Many women have black hair."

Quinn nodded. He'd caught but a glimpse of her face, but in that moment he had been sure. "Aye, but do many have eyes so pale a blue?"

Lucan's gaze snapped to the woman. He shifted and moved between two of the cottages to get closer.

Quinn hurried to follow him. He couldn't remember where he had seen Isla, but he knew he had. If only he could remember where. And when.

Isla turned her face, devoid of any expression, to the MacClure laird. "I'm saying Allan is correct. The MacLeods were executed here. Just as your people were."

The MacClure laird fisted his hands, and Quinn didn't know if he would hit Isla or not. "Enough."

"To send your men out is foolhardy," Isla continued as though she hadn't heard him. "Keep them close, laird."

Quinn stopped Lucan when he would have gotten closer. Isla turned and walked away from the group of men. She halted midstride and suddenly turned and looked over her shoulder at the castle, and for the first time there was a hint of emotion on her face.

It was hatred.

CHAPTER THIRTEEN

Cara jerked away from the window, her hand at her throat. The raven-haired woman had seen Cara; of that she was sure. A shudder went through Cara, for she was certain the woman held malice in her gaze.

"Cara?"

She jumped at the sound of Fallon's voice.

"What are you doing up here? Lucan will have my head if you harm yourself."

She couldn't tear her gaze from the black-headed woman, her long, straight locks blowing in the wind.

Fallon navigated the broken stones and wood and grasped Cara's arm. "Cara."

"Look, Fallon," she said, and pointed.

He glanced out the window and swore under his breath. "Did she see you?"

"Aye."

"How?"

Cara tore her gaze from the woman. "I don't know. I kept to the shadows. I just wanted to see what was going on at the village. I didn't make a sound, didn't move."

"I believe you. Do you know that woman?"

"I've never seen her before in my life, but there was something . . . familiar about her."

Fallon's dark green eyes narrowed on Cara. "Don't come up here again. You could fall through the boards."

"I was very careful."

Cara turned to look back at the way she had come. It had been much easier crossing the rubble on her way to the window since most of the stones acted as steps of sorts. Then there had been the board that she had walked over. Her gaze had been on the village, so she hadn't noticed the gaping hole the board covered or how far down she would fall if she slipped.

"Lucan is going to rip my head off," Fallon mumbled beneath his breath.

She had been more than confident in her ability to climb over the rocks in her haste to get to the window. Now she wasn't so sure about getting back.

"Is there another way?"

Fallon shook his head. "This is it."

"I see."

"Let me go first so I can make sure everything is stable before you cross."

Cara nodded, not at all ready to walk over the gap. She had never been afraid of heights, but after her fall over the cliff she had a new appreciation for them.

Fallon walked over the thick board, his arms outstretched. If it had been Lucan, he would have jumped over the gap. But Fallon wouldn't let his god free for even that.

There was a loud crack in the silence. Cara froze, her gaze on the wood. Fallon stilled for a heartbeat, then jumped to the other side. He landed in the rocks, his boots sliding in the wreckage toward the hole. His hands gripped stones in the pile as he hastened to stop slipping.

When he righted himself, he checked the board and nodded. "It's secure."

"Is it going to break?"

He licked his lips and held out his hand. "The hole isn't that big. Get to the center, and I can grab your hand and pull you over."

It sounded like a good plan except for the fact that she had to get to the center without the wood breaking. She had faced the dark. She could do this.

She placed one foot on the board. After a deep breath, she put her other foot in front of the first.

"Good," Fallon said, and smiled at her.

"You are really quite handsome when you smile."

He chuckled. "Is that so? Are you saying I should smile more?"

"I'm saying you should attempt it."

"I'll give it a try. Keep coming."

She hadn't realized she had taken several more steps until he said something, but she refused to stop now. Her legs shook, causing her to wobble.

"You're going to make it," Fallon said. "Look at me, Cara. Keep your eyes on me."

She tried, but how would she know her feet weren't staying on the board if she didn't look at it? She glanced down and groaned when her gaze fell on the hole. It was a significant way down. Five levels to be exact.

"Cara," Fallon called.

She lifted her gaze to him. She was nearly to the center. His outstretched hand was almost within her grasp. Just . . . a . . . few . . . more. . . .

She shrieked as the board gave a loud crack before

it split. Cara felt herself falling, saw Fallon's eyes widen. And just as suddenly as she had dropped, she was jerked to a stop. When she looked up into Lucan's sea green eyes, she felt like crying.

"What in the name of all that is holy are you doing?" Lucan ground out.

He lifted her out of the gap and set her on her feet beside him. His arms wrapped around her, holding her close. She clung to him, her entire body shaking.

"That's the second time I rescued you from a fall," he whispered into her hair.

"I didn't mean it," she said, her face in his chest. "I just wanted to see the village."

She heard stones sliding as Fallon moved over to them. "I came to get her," he said.

"And you would have let her die!" Lucan bellowed.

"Nay," Cara said, and put her hand on his chest as she pulled back. "Had I done what Fallon said, I would have been all right."

"Had you done what I said, you would never have been up here," Fallon argued.

She cut him a glare, then looked back at Lucan. "Thank you. Again."

He gave her a curt nod and took her hand. He was tender as he helped her out of the chamber and down the corridor. All the while Fallon grumbled behind them about how the hallway should have been sealed off, but that even the village idiot would have known not to go up there.

Cara was duly chastised, and she was glad to have Lucan touching her again. It was the first she had seen of him all morning. She hadn't realized how much she craved the sight of him until he wasn't with her.

She clung to his hand and followed him to the great hall. But once there, he released her hand and stalked from the castle.

Cara looked behind her to Fallon, who was staring after Lucan as well. The realization that Lucan really didn't want her, that she was just something else he could fix like his brothers, made her throat burn.

"It has been a long time since Lucan has had his life turned upside down," Quinn said from the table. "I quite like this."

"Quinn," Fallon admonished as he walked past her. "Doona pay any heed to Quinn, Cara."

She wrung her hands. Sister Abigail said idle hands were the devil's work. "I need to do something."

Quinn rose and unsheathed a dagger he kept in his boot. He handed it to her hilt first. "I was just about to skin and clean the deer."

Cara took the dagger, grateful that she had something to do. "I'll help."

She and Quinn got to work quickly, and though her hands were busy, her mind wandered. To Lucan. She didn't know much of men, but she had been sure Lucan desired her. It was there in the way he looked at her and in his kisses. At least, she had thought it was. Now she wasn't sure of anything anymore.

Her life was in disarray again, all because of the Demon's Kiss. Her mother's blood. Her blood. What was so important about it? There was no one alive who could tell Cara the truth. She would have to carry her question with her until Deirdre found her.

For Cara had no doubt, despite Lucan's efforts, that Deirdre would take her. To what end, Cara wasn't sure.

Death most likely.

She dropped the dagger and looked at the blood that soaked her hands and forearms. "I need to leave."

Quinn paused on his knees and lifted his face to her, his brow furrowed. "It's just blood. It'll wash away."

"I need to leave. Everywhere I go people die. My parents and now the village. If I stay here, you and your brothers will die as well."

Quinn sat and regarded her. "We're immortal, Cara."

"But you can still die. Lucan told me that."

Quinn's lips twisted wryly. "And I'm sure Lucan told you your safest place is with us."

"You have your own battle with Deirdre. You would still be safe had she not come looking for me."

"Stay here, Cara. You have no idea what's out in the world."

She laughed, the sound brittle to her ears. "I had thought living in the nunnery and giving my life to God would keep me safe from the evil."

"No one is safe. No one. The evil strikes where it will."

She swallowed back tears. "You're right, of course. I'm going to go wash the blood off."

"Follow the path," Quinn said as he pointed out the kitchen doorway. "It'll lead you to the sea."

How he knew she needed a moment alone she didn't know. She gave him a nod and kept her pace slow as she left the kitchen. She didn't want Quinn to know what she planned. Not yet anyway.

The path down to the sea was steep. Many times she had to grab hold of the rocks to keep from sliding as her feet came out from underneath her. It would be a dangerous climb back, but then she had no intentions of returning to the castle.

She had tried to tell Quinn, tried to make him understand. She couldn't stay there. Not any longer. It wasn't just her feelings for Lucan. It was because she didn't want them to die. They had survived so much. They didn't deserve death.

And she knew she couldn't stay around Lucan and see his dismissal of her. It hurt too much.

Cara had never been to this part of the sea. No one had known about the path from the castle since no one went near the ruins, and with the cliffs the villagers had to go a different route when they wanted to fish. Which meant this bay had been kept isolated for three hundred years.

She knelt by the water and washed her hands. Her shoes and hem were soaked by the time she was done, but she didn't care. Her mind was on a way to slip away unnoticed.

Quinn was busy with the deer. Fallon was busy with his wine. And Lucan was most likely watching the village. It was the perfect time for her to disappear.

She stared over the water, watching the waves roll in. The repetitive movement of the water had always soothed her. She took a deep breath and looked around. The cliffs were too high for her to climb, and the rocks that jutted out around the bay would be impossible to cross in her gown. Her only option was to return the way she had come and find some other route on the other side of the castle.

Cara lifted her skirts and started back up the path. She was halfway up and out of breath, her lungs burning, when she spotted another pathway that jutted to the left.

With a glance at the castle, she took it. The trail wasn't near as steep, and it veered away from the castle, taking her along the coast. Cara lifted her skirts to her knees and lengthened her stride until she was running.

The farther away from the MacLeods she was, the better chance they had to live. When the ache in her side became unbearable, she stopped and leaned her hands on her knees. She glanced over her shoulder, amazed she had put so much distance between her and the castle.

Part of her wanted to return, wanted to make Lucan face the attraction between them. But she couldn't. She would rather stay away and have him safe than risk his life.

She looked at the sun. It was almost midday. She needed to hurry if she wanted to get away before dark.

"Farewell, Lucan MacLeod."

With one last, lingering look at the castle she took her skirts in hand and ran.

CHAPTER FOURTEEN

Lucan clenched his hand into a fist and punched the stone wall in the bailey. The stones shattered and crumbled. His hand throbbed, but it only lasted a moment before he began to heal. He looked down at the rocks that fell to his feet and sighed.

His mother would have shaken her head for letting his temper get the better of him. For so many years he had kept his emotions in check. His control had been legendary in his clan. Yet one slender girl had shattered everything.

Lucan hadn't asked for a woman, hadn't wanted a woman.

Liar.

He placed his hands on the walls and let his head hang between his shoulders. So he might have wanted a woman, but he never asked to feel such hunger for one as he did for Cara. His body craved the release found in a woman's willing body. He yearned to hold a woman in his arms and thrust into her wet heat.

With Cara he felt so much more than the physical longing. And with those more complex feelings came hope. Lucan knew all too well there was no hope for him, no salvation for his brothers. They were destined to live as they were—isolated and alone, watching the world from the castle.

And when you canna hide in the castle any longer? What then?

He didn't have any answers; he never had. Returning to their home had been the one thing that kept the brothers together. In many ways, Lucan hadn't wanted to live at the castle. There were too many memories, too much anger and resentment, in the stones to find any measure of peace. Yet it had calmed Quinn to a degree. In that instance, it had been worth it.

Somehow, someway, if they managed to escape Deirdre again, they were going to have to go out into the world and find a place. They couldn't hide any longer. Too much had changed. They were Highlanders, yet they no longer fit in the Highlands.

Cara can teach you.

Lucan squeezed his eyes closed. Cara was never far from his thoughts. He found himself thinking of her constantly. It had been the mere thought of her as he and Quinn had returned from the village that made Lucan search her out. When he had found her and Fallon in one of the crumbling towers, the board breaking under her, Lucan had known a moment of sheer panic.

Time had slowed to a crawl as she screamed and fell. He had been at the doorway, a good twenty strides from her, but he had leapt and grabbed her arm.

He had wanted to shake her and pummel Fallon for letting her fall. Lucan couldn't let Cara out of his sight without her getting into some kind of trouble.

Fallon, however, proved once again that he would rather let someone die than release his god.

Despite Lucan's anger, he couldn't fault Fallon. He had his own problems to deal with, just as they all did. Maybe someday Fallon would be able to face his.

Lucan pushed away from the wall and walked to the blacksmith shop. The last time he had used it was about a decade ago when he had made Fallon a new sword. Since Lucan needed to do something to occupy his mind and his body, he started the fire in the forge and reached for some iron. Cara needed a dagger.

Cara berated herself for leaving the castle without any food or water. She knew the area enough to know there was a stream nearby, but that would mean she would have to follow it instead of striking out across the land.

She had no idea where she was going, only that she wanted to put as much distance between her and the MacLeods as she could.

No food, no water, and no weapons. What about shelter for the night?

She wrapped her arms around herself. In her haste to leave, she had acted rashly and not prepared for a journey. She hadn't thought about the nighttime and being alone in the dark. Without Lucan by her side would the demons haunt her again? The first thing she thought of was a fire, but it would attract unwanted attention.

Cara had veered from the sea about an hour ago. The landscape undulated, rocks cropping up everywhere but giving her no place to hide. There was a forest about two leagues away where many of the village men went to hunt on occasion. That would be her first destination.

She wondered how long it would take before the brothers realized she was gone. Would Lucan come for her? Her heart sped up at the prospect, but in reality she knew the answer was nay. They didn't leave the castle. Especially not for someone who had brought Deirdre upon them.

Cara couldn't wait to meet this woman. Lucan had said she was beautiful, and Cara hated Deirdre for that. The jealousy that raged within Cara was pointless, chiefly because she knew how much Lucan hated Deirdre. But the envy stayed nonetheless.

"Idiot, idiot, idiot," Cara mumbled to herself.

Lucan was drenched in sweat from the exertion of pounding on the steel and the heat from the forge. The shape of the dagger had come along nicely. He lifted the iron in the tongs and inspected it. He had curved the blade, giving it a vicious point at the end of the weapon. The weight was good and light enough for Cara to wield.

He set down the tongs and reached for his tunic he had taken off hours earlier. He wiped the sweat from his face with his tunic and extinguished the forge. When he walked out of the blacksmith shop it was to find it well past midday. Which explained his hunger.

Lucan walked around the bailey to the kitchen and the well-worn path that would take him to the sea. He was surprised to find the gate that led out of the castle wall open but didn't think much of it, since Quinn often went down to the water.

As Lucan made his way down the path, memories arose of him chasing after his father as they ran from the castle before Lucan's mother caught them. The sky had been bright blue that day with occasional white, fluffy clouds that floated past. He and his father had spent the afternoon fishing and lying in the sand. It had been a glorious day.

When Lucan's feet hit the sand he stopped and stared at the rock his father had stood on when he cast the net into the sea. He had seemed a giant then, tall and imposing.

With a shake of his head Lucan pushed aside those memories and removed his boots and trousers before he ran and dove into the sea. The cool water was wonderful against his heated flesh that had stood next to the forge for too long. Yet his muscles felt good and his control was back in place. He would be able to face Cara now and keep a tight rein on his desire.

Once he was cooled, Lucan moved to one of the boulders. He lay back, his skin touching the warm rock. A thread of smoke drifted through the sky from the village where the MacClures had burned the bodies of their clan. Lucan threw an arm over his eyes against the bright sun. He couldn't stay long, but he would take what little time he had to himself.

After half an hour, Lucan rose and pulled on his clothes. When he walked into the castle he found Quinn had butchered the deer and was roasting some meat in one of the ovens. Lucan's mouth watered as his stomach growled.

He grabbed an oatcake and strode into the great hall where, predictably, Fallon lay on the bench, his wine bottle in his hand.

"Where have you been?" Fallon asked through half-open lids.

Lucan slid onto the other bench. "Working."

"On what?"

"Cara needed a dagger that would fit her hand."

Fallon raised himself on his elbows and peered at Lucan over the table. "Is that so?"

"Aye."

After a moment Fallon sat up and rested his forearms on the table. "Are you still angry with me?"

Lucan knew he referred to Cara falling. "Nay. You had gone up there to get her. She needs to know most of the castle isn't safe. One wrong step and she could die."

"I tried to tell her."

He patted Fallon's arm. "She'll learn."

Quinn walked into the hall from the bailey and kicked the door shut behind him. "I suppose you're talking about Cara."

"You don't have to say her name like it sours your stomach," Lucan said.

Quinn twisted his lips in a wry smile. "I don't. She helped me clean the deer. Said she needed something to do."

"That's good. Where is she now?"

"I don't know," Quinn said. "The last time I saw her she was going down to the sea to wash the blood off her hands."

Lucan frowned. "I was just at the beach. She wasn't there."

"That was hours ago."

"Then where is she?"

"Easy, Lucan," Fallon said. "I'm sure she's around somewhere. She has nowhere else to go."

Lucan took a deep breath to calm the prickles of

fear that raced through him. Then he caught a look at Quinn deep in thought. "What is it?"

Quinn's gaze jerked to his. "I didna think anything of it at the time, just thought she was talking as most women do."

"Quinn," Fallon growled.

"She said she needed to get away. That everyone around her died, and she didn't want us to follow the same fate," Quinn said. "I told her that was foolish because we were immortal."

Lucan gripped the table until his knuckles turned white. He heard the wood begin to splinter, but he didn't care. "What did she say after that?"

"Nothing. She went down to the beach."

Lucan jumped from the table and raced up the stairs to Cara's chamber. When he didn't find her in there, he started shouting her name.

A moment later Quinn and Fallon were calling for her as well. After fifteen minutes when they hadn't found her, Lucan knew she was gone. He met his brothers back in the great hall.

"I'm going after her," he declared.

Quinn shook his head. "That's not wise. Deirdre could attack tonight."

"She could. She could also send Warriors. I promised Cara I would protect her."

"She obviously doesn't want your protection if she's left," Fallon said. "Think about that."

Lucan heard his brothers, but he wasn't going to spend time arguing. "I'm going after her. Either you can help me, therefore getting me home faster, or you can hinder me. Your choice."

Fallon and Quinn shared a look before Quinn said, "All right. What do you want us to do?"

"I need to find which way she has gone."

Fallon walked to the castle door. "I don't imagine she'll have gone to the village, but I'll head there to look."

"I'll take the cliffs where you saved her," Quinn said.

Lucan's chest tightened in frustration. "I'll go to the beach and see if I can find anything."

But no matter how hard Lucan searched, he found nothing of Cara. He was climbing the path back to the castle when Quinn and Fallon came into view.

"Nothing?" Lucan asked.

"Nothing," they replied in unison.

Cara couldn't have just disappeared.

"Did she try to swim, you think?" Quinn asked.

Lucan glanced at the water over his shoulder and shook his head. "Nay, I don't think so."

His foot slipped and he grabbed a larger rock that protruded from the ground to hold him. That's when he saw the spot of grass that had been stepped on.

"What did you find?" Quinn asked.

Lucan shrugged and moved the tall grass out of the way. A smile pulled at his lips when he caught sight of more trampled grass.

"This path hasn't been used in a while," Fallon said. "We used to use it to go hunting bird eggs."

"It's also the way Cara went," Lucan said. He looked at his brothers. "We'll be back tonight."

"If she wants to come back."

Lucan glared at Fallon. "She's not thinking straight. Once I talk to her, she'll come back."

Quinn crossed his arms over his chest. "She's not a child, Lucan. She's a grown woman."

"Who needs us. We don't know what Deirdre has planned for her."

"So you want to keep her locked away just as

Deirdre kept us?" Fallon asked. "Think, Lucan. You cannot make her return."

Lucan hated that they were right. He wanted Cara with him, even if having her near was the cruelest torture imaginable. "All right. I just want to find her and make sure she's safe. If she doesn't want to return, I won't make her."

"Do you want me to come with you?" Quinn asked.

"Nay. Stay here in case we're attacked."

Lucan turned away and started down the path at a jog. The urge to run full out, the ground falling behind him, and find Cara was strong. So strong he didn't want his brothers to see it.

But once the castle was out of sight, Lucan stretched his legs into a run. With his heart pounding in his chest and his mind racing with possibilities, he pushed himself harder.

Every once in a while he would stop and track Cara. He knew as soon as she headed away from the coast that she was going to the forest.

There was nothing that was going to stop him from finding her now.

CHAPTER FIFTEEN

Cara stopped to rest against one of the tall pines of the forest. She looked behind her, her gaze scanning the trees. For almost two hours now she had the suspicion something was watching her. And following her.

She tried to stamp down the fear that continued to grow but was helpless against it. Deirdre's wyrran could be tracking her. Her heart thumped in her chest, beating double time when she saw something move in the trees.

The urge to run was strong, but Lucan had told her to stand her ground, to know what she was fighting. If there was a chance to win, she had to get the upper hand.

Upper hand with what, you fool? You have no weapon.

Cara still couldn't believe she had left with nothing. She glanced at her feet and saw a stick that was long enough and thick enough for her to use as a weapon.

She drew her mother's vial from beneath her gown

and wrapped her fingers around it. Prayers tumbled from her lips, but nothing could ease the terror inside her. She tried to recall everything that Lucan had taught her, but one afternoon of training a warrior she did not make.

A twig snapped to her right, and she jerked her head around, the stick raised in her hand. Only there was nothing. She knew her imagination was running away with her, that she was envisioning monsters where there weren't any.

She gasped when she turned back around to find a man standing before her. He had dark hair held back in a queue at his neck. The saffron shirt beneath his kilt of bold green and blue with black was threadbare but clean. His tartan wasn't one she recognized, which meant he wasn't from a neighboring clan.

"Are you lost?"

She started at his deep, rich voice.

"I can help you," he continued. "The forest is easy to become lost in."

She licked her lips. "You've been following me."

"Aye," he answered with a small nod. Blue eyes watched her with patience. "I saw you come into the forest as if you were running from something."

"What clan are you from?"

His gaze dropped from hers for a moment. "Shaw."

There were no Shaws anywhere near them. She didn't know if he had been banished or left his clan on his own, and she wasn't sure she wanted to know which. "I'll be fine. Thank you for your offer."

"You don't look as though you'll be all right, lass. There are many wild creatures in the woods, and that stick in your hands willna keep them at bay."

"I know all about wild creatures," she mumbled.

She would much rather face a boar than one of the Warriors.

He lifted his hands. "I have no weapons, and I mean you no harm. I only want to see you safely out of the forest."

She glanced at the sky. It would be dark soon. And the night brought all kinds of things she wasn't ready to face. Not without Lucan. "Is there somewhere I can stay the night?"

"There is a shelter," he said slowly, his eyes narrowed as if he wasn't sure he should have told her. "I can take you there."

Cara dropped her head back against the tree. She didn't know what to do. Sister Abigail had always told her she was too trusting. The stranger, Shaw, didn't look as if he meant her any harm, but that didn't mean anything.

"You don't trust me." It wasn't a question.

Cara shook her head.

"You are right not to trust," Shaw said. "There are too many . . . things . . . to be wary of."

It was the way he said it that made her take another look at him. In his blue gaze she saw pain and weariness and . . . something else that looked almost familiar.

"What's in the forest?" she asked. She had to know.

He shifted his gaze to the trees over her shoulder. "Nothing too scary."

Cara thought of Lucan and how she wished he were beside her. She felt chilled to her soul and only Lucan's heat could warm her. The only scary things she knew were the wyrrans and Warriors. As long as they weren't in the forest, she would make it.

"Who do you run from?" Shaw asked.

She shrugged. "Myself."

"Ah," he said, and nodded. "I understand."

There was a loud growl to her left. Cara turned her head to see something dark crashing through the trees at an alarming rate. She caught sight of claws and teeth amid what looked like shadows.

Nay!

She turned back to Shaw to find the man vanished and in his place was a Warrior. He faced her threat crashing toward them, his lips peeled back to show his fangs. Cara couldn't take her eyes off his skin, which had turned a dark green that could easily cloak him in the forest.

The brothers had been wondering how to find other Warriors, and she had discovered one by accident. Was he friend or foe? More important, could he beat whatever was about to attack them?

The thought had barely gone through her mind before Shaw crashed backward to the ground, flipping over and over with the force of the other Warrior upon him. Cara turned to run when she saw something gleam gold against the black skin of the attacker's neck.

Lucan.

He straddled Shaw and raised his hand. She winced when his claws slashed Shaw's chest. The other Warrior howled in pain and kicked Lucan in the back, knocking him over Shaw's head.

Both jumped to their feet, circling each other. Around Lucan she saw darkness follow him, as if it waited for his call.

He had said he controlled shadows and darkness.

Cara couldn't let this continue.

"Lucan! Stop. He was helping me," she cried.

Lucan paused and glanced at her. "Are you hurt?"

"Nay."

"Lucan?" Shaw said. "Lucan MacLeod?"

Cara's gaze jerked to Shaw, who stared hard at Lucan.

"Who wants to know?" Lucan asked.

Shaw lowered his arms. In a blink his skin returned to normal, all traces of the Warrior gone. "I'm Galen Shaw. Deirdre unbound my god not long after she found you and your brothers."

Cara took a step toward the men, but Lucan held up a hand to stop her. He kept in his Warrior form, his black skin gleaming in the fading sunlight that filtered through the trees. She was fascinated by the change in him and how easily he wore the dual responsibility.

"All the Warriors I've encountered have tried to force me back to Deirdre," Lucan said.

Galen shook his head. "Word of how you and your brothers escaped Deirdre is what gave many of us the courage we needed to break free ourselves. But that was long ago when she thought fear would keep us in the mountain. She has a different dungeon now, one that no one comes back from."

"You could be lying."

"I could," Galen agreed. "But I'm not. Every Warrior knows of the MacLeods. Every Highlander knows of the MacLeods. You and your brothers are legendary, Lucan. I've been searching for you for over a century."

Lucan stiffened. "You want to be the one to try and take me back to Deirdre's?"

Galen sighed. "Haven't you listened to anything I've said? You and your brothers aren't the only ones fighting Deirdre and her plan for dominance. We need to band together."

"Aye," Cara said. "I agree."

Lucan ignored her, his gaze boring into Galen.

Finally Galen sighed. "Think on it, MacLeod. Deirdre will find you someday."

"She already has," Lucan said.

Galen's body jerked as if he'd been shot with an arrow. "You already fought her?"

"Not yet. She sent her wyrran and a few Warriors looking for . . . something else. They found me instead."

Cara wondered why he didn't tell Galen that Deirdre wanted her.

Galen's blue eyes shone with anticipation. "You killed the Warriors."

"There were two. One got away."

"So Deirdre will be coming for you."

Lucan shrugged. "Probably."

"I can be of service," Galen said. "You'll need all the Warriors you can get."

"My brothers and I didn't survive this long because we trusted people. The answer is nay."

Galen glanced at her. "If you change your mind, you know where to find me."

With that, he disappeared into the forest. Cara released the stick and blew out a breath. Then Lucan turned to her.

"You ran," he said, his jaw clenching in anger. The shadows moved closer to him.

Cara nodded. She had hurt him by leaving. She could see it in his eyes. "I did, Lucan, but only to protect you."

His forehead furrowed. "You didn't run because you fear me?"

"Nay." She walked to him and put her hands on his chest. Warmth enveloped her. "I ran because everyone around me dies. I don't want you to die."

"Look at me, Cara."

"I am."

"Nay!" he shouted. "Look at me. Look at what I am."

She smiled and ran her fingers over his lips, her thumb brushing one of his fangs. "I see you, Lucan. I see the god that gives you immortality and strength beyond my reckoning. I also see the man who has saved me many times and who continues to protect me despite everything. I see the man who desires me, but denies that desire because of what he is."

"Cara."

She ignored his warning and let her hands roam over his chest. She wished his tunic was gone so she could feel his skin beneath her hands. "You came for me."

"I vowed to keep you safe. I just wonder who will keep you safe from me?"

"I don't want to be safe from you," she whispered.

His hands wrapped around her arms and pushed her back against the tree. She sighed in anticipation when his body slammed against hers.

"Walk away, Cara. Please."

"I can't," she murmured. "I want this, Lucan. I've wanted this from the moment I first looked into your eyes."

He closed his eyes. "You doona know what you're saying."

"I do," she argued. It excited her when he was in his Warrior form. He was dangerous and unpredictable. And he was hers.

She rose up on her tiptoes and placed her lips over his. He groaned and slanted his mouth over hers, his tongue slipping between her lips to plunder her mouth with wicked pleasure. His hands gripped her hips as her tongue touched his fangs.

"Ah, God, Cara. What you do to me," he mumbled against her neck as he placed hot, wet kisses on her skin.

She grinned and opened her eyes long enough to see he had returned to normal. He lifted his head, his sea green eyes holding hers.

"Are you sure? I don't think I can stop this time."

She put her hands under his tunic to touch his muscular torso and felt his stomach jump. "I never wanted you to stop before."

There were no more words as he claimed her mouth. His lips were soft, smooth, and firm and his taste heavenly. It was what she had needed, this delicious, alluring taste of him. But she wanted more. She wanted to understand the emotion that unfurled low in her belly and made her sex throb when Lucan touched her.

She pushed his tunic up to reveal more of his sculpted body. He broke the kiss long enough to jerk the tunic over his head and toss it aside. Then his mouth was on hers again, coaxing her passion higher, promising infinite pleasure.

He held her as if he was scared she might run away. She smiled inwardly. She wasn't running anywhere, and there was no way he was this time, either. She would see where their desire took them.

Lucan clutched Cara against him. Her hands caressed his chest, his shoulders, and his neck, all the while she was kissing him with an abandon that drove his hunger higher.

He had fought his need for her and he had lost. She was in his arms, and he was going to relish every moment with her. Her soft moan made his heart pump faster.

"I want to feel you," he said.

She nodded her head with a smile. He took a half step back and helped her to disrobe. He knelt before her and lifted one small foot to remove her shoe before he slowly unrolled her thick woolen hose down her leg. His fingers grazed her skin, marveling at its soft texture.

He looked up as he began to repeat the process on the other leg and saw her hands grip the tree, her eyes closed and her lips parted. Her pulse beat rapidly at her neck, letting him know she enjoyed his touch.

Lucan kissed the top of her foot and set it on the ground. He straightened and jerked off his boots, but when he reached for his breeches, her hands stopped him.

"I want to," she said.

He looked into her dark eyes and saw a hunger that matched his own. Lucan nodded, his balls tightening in excitement. She unlaced his breeches and tugged them over his hips. His cock sprang free, hard and wanting.

There was a soft intake of breath before she wrapped her fingers around him. Lucan dropped his head back and fisted his hands. Her touch was soft and sensual, innocent and erotic. Up and down she moved her hand over his length, learning the feel of him.

"You're so hard and hot, but so smooth."

He thought he would die. He had gone without too long. There was no way he would be able to bring her to climax without spilling, not if she kept touching him.

"No more," he whispered, and looked at her. "It's my turn."

He spread her gown and his tunic on the ground and then held out his hand for her. Cara didn't hesitate in taking his hand and letting him lay her down.

His gaze roamed over her body, perfection in every detail from her full dark-tipped breasts, to her narrow waist and flared hips, to her slender legs.

She lifted her arms for him, wrapping them around his neck. The smile on her lips was all seduction. If he had any thoughts of trying to stop what was between them, he knew she wouldn't let him. The fact that she had seen him, really seen him for the monster he was, and still wanted him boggled his mind.

"Don't make me wait," she whispered. "I've dreamed of this since our first kiss. Show me the passion, Lucan. Show me the promise of pleasure I see in your eyes."

Lucan was humbled beyond words. He cradled her face in his hands and kissed her, running his lips lightly over hers. He wanted to take this slow, since it was her first time. But Cara was having none of that. She licked his lips and moaned. He was lost then. He would give her anything she wanted, no matter the cost.

He sank into her kiss, devouring her taste and her scent. His hands roamed her body as he learned every curve and sensitive spot of her skin. With his rod nestled between her legs, he felt her heat and her moisture. He wanted to plunge inside her, but she wasn't ready. Not yet.

He cupped her breast and massaged it while his

thumb moved back and forth over her nipple. Her nails sank into his back when the little nub turned hard. He leaned down and closed his lips over the nipple. He teased the peak with his teeth, biting gently before he laved the tip and suckled it deep in his mouth.

Her breaths were coming in great gulps, her hips rising against his, seeking the fulfillment she didn't understand yet. Lucan moved to her other breast and repeated his ministrations. She writhed beneath him and murmured his name.

Already Lucan was at his breaking point. He *had* to be inside her. He shifted his hand between their bodies until his fingers parted her dark curls. A smile pulled at his lips when he felt how wet she was.

She jerked when his fingers smoothed over her sex, touching a part of her no one else ever had. Or ever would.

"Lucan," she whispered.

He slipped a finger inside her. God's blood, she was tight. He clenched his jaw to hold back his desire as he prepared her. In and out his finger pumped and soon her hips rocked against him. He moved another finger to join the first. She moaned and arched her back. Her hard nipples gleamed in the afternoon sun, begging him to take them again.

Unable to resist, he suckled a taut peak and moved a third finger inside her. She cried out, the tempo of her hips moving faster.

His rod ached, the need too great. He removed his hand. Cara's eyes flew open to meet his. Excitement flashed in her depths when the head of his cock rubbed against her sensitive sex. He pushed inside her and closed his eyes at the exquisite pleasure.

He pulled out and then sank deeper inside her

heat. When he met her barrier, he withdrew until just the tip of him was inside her. With one thrust, he pressed through her maidenhead.

Her body tensed and she jerked. Lucan stilled to give her body time to adjust to him.

"Is it over?"

A laugh bubbled inside him at her annoyed tone. He looked into her eyes and gave her a kiss. "Not in the least."

"Good."

The need to move, to plunge into her hard and deep, filled him. He held himself in check and began to move with slow, short thrusts. It didn't take long for her body to relax and soft sighs to reach his ears.

"Put your legs around my waist," he said.

As soon as she did, he sank deeper. He couldn't hold back the groan at the feel of her taking all of him. Their pace quickened, his thrusts going deeper, harder, as she lifted her hips against him.

The pleasure was too much, too intense. He knew he was about to orgasm, but he refused to reach completion before Cara. He shifted his weight to one hand and reached between them until his finger stroked her clitoris. She cried out and clawed his back as he caressed her.

He kept a steady rhythm, watching the emotions on her face as her body tensed. A heartbeat later she cried out as she peaked. Lucan was powerless to hold back his climax any longer. With her body clenching around his, he buried himself inside her and let her milk him dry.

For long moments they stayed as they were, their breaths mixing, their hearts racing. He parted his lids to find her watching him with bright eyes.

"That was . . ." She trailed off with a shrug.

He knew what she meant. Words for what had happened, the feelings that had washed over him, were missing. Then he thought of one that captured the moment. "It was perfect."

A slow smile pulled at her lips. "Aye. It was most assuredly perfect."

He put his forehead to hers. "Will you come back with me to the castle?"

"I'd go anywhere with you, Lucan, even to the fires of Hell."

"Let's hope it doesna come to that," he said with a kiss on her nose.

He rolled to his back and pulled her against him. He gazed at the tops of the trees and the pink and orange sky of the setting sun.

With his body sated, he found himself thinking of when he had come upon Cara talking to Galen. The need to kill had never been so strong. Galen hadn't been hurting Cara, but he had been near her. It was enough for Lucan.

What he still didn't understand was why she wanted him. Lucan had stayed in his Warrior form so she could see what he was, take in his anger and the danger that surrounded him. Instead of pushing her away, it seemed to excite her. That should have worried him, but it pleased him more than he wanted to admit.

"What are you thinking?" she asked sleepily.

"About you."

She chuckled. "I hope it's good."

"I wish you hadn't run, Cara."

With a sigh she rose up on her elbow to look at him. "I did what I thought was best."

"You knew running would make you an easy target for Deirdre."

"I did."

"And you did it anyway."

"You told me yourself Deirdre wouldn't stop coming after me. I figured if I let her have me it would give you and your brothers a chance to get free of her."

He cupped her face. "You are the bravest woman I know."

"Nay," she said with a slight shake of her head. "Just one that is starving."

CHAPTER SIXTEEN

Cara wanted to stay in Lucan's arms forever. It didn't bother her that night was approaching. As long as she was with Lucan she was safe. But with the way he kept glancing at the sun, she knew their time had come to an end.

She sat up and looked down at his luscious, hard body and wanted to explore him to her heart's content. Next time, and she was sure there would be a next time, she was going to run her hands all over him.

He smiled at her, unabashed in his nudity. She glanced at his flaccid rod, amazed at how it had felt in her hands. She supposed she should be embarrassed about her own nakedness, but she liked how he looked at her. The stark hunger in his eyes made her stomach flutter.

"I need to get you cleaned up," he said as he rose in one fluid motion to his feet.

Cara saw her virgin's blood on him. A glance between her legs showed a few spots of blood had gotten on her gown. The ripping of material drew her gaze to him. Lucan had torn his tunic in half and knelt between her legs.

"I'd wet it if there was water."

She shrugged and reached for the material. "It's no matter."

He held it away from her. "Lay back. I'll clean you."

She nodded and leaned back on her elbows. His hands were gentle as he cleaned off her blood and his seed from between her thighs. Only once she was clean did he wipe himself. He buried the tunic some distance away and returned to her standing in profile as he pulled on his breeches and boots.

Cara couldn't take her eyes off him. He was a glorious specimen, a Highlander in every sense of the word. He fit into nature as well as any animal, and the danger that surrounded him only added to his allure.

He was a man every mother would warn her daughter about. But he was a man whom every daughter would want for her own.

Lucan turned his head to Cara and raised a brow. "Something wrong?"

She ran her gaze down his lean buttocks and powerful legs. For a man chiseled in perfection, he was amazingly gentle with her.

Cara licked her lips. "Everything is just right."

"Need some help getting dressed?" His eyes darkened with desire.

If she didn't dress now, they would never leave, and she knew how much Lucan wanted to return to the castle. She shook her head and reached for a stocking. "Not this time."

Lucan leaned against a tree, his arms crossed

over his chest, watching her when she turned around from dressing. "Women wear too many clothes."

"I could say the same as you. Highlanders now wear kilts."

He shrugged one shoulder. "I might have to get one. It would make it easier to get to you when I wanted to make love."

A warm heat stole over her body. "So you will take me again?"

"I will take you many times, Cara. I may have fought what was between us, but know this: you are mine."

When he held out his hand, she took it, accepting whatever the future held for her. "And you are mine," she said when she pulled even with him.

He nodded. "Aye."

They walked through the woods in a companionable silence. That morning Cara had thought everything lost to her, and now she had it all. Well, almost, if Deirdre would stop looking for her.

"We found another Warrior," she said.

"Maybe."

"I understand why you don't trust people, Lucan, but I feel that he's telling the truth."

"Maybe," Lucan said again.

She rolled her eyes. Night was approaching quickly, and as they reached the edge of the forest, Cara found she was anxious to get back to the castle.

Suddenly Lucan stopped, his arm drawing her to a halt. Cara stilled and listened.

"What is it?" she whispered.

Lucan shook his head to quiet her. Then she saw movement in the shadow of a tree and Galen stepped into their path. She felt Lucan's nails growing as she clung to his hand.

"What do you want, Shaw?" Lucan demanded.

But Galen's eyes were riveted on her. "You wear it for all the world to see?" he asked, his voice low and angry.

Lucan shoved her behind him. "What are you talking about?"

Galen pointed to her. "The vial. The Demon's Kiss. It should be hidden."

Cara glanced down to find her mother's necklace was indeed outside her gown. "I usually keep it hidden, but only because people thought it odd."

"Where did you get it?" Galen demanded.

"None of your damned concern," Lucan growled.

Cara, however, realized Galen might know about the vial. She stepped around Lucan. "From my mother when I was just a child."

"The wyrran killed her, didn't they?" Galen asked.

She nodded. "My parents hid me, which was the only reason I escaped."

"Do you know what it is you hold, what you are?"

"Nay."

"Cara," Lucan warned.

She looked at Lucan and touched his arm. "I've wanted to know what this necklace was for as long as I can remember. I no longer have my mother to tell me. Would you deny me the information if Galen has it?"

Lucan sighed and shook his head. "Of course not."

She turned to Galen. "What is this necklace?"

"That blood you carry is from a *drough*."

Cara recalled how Lucan had told her there were two sects of Druids, the *mie*, or good Druids, and the *drough*, or evil Druids. "My family was good and decent. They weren't evil."

Lucan's arm wrapped around her waist and pulled her against his side. "Go on," he told Galen.

"The blood ritual is a ceremony every *drough* performs on their eighteenth year. The bloodletting is supposed to open them up to receive black magic."

"Nay," Cara said. "My parents were good people."

"Did you move around often?" Galen asked.

She opened her mouth to deny it when a memory of them walking into the cottage surfaced. How pleased her father had been, and how her mother had said they hoped they could stay longer than the last village.

"You did, didn't you?"

She nodded to Galen, her chest tightening. "Why did we move so often?"

"Because of Deirdre," Lucan answered.

Galen gave a curt nod. "Deirdre has been gathering up every Druid, *mie* or *drough*, she can find. She kills them for more power. The *drough* pose a threat to her magic, and it is said that some *mie* know how to bind the gods."

She glanced at Lucan to see if he had heard Galen. Lucan's gaze touched her, wariness filling his gaze. If a *mie* could bind the god inside Lucan, Cara would find a *mie* for him.

Cara touched the vial. "A Warrior said Deirdre wanted the blood. Why?"

"A *drough's* blood holds great magic, especially to the one who either spills the blood or captures it." Galen's gaze narrowed as if something just dawned on him. "You're what Deirdre is looking for."

She glanced at Lucan. "I am."

"Then you're going to need as many Warriors as you can find, MacLeod. Deirdre wants your woman more than she wants any Warrior."

"Why?" Lucan asked.

"The power of Cara's blood mixed with her mother's is heady for one such as Deirdre to ignore. The jolt of power she would get would be immense. It is rare indeed to find a Druid with her mother's *drough* blood around her neck."

Cara pulled the necklace over her head. "Then I will pour out my mother's blood."

"Nay," Galen said, and held out a hand to stop her. "Don't."

"What aren't you telling us?" Lucan demanded. "The *droughs* were evil. They would be a benefit to Deirdre, and since blood is let as a ritual, it would be easy for Deirdre to gain their blood. Why kill them when she could have them on her side?"

Galen sighed and ran a hand down his face. "Deirdre is a *drough*. She has kept herself alive using her brethren's blood for over five hundred years. Each time she kills a *drough* and gains their blood, she grows stronger. She wants no *drough* around that might usurp her power."

Lucan cursed long and low.

"Your woman needs to be kept away from Deirdre at all costs. She must keep the vial safe as well, for she may need her mother's blood one day."

"I'm seeing to that," Lucan said.

Galen leaned his shoulder against a tree. "Cara could fight Deirdre with her magic."

"I know nothing of the Druids and their ways," Cara said with a shake of her head. "I didn't even know what a *drough* was until Lucan told me. I have no magic."

"Not true," Galen said. "Every descendent of the Druids has magic. The *mie* turn to nature for theirs. The *drough* take their own blood, thereby sacrificing a part of themselves to evil. Once that is done, the black magic takes over."

She put her hand on Lucan's chest. "I don't want to use black magic."

"You willna have to," he promised her. "We'll find a way."

When they looked up, Galen was gone. "You're going to need more than your brothers, MacLeod," Galen's voice echoed in the trees.

"He moves like the wind," Cara said.

"Come," Lucan said, and took her hand. "We need to get back to the castle."

She gathered her skirts in one hand while Lucan held her other and they ran. He slowed his pace so she could keep up, but she was no match for his strength. Night soon blanketed the land. When she could go no farther, Lucan lifted her in his arms without breaking stride and kept running.

Cara laid her head on his shoulder and closed her eyes as her mind ran over everything Galen had told her. She didn't want to believe her mother had practiced black magic. There had been too much laughter, too much good, in Cara's life for her to believe her parents had been evil.

But the vial of her mother's blood around Cara's neck spoke otherwise. How she wished her mother were there so she could ask.

"We'll get through this," Lucan said.

She nodded, unable to reply. His words were meant to comfort and reassure, but she knew the truth of the situation, and it would take more than promises to keep her alive.

CHAPTER SEVENTEEN

Fallon stood on the battlements, his gaze to the east where they had last seen Lucan.

"He should have returned by now," Quinn said.

"He'll be here." Fallon hoped Quinn didn't hear the fear in his voice.

"I should have gone with him."

"He wanted us to stay here."

Quinn leaned his hands on the stones and blew out a breath. "We aren't prepared, Fallon. Deirdre will strike, and we'll find ourselves as her prisoners in the mountain once more."

"We'll be ready."

"Stop!" Quinn bellowed, his voice echoing in the silence. "Just stop," he said more quietly. "Admit that you're afraid. Admit that we don't stand a chance."

Fallon faced his youngest brother and wished to hell he'd been the man his brothers had needed him to be. "There is always a chance."

"Don't try and sound like Da."

Fallon was walking past his brother to return to the great hall when Quinn's voice stopped him.

"What is that?" Quinn asked.

Fallon turned and followed Quinn's gaze. He saw someone running toward the castle with something in their arms. Then there was a familiar whistle. "It's Lucan. And he has Cara."

Before Fallon finished talking, Quinn had jumped over the battlements to land on the outside of the castle wall and raced toward Lucan. Fallon sagged against the stones. He stayed there but a moment more before he started toward the stairs that would take him to the bailey.

Fallon paused and looked at the bailey. He could jump it. He knew if he let his god out, he would land safely. It would be a small sacrifice, something to test himself and his god. Fallon hesitated a moment too long and stepped away from the edge.

He was a fool to think he was strong enough to control the god as Lucan did. Fallon was too much of a coward to even try. He ran down the stairs and met Lucan and Quinn in the bailey.

"Is she hurt?" Fallon asked when he saw that Lucan carried Cara.

"Nay," she answered. "He won't let me down."

Lucan grunted. "She's tired."

Fallon followed Lucan inside the castle. He didn't miss the look between Lucan and Cara when he sat her in one of the chairs before the hearth. Something had changed between them, and it wasn't difficult to figure out what it was. Fallon was glad for his brother. After all they had been through, Lucan deserved some happiness.

Cara lifted her gaze to Fallon, then shifted to Quinn. "I'm sorry. I really thought I was doing the right thing in leaving."

"You are welcome here as long as you need to stay," Fallon said.

Her smile was genuine. "Thank you."

"I have news," Lucan said as he built a fire.

That got Quinn's interest. "What kind of news?"

"A lot, actually," Cara said. "I found another Warrior."

Fallon glanced at Lucan. His tunic was gone and could have been torn in battle. "Did he attack?"

"Nay." Lucan dusted off his hands and stood when he finished. "He knows of us, of how we escaped Deirdre. He said he's been hiding from Deirdre as well, and there are others like him."

"Others?" Quinn repeated.

"Aye, others," Lucan said. "He said we're going to need him and the other Warriors when Deirdre attacks."

"I don't know," Fallon said, and ran a hand down his face. "All this time we've thought we were alone."

"Galen said he's been searching for all of you," Cara said. "He could be a way to win against Deirdre."

Quinn gave a snort. "Or he could be a way to utter defeat."

"Do you have another option?"

Fallon hated to admit it, but Cara was right. One look at Lucan, though, and Fallon knew there was more. "What else happened?"

Lucan sighed. "First, I must get food for Cara. She hasn't eaten since this morn."

He stalked to the kitchen and pulled some of the roasted deer from the pit and put it on a trencher. There was a little bread left that he added as well.

For a moment he stared at the food. There had been a time when his trencher had been piled with various foods. He missed the meals he had taken for granted.

When he walked back into the great hall Cara was at the table pouring herself some wine from Fallon's bottle. Lucan lifted a brow at his elder brother. Fallon didn't share his wine easily.

"She looked as though she needed it," Fallon said in way of an explanation.

Lucan placed the trencher between him and Cara and motioned for her to eat. Once she had selected a piece of meat, he took one for himself. He watched her eat, the way her lips closed over the meat and pulled the bite into her mouth, and the way her tongue licked the juice from her lips. He grew hard just watching her.

She glanced at him. By the way she smiled, she saw his hunger. If they were alone, he would haul her on top of the table and make love to her again.

But they weren't alone, and if Quinn's glare was any indication, everyone knew how much Lucan wanted her. The question was did they know he had already tasted her? Did they know he had sampled a slice of heaven that he didn't plan to ever let go?

"Lucan," Fallon urged.

He finished chewing his bite and put his elbows on the table. "Galen also knew of the Demon's Kiss."

"What?" Quinn demanded as he moved to stand at the foot of the table near him. "How?"

Lucan shook his head. "I don't know."

Fallon slid onto the bench across from him. "What did you learn?"

Cara's hand slipped under the table and rested on his leg. She was afraid to tell them, afraid of what they would say. He covered her hand with his own and gave her a little squeeze of reassurance.

"We know why Deirdre wants Cara," Lucan answered. "Deirdre, it seems, is a *drough*."

Quinn crossed his arms over his chest and cursed. "A *drough*. Why didn't we ever think of that?"

"We had other things on our minds," Fallon said.

It was true, but they should have recognized Deirdre for what she was. "Her use of black magic should have told us then."

"But *droughs* have been gone for centuries," Quinn argued.

Lucan looked at his younger brother. "Have they?"

"They've been hiding from Deirdre," Cara said. "Deirdre uses their blood, the blood of all Druids actually, to become stronger as well as immortal."

Fallon's and Quinn's gaze moved to the vial hanging around Cara's neck. Lucan entwined his fingers with hers.

"You're *drough*," Quinn said into the silence.

"Nay," Lucan said. "She is a descendent from Druids. A Druid, by nature, is a *mie*."

Cara's fingers tightened in his. "To become *drough*, Druids give a part of their blood in a ritual that lets the black magic in and thereby the evil. The ritual is supposed to be performed on a Druid's eighteenth year."

"Holy hell," Quinn cursed. "Have you, Cara?"

She shook her head.

"But your mother was a *drough*," Fallon said.

"It appears so."

Lucan ran his thumb over the back of Cara's hand. "Galen also informed us that a *mie* has the power to bind our god. We wanted to find other Warriors and a Druid. It appears we've found both."

"I canna bind the god," Cara said. "I know nothing of magic."

"Galen said it came naturally."

"Have you seen me do anything magical, Lucan?" she argued. "I'm not your Druid, but I will find you one."

Fallon lifted the wine to his lips and took a long drink. He wiped his mouth with the back of his hand. "Let me see if I understand this. Cara is a Druid. Her mother was a *drough*, and Deirdre killed her."

Lucan gave a nod.

"Deirdre is killing all the *droughs* for their magic."

"We've no idea how old she is," Lucan said. "With the growth of her magic, she's able to become immortal."

"Wonderful," Quinn murmured.

Fallon scratched his chin. "Deirdre wants Cara, and I gather she's something special because she has a Demon's Kiss."

"Aye. Deirdre would get the blood of Cara's mother as well as her own."

"Wait," Quinn said. "If it was Deirdre that killed Cara's parents, wouldn't she have already gotten her mother's blood?"

Lucan looked at Cara for an answer.

Cara took a deep breath. "I thought about that as we traveled back to the castle. I don't think Deirdre needs the blood of a *drough*. I think she needs the blood in the Demon's Kiss."

"I agree," Lucan said. "Innocent *mie* blood freely given in a black magic ritual that draws evil. I cannot imagine what kind of powers the blood in a Demon's Kiss would hold."

Quinn ran a hand through his hair. "This just gets better and better."

"Does it matter that Cara hasn't become a *drough*?" Fallon asked.

Lucan looked at Cara, who shrugged. "I don't know," Lucan said. "Galen said Deirdre was hunting all Druids, *droughs* and *mies* alike."

"Is she killing the *mies*?"

Lucan threw up his hands. "I don't know."

"Galen would," Cara said. "He was right, Lucan. We're going to need him, and not just in the coming battle with Deirdre. He could have the answers to the questions we have."

"And he may not," Lucan argued.

Lucan wanted to believe Galen sided with them, but he had spent too many years being wary of everyone to trust so easily.

"We need to keep Cara away from Deirdre," Fallon said.

Quinn nodded. "As well as any other Druid we can find."

Cara rolled onto her back and yawned while she stretched her arms over her head. She hadn't remembered coming to bed. The last thing she recalled was sitting with the brothers in the great hall as they spoke of strategies for the battle. It must have been Lucan who brought her to her chamber.

She glanced at the pillow next to her and frowned. After they had made love, she had expected him to come to her in between his turns keeping watch. It bothered her a great deal that he hadn't. She should have told him she didn't care that he was immortal and she wasn't. She wanted to spend her time with him, however short that time was. Had he changed his mind? Regretted what they had done?

Her stomach clenched nervously. Or worse, did Lucan now believe she was a *drough* and want nothing to do with her? She wasn't a *drough*, and she would prove it to him.

How?

She didn't know. She didn't even know anything of Druids and their sects, much less how to assure Lucan she wasn't evil. But good or evil, Deirdre wanted her.

Galen said you could battle her.

Cara sat up and let the covers fall to her waist. It would take great magic to battle Deirdre. For a Druid who had studied magic all her life, it might seem like a simple idea, but for Cara, it was impossible.

She didn't know the first thing about being a Druid or about magic. Battling Deirdre was out of the question.

And the tingling of your fingers?

Cara threw off the covers and pulled her nightgown over her head. She bathed with the bowl of cold water that had been left for her, then dressed for the day. When she walked to the great hall she found Fallon sharpening spears and other weapons.

"Good morn, Cara," he said when he caught sight of her.

She paused on her way to the kitchen to say, "Good morn." Once in the kitchen Cara rummaged around and found that someone, most likely Quinn, had taken several things from the village homes. She found flour and yeast to make bread.

It was while she was kneading the dough she glanced up to find Lucan standing in the doorway watching her.

"Did you sleep well?" he asked.

"Aye."

He moved into the kitchen to stand across the table from her. His sea green eyes were warm as they raked over her body. "I remember coming in here as a lad and watching Cook make bread."

Cara smiled. "I imagine she gave you a slice as soon as it came out of the oven."

"Oh, aye. Even at such a young age women were susceptible to my charms."

She paused. He was handsome, but when he smiled, he was devastating. "I love it when you smile."

He walked around the table and pulled her against him. She tried to keep her hands that were full of flour away from him, but he didn't seem to care.

"Ask me," he demanded in a rough voice.

"Ask you what?"

"Ask me why I didna come to you last night."

Cara looked away. She didn't want him to know how much she had wanted his arms around her.

He gave her a little shake. "Ask me, Cara."

"All right." She forced her gaze to his. "Why didn't you come to me last night?"

"Because I knew if I did I would take you again, and your body needs time to heal. It took everything I had not to go to you."

Of all the reasons she imagined he would come up with, her welfare hadn't been one of them. "You could have just held me."

"Nay," he said with a small shake of his head. "It's not enough. I need you in ways that leave me baffled. I couldn't chance hurting you."

"Even if I wanted you again?"

He groaned and briefly closed his eyes. "Och, lass, you're killing me."

Cara moaned into his mouth as he kissed her. The tight feeling in her chest disappeared at Lucan's words. He hadn't changed his mind. He had only been thinking of her.

He grabbed her hips and pulled her against him as he ground his hard arousal against her. "If I don't stop now, I won't."

"And the bread will ruin," she said between kisses.

Lucan ended their kiss. "You thought I didn't want you."

Cara thought about lying, but she realized to do so now would alter their relationship. They had been honest with each other from the beginning. "Aye. I did."

"I told you yesterday you were mine."

"Even though you found out I'm descended from *droughs*?"

"You're descended from Druids, Cara. There's a difference. Your ancestors chose to be *droughs*. You don't have to make that choice."

But in the back of her mind, Cara knew that she would have to make a choice.

"When you finish here, come out to the bailey. I would like to have you practice more with the weapons."

She laughed as he slapped her on the bottom when he walked past. She turned and shook her head. "My same argument stands. Mortal weapons won't do me any good against magic."

"You never know," he called over his shoulder.

Cara watched him until he disappeared into the great hall. Her smile never wavered as she finished with the bread and set it to rise.

She rinsed her hands and had started toward the

great hall when the garden caught her eye. With one look at the plants, her fingers began that now familiar tingle. Herbs still grew in the weeds; at least the ones that hadn't been choked out were still growing. With a little care, they could return.

Cara walked out of the kitchen and knelt in the garden. As soon as her hands touched the plants, a warm, contented feeling stole over her. She began to pull the thick, mature weeds out of the ground. It felt good to get her hands in the soil, even when the dirt got under her fingernails. There was something natural and *right* about it. She didn't question her feeling, only followed it.

She paused in her task only long enough to put the bread in the oven, and then she was back in the garden. By the time noon came, the garden was half-weeded and the smell of fresh-baked bread filled the air.

With a slap of her hands together, she dusted them off and rose to rinse them. She turned to find Lucan leaning against the castle watching her much as he had done earlier in the kitchen.

"I couldn't let the bread burn," she said when he raised his brows.

"Nay, I suppose you couldn't. And the garden?"

She glanced at the ground, happy to see many of the herbs were still in place. "I couldn't stand around doing nothing."

"I didn't think the herbs still survived."

She shrugged. "They may not. Most were overtaken by weeds, but I've given them a fighting chance now."

"Hm," he said, and held out his hand. "Fallon and Quinn are waiting."

Cara didn't miss the curious glance he gave the

garden. She gathered the bread and took it into the great hall, where even Quinn smiled when he saw the fresh bread. The brothers eagerly cut into the bread, but Cara found her attention returning again and again to the garden.

And when she began to wonder if she could slip away unnoticed to return to the herbs, she knew something had changed.

CHAPTER EIGHTEEN

"Keep your sword up," Lucan told Cara. Her arms were tiring and her lips were pinched, but he couldn't let up on his instructions. There was so much she needed to know, and so little time to learn it.

Fallon and Quinn had taken turns with him instructing her. Cara didn't complain once, though he knew she didn't see the need in it.

"Watch my eyes," he reminded her. He lunged, and the end of his wooden sword hit her between her breasts. "You weren't watching."

She sighed and took a step back as she lowered her sword. "You had years of training, Lucan. I can only learn so much in a few days."

"But you've done well considering," Fallon said.

Lucan noticed Fallon had left his wine in the castle. For the past few hours, Fallon had drunk nothing but water. Lucan couldn't recall the last time Fallon had gone so long without his wine.

Quinn sat beside Fallon on the steps. "It's her skirts. They hamper her."

Lucan nodded. "There's nothing to be done about it, though."

"I could wear breeches as you do," she said.

Lucan choked on his spit. As he coughed, he imagined what she would look like walking around the castle with breeches molding to her body. He would like nothing more than to see that, but he didn't want anyone else to see.

"Nay," he said when he stopped coughing. "No breeches for you."

She rolled her eyes. "Any other suggestions?"

"Stay near one of us," Quinn said.

"Easier said than done," she retorted. "It's not that I don't want to learn. It's that I don't think I can."

"Aye, you can," Lucan said. "You've come a long way already. Before, you could barely hold the sword. With a tap of my blade against yours I could knock your weapon out of your hand. Now, you hold it with a firm grip."

Fallon nodded. "And you're quick despite your skirts."

"The Warriors will use their strength," Lucan said. "They will try to overpower you, but with your swiftness, you can keep away from them."

Her head cocked to the side. "You have such faith in me."

"You're learning from a MacLeod. Of course I have faith in you."

She laughed, the sound music to his ears. When was the last time the bailey had heard laughter? By the looks on his brothers' faces, they were thinking the same thing.

"All right," Cara said, and lifted her sword and dagger. "Let us continue."

"This time, don't engage me. Stay out of my reach. Only use your weapons to deflect mine if I get close."

"Remember," Fallon said. "The Warriors and wyr-ran will be striking out with their claws."

Lucan nodded. "I want to get her used to evading the sword first."

Cara's stance had widened, her knees slightly bent as she stared into his eyes. He was more than impressed with how much she had learned in the short time she had trained. At first, he had done it merely to give her the idea that she could defend herself. They had all known she didn't stand a chance against a Warrior.

But the more time Lucan watched her, the more he realized she stood a very good chance of keeping a Warrior or wyrran off her until he or his brothers could get to her.

He circled her, her steps matching his. He lunged forward and smiled when she spun out of his reach, her dagger touching his arm. Had she not put the flat of the blade against him, she would have sliced him open.

"Very good," Quinn called, approval in his voice. "He'll be expecting that from now on, though."

Lucan feinted to his right, then moved toward her on the left. She didn't realize his ploy until it was too late, but instead of being caught, she ducked and rolled out of his reach. When she came to her feet, her dagger touched the back of his knee.

Fallon clapped. "Impressive, Cara. You would have made a great MacLeod warrior."

Lucan couldn't agree more. She had the spirit of the Highlands inside her. That would be an advantage to her. He faced her and gave her a small nod. She beamed but readied herself lest he catch her unawares.

He gave her little time to prepare as he fell on one

knee and swept his sword at her ankles. She jumped in time to avoid being hit, and before Lucan could stand, her sword was at his throat.

"Either you're moving slowly to give me time or . . . ," she trailed off.

He saw the wariness in her mahogany eyes. "Or what? It comes natural to you?"

"I'm a woman."

He grinned. "I've noticed."

She looked at the weapons in her hands. "Women don't battle, Lucan."

"Why not?" Quinn said. "Maybe if I had taught Elspeth she could have gotten our son away."

"I wasn't moving at my normal speed," Lucan said. "But I wasn't moving slow, either."

He took her hand and guided her to the steps. Fallon held out a jug of water to Cara. She drank her fill and handed it to Lucan.

"They didn't attack last night," Cara said.

Lucan met his brothers' gazes. "Nay."

Which meant Deirdre was taking more time to gather her forces. Deirdre was nothing if not intelligent. She wouldn't react until she had everything in place. She wasn't going to give up so easily on Cara, either, and if Deirdre could capture the MacLeods at the same time, it would be an added benefit.

"What does it mean?" Cara asked.

"Trouble," Quinn answered. "It means trouble, Cara."

Her dark gaze met Lucan's. "You know what we need to do."

He knew exactly what she wanted. "We doona know if we can trust Galen."

"And you won't until you talk to him. How much time do we have before Deirdre strikes?"

Fallon shrugged. "She could attack at any time."

Cara lifted her brows. "Just talk to Galen."

"Maybe she's right," Quinn said. "We can hold our own against Deirdre's army, but the more Warriors we have on our side the better."

"You said he knew of more Warriors, right?" Fallon asked.

Lucan shrugged. "So he said."

"What choice do we have? We need to find out."

Lucan still wasn't convinced. If they let Galen inside their castle, he could easily take Cara away the moment Lucan's back was turned.

"You want to keep Cara safe, don't you?" Quinn asked.

Lucan clenched his jaw. "You know I do."

"Then we need to talk to Galen."

Lucan blew out a breath. "Fine. I'll go find him first thing in the morning." When they started to argue he pointed to the sun. "We don't have time now. The sun will set in a few hours."

With his speed he could find Galen and return before dark, and his brothers knew it.

Cara stood and wiped strands of hair from her face. "I'm going to wash up and get supper ready."

He watched her walk into the castle. As soon as the door closed behind her Fallon rose to his feet.

"We cannot wait, Lucan. You know this."

Quinn glared at him. "You're always the one telling us we need to see what we are and adjust. Look around you, Lucan. We need to adjust to what's coming."

"I know," he admitted.

"It's not easy, is it?" Fallon asked.

Lucan frowned. "What?"

"Making decisions that affect someone you care about."

"I've been making decisions for you and Quinn for three hundred years."

"Aye." Quinn nodded. "But we aren't the woman you want to claim as your own, which is folly in itself."

Lucan didn't want to hear why he and Cara couldn't be together. He knew the arguments since he had used them on himself without success.

"First things first," Fallon said. "We get Galen. Now."

Lucan shifted his gaze to his older brother. For just a moment he sounded like the Fallon of old, the Fallon before their clan was butchered. "Are you ordering me, Brother?"

Fallon nodded. "I am the eldest."

Lucan had wanted Fallon to accept his role as head of their family for a long time. He had thought it would never happen, so had resigned himself to being in charge. Now that Fallon had stepped forward, Lucan found he didn't care for it.

"If you want to win against Deirdre, we have to take chances," Quinn said. "We'll all keep an eye on Galen. That I vow, Lucan."

He ran a hand down his face. There was no use in arguing. If he didn't go, Quinn would. "I'll return as soon as I can."

"Godspeed," Fallon said.

"Don't let Cara out of your sight," Lucan told them.

At the nods of his brothers, he turned on his heel and ran out of the bailey. As he passed the gatehouse he lamented the fact that they didn't have a gate. Not that it would keep the Warriors out, but to keep anyone else from coming inside.

Quinn sighed as Lucan's long strides took him out of the bailey. "Lucan was always wary of people, but it has gotten worse over the years."

"We've all gotten worse over the years, little brother."

"Have you seen the way he looks at Cara?"

Fallon chuckled. "That would be difficult to miss."

"Aren't you worried?" Quinn couldn't believe Fallon was so calm about it.

"There is nothing you can say that will change Lucan's mind. He tried to stay away from her and failed. Surely you remember what it was to desire a woman. We've been here alone without a woman for too many years. I'm not surprised that Cara has awoken something inside him."

Quinn shook his head. "It will only cause him more heartache. Cara is mortal. We're immortal. There is no hope for them."

"Right now Lucan is happy. Doona take that away from him."

"It will destroy him," Quinn argued, feeling the anger rise inside him. "You know this. He survived so much, but if he falls in love with Cara and loses her . . . we'll lose Lucan."

Fallon closed his eyes and nodded. "I know, but how can I tell him to stay away from her?" He lifted his lids and his gaze settled on Quinn. "I would no more warn you away from a woman, either. We live in Hell. Why not take a bit of joy that comes our way, since it is so few and far between?"

"You know as well as I that Lucan holds us together."

"Then when the time comes, we'll be the ones that hold him together."

Quinn stared at his older brother, seeing their father in Fallon's dark green gaze.

"Do you not think we can?" Fallon asked.

Quinn shrugged. "I don't know."

"I don't mean to pry, but you know what it is to lose a wife, Quinn. If anyone could be there for Lucan, it's you."

"It may be a moot point." He didn't want to talk about Elspeth and his marriage. He wouldn't. "Deirdre could come tonight and take Cara. I don't think it matters what we do. He's going to lose Cara to that evil bitch."

Fallon crossed his arms over his chest and shrugged. "Maybe."

Quinn took the stairs two at a time to the top. "Since you're the one who sent Lucan to get Galen, you're the one that gets to tell Cara he's gone."

"She's the one that wanted Galen to come. She'll understand."

"Uh-huh. And that just proves you know nothing of women," Quinn said as he walked into the castle.

CHAPTER NINETEEN

Cara splashed water on her face to remove the sweat and grime. Once she dried off, she looked around the kitchen to gather food for the evening meal. The way the brothers had been staring at each other she knew Fallon and Quinn were trying to talk Lucan into finding Galen. It was the reason she had gone inside. They could be out there until the sun set, which gave her the time she needed to weed more of the garden.

The light was fading fast, but she didn't need a lot to pull weeds. The tips of her fingers began to prickle as she walked into the garden. As soon as her hands plunged into the dirt, a quiet calm descended on her soul. She wished she would have helped the nuns tend their garden. Maybe she would have found peace years ago.

As it was, the nuns only let her go out and pick the vegetables or herbs. Nothing more.

She yanked a stubborn weed from the ground and tossed it aside as she thought of how easy she found Lucan's training. Well, "easy" wasn't the right word. She liked the time she spent with Lucan and being able to see a part of their world. But it was like her body knew what she needed to do to avoid an attack before her mind did.

Half the time she didn't know how she was going to avoid Lucan; she just ended up doing it. She had thought he was moving slowly at first, but the more they trained the more she realized she was the one moving faster.

She gasped when her gaze landed on a parsley plant. It was like finding treasure. The small, green leaves were barely visible through the weeds. Cara carefully plucked the weeds away from the herb and marveled at how well the little plant was doing.

Her fingers traced the edges of the leaves, silently urging it to grow, to taste the sun and soil and water.

"Cara."

She looked over her shoulder to find Fallon and Quinn behind her. "I'll be there in just a moment."

"I . . . um . . . I came to tell you something," Fallon mumbled.

"Just tell me." With Fallon she never knew if he was drunk or hesitant about speaking about something he thought sensitive. Besides, she had her lovely new find at her fingertips. She smiled and blew dirt off the little leaves, eager to see it develop, imagining the flavor it would add to their simple food.

"Lucan left to get Galen," Quinn stated.

The smile faded from Cara's lips. "Left? You mean he went alone?"

"Aye," Fallon answered.

Cara looked at the brothers over her shoulder. "When I said Galen needed to be brought here, I expected all of us to get him. It isn't safe for Lucan to be out alone, nor is it safe for you three to be separated."

Fallon raised his hands. "We'll keep you safe, Cara."

"I'm not concerned for me. I'm worried about Lucan. Have either of you thought what would happen if Deirdre captured him?"

Quinn had the good grace to lower his gaze and kick the dirt with the toe of his boot. "We thought it would be better to have Galen return tonight than for all of us to leave."

Anger churned through Cara. She turned back around and closed her eyes as she took several deep breaths to calm herself. When she opened her eyes and saw the edges of the parsley's leaves brown and withering she cried out and jerked away from the plant. In a heartbeat, Fallon and Quinn were at her side.

"What is it?" Fallon asked.

She pointed to the herb. "It was healthy just a moment ago, the leaves bright green and thriving."

Quinn wiped his hand down his face. "Holy hell."

Lucan kept at a steady, even run over the land in a straight line to the forest. He wanted to be back as quick as he could, so he hoped for Galen's sake he would be easy to find.

Lucan was about halfway to the forest when he saw someone walking his way. He slowed, his senses wary. The man stopped as he caught sight of Lucan. A moment later, he lifted his hand in greeting.

Lucan spotted the worn Shaw tartan and sighed. He crossed his arms over his chest and waited as Galen ran toward him.

When Galen approached, a small smile lifted one corner of his mouth. "I knew you'd come."

Lucan turned back to the castle. "You didn't. You got lucky is what you did."

"I could argue the point with you, Lucan, but I willna bother. We all have our powers."

"Where were you going?" Lucan asked.

"I knew you and Cara had headed in this direction. I was coming to find you. Shall we go? I sense you're in a hurry."

Lucan hesitated. "I didn't want to come."

"You don't trust me."

"Nay."

Galen stared at him, their gazes locked. "You are right to be wary. I am just one man against three brothers. You could easily kill me."

"I know that. I'm more concerned about Cara."

"She's to be protected above all else," Galen said. "Deirdre cannot get her hands on Cara."

"I agree. Still, Shaw, I'm leery of bringing you back with me."

Galen nodded. "I could tell you what Deirdre did to me and why I escaped her, but you would only think it a lie. The fact you cannot ignore is that to keep Cara safe you need all the Warriors you can get."

Lucan didn't want to admit Galen was right. He should be the one protecting Cara, but Deirdre wouldn't send a few Warriors. She wanted Cara, and if he knew anything about Deirdre it was that she didn't give up on her hunt easily.

"All right," he said after a moment. "But be warned, Shaw, we will be watching you."

"You have my word, MacLeod, that I am against Deirdre in all matters. I will stand in opposition to her always, protecting everyone who has gained her attention."

It was all Lucan could ask for. He didn't want to

like Galen, but the honesty and determination in the Warrior's blue eyes was hard to mistake. Lucan was taking a huge risk bringing Galen back with him, but to save Cara he would take that chance.

"Come." Lucan turned and lengthened his strides until he was running again. Galen easily kept up, but Lucan expected no less with a god inside Shaw.

"How many others are there?" Lucan asked.

Galen shrugged. "We're spread out in the Highlands. Many do as I do and find other Warriors to try and turn them on our side."

"Just to fight Deirdre? Why not hide?"

"You know there is no hiding from Deirdre. Besides, there is much you do not know. You and your brothers thought you were doing the right thing in hiding, but you've only hurt yourselves, I think."

Lucan clenched his fists, hating that they were at a disadvantage because they had stayed hidden. "Just what don't I know?"

"I'd rather only do the telling once, if you don't mind. Once we gather with your brothers, as well as Cara, I'll tell you everything."

Lucan halted and glared at Galen. "What has Cara got to do with this?"

A few strides later Galen stopped and faced him. "A lot. She doesn't want to acknowledge it, and you want to keep her out of sight."

"She's just a lass. Nothing more."

Galen shook his head. "Deny it all you want, Lucan, but you'll see for yourself."

He wanted to hit Galen. Hard. Then leave him. But Lucan couldn't. He had promised his brothers he would bring Galen back to the castle.

"Go ahead and hit me," Galen said. He held his arms outstretched and waited.

Lucan was instantly cautious. "What makes you think I want to hit you?"

Galen burst out laughing. "Your eyes, MacLeod. They're black. Now hit me. You'll feel better."

"Aye, I would, but I'm not going to. Keep up if you can."

Lucan leapt into a run, pumping his legs faster and faster, his heart pounding in his chest. It had been so long since he'd felt such freedom that he exhilarated in the rush of wind over his face, the ground blurring beneath his feet.

He had run just as fast when he followed Cara, but he'd been worried about her safety. Now, he enjoyed the moment, since he didn't know how long it would be until he had another.

It wasn't long before the castle came into view. Lucan's gaze moved over the towers, but he didn't see Quinn's shadow. A glance at the battlements showed that Fallon didn't wait for him. It wasn't like them not to be watching. Where were his brothers?

"You came back to your castle?" Galen's voice was heavy with surprise. "We never thought to look here."

Lucan didn't bother answering. There was only one reason his brothers wouldn't be standing guard and that was Cara. He pushed himself harder. The sound of Galen shouting his name was blurred with the wind.

When he reached the castle he didn't stop in the bailey but went straight into the great hall. He slid to a halt when he saw Cara sitting at the table staring at her hands while his brothers paced around her.

"Lucan. Thank God," Fallon said as he stalked toward him.

There was a sound behind Lucan. He turned and

saw Galen fill the doorway. Lucan motioned Shaw inside. Just as Lucan opened his mouth to ask what was going on, Cara's dark gaze turned to him. There was such hopelessness and fear in her depths that it chilled him.

He started toward her, but Fallon's hand on Lucan's chest blocked him. He pushed Fallon's hand off, but Fallon grabbed his arm.

"Lucan," Fallon growled.

He jerked his head to Fallon. "She needs me."

"And you need to hear what has happened."

That stopped Lucan cold. "Is she hurt?"

Fallon shook his head. "Nay. Not hurt exactly."

"If you don't tell me what has happened to her, Fallon, I'm going to rip you limb from limb." Lucan was holding on to his anger by a thin thread. Something had happened to Cara, and by God, he would know what it was so he could fix it.

"Well, at least we know how to get him to show emotion," Quinn said as he walked over. "I'm Quinn," he said to Galen. "The one glaring at Lucan is Fallon."

"And I'm Galen Shaw. It's nice to finally find the three of you."

Lucan knew he should have made the introductions, but his mind was occupied with Cara. "Fallon."

Fallon nodded. "She was pulling weeds when I went to tell her you had gone."

"It was green," Cara murmured.

Lucan shifted his gaze to her. Her elbows were on the table, her palms facing her. She ran her thumbs over the pads of her fingers from her pinkies to her forefingers over and over again.

Quinn took a step closer to Lucan. "She got angry

that we let you go alone. She said we needed to stay together, that none of us were safe apart."

"She's right," Galen said.

Lucan threw Galen a dark look. "What happened next?"

Fallon shrugged. "She cried out. When we went to see what had happened, the plant she had been weeding around had begun to wither and die."

Lucan was at a loss. "I doona understand."

"I do," Galen said. "I warned you she was a Druid. She doesn't know how to control her magic yet."

At this point Lucan was willing to hear and try anything. "Can you help her?"

"I can try."

The four of them walked to the table. Galen sat opposite Cara, and Lucan slid onto the bench beside her. He reached for her hand. Thankfully, she let him have it, but she continued to stare at the other.

"Hello, Cara," Galen said.

She gave him a weak smile. "I'm glad Lucan found you."

"You know what happened in the garden, don't you?"

She blinked rapidly, but it didn't stop the tear that trailed down her cheek. Lucan pulled her against him and breathed in her scent of heather and earth.

"I killed the plant." She spoke so softly Lucan almost didn't hear her.

Galen nodded. "You are a Druid."

"Explain," Lucan bade him.

"Druids were born of this earth with the magic of all things natural. It is inherent for Druids to love the feel of the earth between their fingers, to watch— and even help—plants grow. You will find many *mie* walk barefoot to be that much closer to the earth."

Cara laid her free hand palm down on the table. Lucan's warmth had helped to stop her mind in its whirlwind. Now, as she listened to Galen, she began to understand.

"The *mie* get their magic from the earth," she said.

Galen nodded. "Just as the *drough* get their magic from Hell and the blood of other Druids."

"Does that mean I have the power to make a plant grow as well as kill it?"

"You were angry and you were touching the plant. The herb took your anger into itself, which caused it to wilt."

Cara closed her eyes. "How is this possible? Druids and Warriors and wyrran and *droughs*. A few days ago none of this existed."

Lucan's hand squeezed hers. She looked into his sea green eyes and tried to smile. It was odd, and a bit disconcerting, to find herself so attached to a man after so short a period, but there was no denying Lucan comforted her just as the soil between her fingers had done.

"Don't leave again without saying good-bye."

He nodded. "You have my word."

She turned her head to Galen. "What now? I know nothing of being a Druid."

"I can tell you all I know," Galen said.

Quinn leaned his hands on the table, his lips curled in a sneer. "And just how is it you know so much about Druids?"

Galen cut his eyes to Quinn and held his gaze. "I know so much because I was imprisoned with one in Deirdre's mountain. She had him tortured daily. When he was brought back to the cell, he would be out of his mind with pain. In order to keep his mind sharp, and keep the pain to a minimum, he would tell me stories."

Galen's tale caused Cara's stomach to churn. "What did Deirdre want with the Druid?"

"What does she want with any of us?" Galen gave his head a little shake. "As I told you before, it is the *mie* who knew the spell to bind the gods inside us. Deirdre wants the spell, and she wants to ensure no *mie* binds what she has undone."

"Why?" Fallon asked. He stood at the other end of the table, his arms crossed over his chest. "She knows how to release the gods. Isn't that enough?"

Galen shrugged. "I don't know."

"Unless she didn't release the god," Cara said.

Quinn snorted. "Trust me, Cara. Deirdre released the god inside us. I was there. I experienced it."

She turned to Lucan. "What if she didn't, at least not fully? What if she only awakened it? Didn't you tell me in the story that the Warriors ceased being men at all and became monsters?"

Lucan nodded. "Aye. There was no trace of the men they were. They couldn't distinguish loved ones from enemies after Rome was gone."

Cara bit her lips as she looked at the men around her. "I think I know why Deirdre wants the spell."

"Tell us," Fallon said, his voice dripping with impatience.

"When the gods were first put in the men, the *droughs* gave them orders to drive Rome from our lands. Once Rome was gone, these Warriors turned on their own people."

"Aye," Galen said. "They killed others as well as themselves. They couldn't stop fighting if they wanted to."

She clasped her other hand around Lucan's larger

one that held hers. "Deirdre is a *drough*, which means she knows how to call up spells. Except my guess is both the *drough* and the *mie* realized once they were able to bind the gods that they would be better served to banish the spells forever."

Quinn was shaking his head before she finished. "I don't think so. The Druids would realize they had the power to release and bind a very powerful weapon at any time."

"Then why didn't they?" she argued. "When the Saxons landed, why didn't they call forth the Warriors? I think the Druids feared what they had done, feared it so much they wanted no part of it."

"Even the *droughs*?" Galen asked. "The *drough* fear very few things."

Cara glanced at Lucan to find his brow furrowed as he listened to her. Fallon tapped a finger on his chin, his gaze on the table. She didn't have any facts to support what she said. All she had was her gut feeling.

"I think," she continued, "that Deirdre, being a *drough* and powerful in her black magic, found a way to unlock the gods, but she didn't fully release them. If she had set the gods free as the ancient Druids had, none of you would be sitting here today."

Lucan hissed out a breath. "God's teeth, I think she's right. All the stories I ever heard of the Warriors was how out of control they were. I'm able to control my god."

"I canna believe it," Galen said. His blue eyes were round, his expression surprised. "I could never piece together why Deirdre wanted the spell to bind us when she knew how to release the god."

Quinn sank onto the bench beside Galen. "Holy hell."

"Now I understand why she's taking so long to

attack," Fallon said as he began to pace. "I thought it was because she wanted to ensure they captured us this time."

"She wants to make sure she captures Cara because of the Demon's Kiss, but also because Cara might know how to bind us," Lucan said.

"But I don't," she argued. Yet none of them heard her.

Quinn looked up at Lucan. "We're going to need more Warriors."

Cara couldn't agree more. "Galen, how soon do you think you could have other Warriors here?"

"A day or two or more," he said. "I had already sent word that I ran into Lucan. As I told you both in the forest, we've been looking for you MacLeods for over a hundred years."

"You keep saying 'we,'" Fallon said. "Do you all live in a village?"

Galen shook his head. "We each went our own way when we escaped Deirdre. Some got out before I did, some after, but there are places across Scotland that we mark, messages we leave the others in the ancient Celtic language that none but us can read."

Lucan leaned on the table with his elbow. "What I want to know is how so many Warriors continued to escape Deirdre? With all her black magic, I would think she would have stopped that."

Cara had wondered the same thing. It didn't make sense that so many got out.

Galen chuckled. "The dungeons in Cairn Toul run the depth of the mountain. Deirdre carved her city inside the mountain and stays at the top in her palace. Rarely does she venture down into the dungeon, and if she does, it's never good."

"You say the dungeons are filled?" Cara asked.

"The entire mountain?" She knew Cairn Toul was a large mountain, stretching high into the clouds, but she couldn't imagine the whole mountain filled with people locked away.

"Aye," Galen said. "Her palace is huge and takes up a large portion of the mountain. She doesn't just keep Druids and men she suspects hold the gods inside them; she imprisons anyone she wants. Many she turns into her slaves, using her magic to control their minds."

Fallon blew out a breath. "How is she choosing the men she thinks have the gods inside them?"

"Mostly I think she's guessing. One of the men she captured said there was a scroll of names the *droughs* had written when the men were first turned to Warriors. Deirdre wants that scroll. She asks everyone she questions about it."

"Does it exist?" Quinn asked.

Galen poured himself some water from the ewer on the table. "I think it does, but no one knows who has it."

Fallon reached down to the floor and then placed a bottle of wine on the table. "Did she get any names from the man?"

Galen drained his water. He set the goblet down and frowned. "Aye, she got five surnames."

Silence reigned in the great hall. After a moment, Cara rose and went into the kitchen to gather some food. The news the MacLeod brothers were getting was taking a toll on them. They were going to need their strength in the days to come.

When she walked into the hall, her arms laden with a tray of food, the men were all deep in thought. She set the tray on the table and motioned to the food.

"Eat. We have much to discuss."

She let out a sigh when the men filled their trenchers. Quinn and Fallon flanked Galen, but he didn't seem to mind. She wanted to hear more about Deirdre and the Warriors. Anything to keep her from thinking about her magic running through her. And a future that grew more uncertain with each passing moment.

CHAPTER TWENTY

Lucan watched Cara carefully. He wasn't fooled by how she maneuvered the conversation to Deirdre and the Warriors. Cara wasn't ready to talk about her Druid powers, but she would have to soon. Too much was at stake for them not to be prepared for any eventuality.

He pulled some of the meat off his trencher and gave it to her. She smiled and ate the roasted venison. They would have to hunt and fish tomorrow, since the meat was almost gone. And with the way Galen ate, they would have to hunt daily.

"You said you let the others know you had found me," Lucan said to Galen. "How will they know where to find you?"

"I left a mark on one of the big oaks in the forest, letting them know I was headed west. They'll come this way."

"*If* they come," Quinn added.

Galen bit into an oatcake and swallowed before he answered. "I only leave the forest if it's important. They'll come."

Fallon set down the wine after pouring a hefty amount into his goblet. "I think the more significant question is if they come in time."

Lucan couldn't argue with him there. "We'll alternate patrols tonight."

Quinn nodded as he ate.

"We need to set up a plan," Fallon said.

Lucan had seen a change in Fallon over the past day. He still drank, but not as heavily. His eyes were more focused, and the authoritative tone Lucan had always hated as a lad was back in Fallon's voice. It didn't bother Lucan now, however.

"I agree," Lucan said. "Do you have something in mind?"

Fallon's gaze met his. "I do. We know this castle. I say we use it to our advantage."

Lucan inhaled deeply, ready for battle. "Excellent idea."

Just like the Fallon of old. Lucan glanced at Quinn to see him watching their older brother with interest. Lucan gave a lift of his goblet to Quinn.

"We might not be able to kill them, but we can set traps," Fallon said. "It will keep both the Warriors and the wyrran occupied until they can get out."

"Meanwhile you can attack others that get past," Cara said. "There are many areas you can set traps not just inside the castle but outside."

Lucan grinned at Cara. "Good suggestion."

While Fallon, Quinn, and Galen talked about the traps, Lucan brought Cara's face around to him. She blinked and tried to smile, but he saw through her attempt.

"I'll get you the information you need on being a Druid. We'll get through this."

She lifted his hand between her own. "If my

mother had lived, she would have shown me the *drough* ways. I could very well be a *drough* now."

"You don't know that. Speculating on how the future could have been will only cause your head to ache."

"And you want to fix everything."

He shrugged. "I suppose I do. I'm good at it."

A real smile pulled at her lips. "You're not conceited, are you?"

"Not in the least." To his joy, he heard her chuckle, but it was short-lived. The smile disappeared and she lowered her gaze from his.

"I need to clean up."

Lucan stopped her from rising. "Cara."

"I'm all right," she said, and put her hand on his cheek. "You talk with the others while I tidy the kitchen."

He let her gather the now empty trenchers and watched her walk from the hall. When he turned back around, three pairs of eyes were on him.

"How is she?" Fallon asked. "She seems better now that you're here."

Quinn shook his head. "She was pale as death when she saw the plant dying. Nothing we could say would calm her, and then she just got quiet and stared at her hands."

"I didna like feeling that helpless," Fallon admitted. "It was awful."

Cara had become part of their family whether she wanted to or not. Lucan was glad his brothers had taken to her so easily. His feelings for Cara grew by the day, and he wanted her in his life. Always.

"She's frightened," Lucan said. "As any of us would be in her position. We know nothing of Druids, but with Galen here maybe he can alleviate some of her fears."

Galen shrugged. "I'll tell her all that I know, but words won't help her learn what magic she has."

"Are you sure the only way she can turn *drough* is the blood ritual?"

"Aye. It is done on a full moon in the Druid's eighteenth year. The ceremony is normally a grand affair, but with Deirdre hunting them, I've been told the rituals are kept secret, with few knowing of them."

"Do you know any *droughs*?" Fallon asked.

Galen gave a small nod. "I met several in Deirdre's dungeons, but as far as I know, none of them escaped."

"Druids aren't practicing as they used to," Quinn said. "If anyone knew of them, they would be burned at the stake. Wherever the Druids are, they're hiding, and not just from Deirdre."

"I agree," Galen said. "The Druid tradition is ingrained in them. Just like Cara's magic. She cannot rid herself of it even if she wants to. It's a part of her."

Lucan glanced at the kitchen doorway. "Just like our gods are a part of us."

"Aye," Fallon mumbled.

Lucan flexed his hands. Cara needed a Druid, someone who could show her the ancient ways and help her learn her magic. The problem was they didn't have time to go looking for a Druid.

"I don't know," Galen said.

Lucan looked at him and frowned. "You don't know what?"

"If I can find a Druid in time."

Lucan raised a brow. "How did you know what I was thinking?"

Galen shrugged. "It doesn't take a mind reader to know. One look at you and I could see you were thinking of Cara. Since Cara is upset over her magic, the next logical conclusion would be that you were thinking of finding a Druid to bring here."

Quinn snorted. Fallon shook his head and raised the wine to his lips. Lucan didn't know whether to believe Galen or wonder if part of his ability was being able to decipher what someone was thinking.

Lucan let it go for now. "You do know where some Druids are, don't you?"

"I did," Galen admitted. "That was a decade or so ago. They've most likely moved on. If we survive Deirdre's attack, I'll take you and Cara to them."

Lucan wasn't sure Cara could wait that long. "In the meantime, tell Cara, and us, all you know of the Druids."

"Both the *mie* and the *drough*," Fallon added.

Galen gave a small nod of his head. "I'll see it done."

Lucan leaned forward. "You know a lot about us, Shaw. Maybe it's time you told us about you."

Galen grinned, no anger in his gaze. "I'm no different from you."

"I beg to differ," Quinn said.

"What god is inside you?" Lucan asked. "When we fought, you turned a dark green. It would have been easy for you to blend in with the surrounding forest."

Galen nodded. "Which is one reason I make it my home."

"Your god," Fallon urged.

Galen's gaze shifted to the table. "Ycewold. The trickster god."

Lucan scratched his jaw. A trickster god. *Just*

what powers does Galen have? "And your family? Your clan?"

"I left."

Just two words, but Lucan heard the anger, the frustration, in Galen's voice.

"Has Deirdre wiped out other clans besides ours?" Quinn asked.

Galen shook his head. "Not that I know of. Mine was untouched. I was taken when I went hunting."

"You returned to them." Fallon stared at his bottle, his fingers wrapped around the neck.

Galen squeezed his eyes closed before he opened them. "Aye. I wanted to make sure they were unharmed. Once I saw my mother and father were all right, I left."

"From what I saw, you can control your god," Lucan said.

"It took me a long time to learn how. I kept to the forest, hidden in the trees."

Quinn rose and strode to the fire. He squatted in front of it and stoked the flames higher. "We stayed in the mountains for a time."

"At least you had each other."

Lucan nodded. Aye, at least they'd had each other. He couldn't imagine going through it alone. He looked at Galen with more respect than before. Lucan still didn't trust him completely but couldn't deny that Galen had his admiration. And despite his worry, Lucan found he liked Galen.

Out of the corner of Lucan's eye he spotted Cara walking from the kitchens to the stairs. She kept her head down and moved quickly. She didn't want to be seen. He started to go after her but thought she might need some time alone. There would be no more run-

ning for her. She knew the safest place for her was
with him.

Cara let out a breath as she made it up the stairs
without Lucan or one of the others stopping her. She
paused long enough to light the candle she carried
before she hurried to her chamber. She came to a
halt at the doorway when she saw the tartan of blue,
green, and black, the MacLeod plaid, draped over
the window.

Lucan must have hung it sometime that morning.
She smiled and walked to the window. She ran her
hand over the thick wool, amazed once more at
Lucan. He surprised her in so many ways.

Cara set the candle down and built a fire with
wood that had been freshly stacked. No doubt Lucan
had taken care of that as well.

She couldn't help but smile. There had been a
time when she was young that she had thought about
finding a husband and having children of her own,
but that dream hadn't lasted long. She had realized
soon that the men of clan MacClure looked at her
differently than the women of their clan. She might
have been allowed to live in the clan, but she had
never been part of them.

That's when she had decided to become a nun. It
hadn't hurt that she felt safe inside the nunnery. She
had thought God and the holy artifacts would keep
out any evil. How wrong she had been. About so many
things.

Now that she had tasted passion, had accepted
Lucan into her body, she could think of nothing more
than being by his side. It was a foolish dream, she

knew, but she couldn't help it. Their lives would be forever connected, and not just because he saved her from death that first day. It went much deeper than that.

Love.

Cara tucked her legs to the side and sat before the fire. She reached up and began to loosen her braid. She used her fingers and massaged her scalp from the weight of her hair. Then she began to comb her long tresses.

Lucan. Her thoughts were never far from the immortal Highlander. She stared into the red-orange flames and sighed. Their lives might be intertwined, but they were destined to be pulled apart. Her death, which was an eventuality if Deirdre captured her, would ensure that, while he lived on forever.

But she couldn't deny the deep emotions Lucan had called forth. Emotions she had never felt for another person before. They frightened her, but at the same time those feelings gave her strength and pulled her closer to him.

A hint of sandalwood touched her senses. When she lifted her gaze to the door it was to find Lucan. He stood with his hands hanging by his sides, his gaze riveted on her.

"You are so beautiful."

She smiled at his compliment. "As are you."

"Nay," he said with a shake of his head. "Women are beautiful. Men just are."

"I would have to disagree with you. I see before me a man of strength and power and magic. A man with rippling muscles, and a body very pleasing to the eye. A man with sea green eyes, and a mouth that does delicious, wicked things to me."

"All that?" He stepped into the chamber and shut the door behind him.

"All that and more."

"There's more?"

She smiled at the teasing glint in his eyes. "Shall I tell you?"

"I think so."

She set aside the comb and bit her lip as he moved toward her. He lowered himself beside her and waited.

Cara reached up and touched the torc around his neck, letting her fingers run over the braided gold bands of the torc. She traced the griffin head and the opened beak. "I find this very beautiful. A griffin. The Celtic beast symbolizing the balance between good and evil."

"Is that so?" His green eyes were crinkled in the corners.

"Ah, but you already knew that. Tell me, Lucan MacLeod, why do you wear this torc?"

He shrugged. "Every male in my family was given a torc by the laird."

"Your father chose yours?"

"Nay. It was my mother. She chose all of her sons'."

Interesting. "Do you think she knew what your future held? That you would be the one brother that learned to control your god?"

"Possibly. My mother seemed to know every-thing."

The griffin head on either side of the torc en-thralled Cara. Highlanders knew what the ancient Celtic symbols meant, so it was no accident that Lucan had been gifted the griffin.

"You have the griffin. Fallon has a . . . boar, aye?"

"Aye," Lucan said with a slight nod. "And Quinn has the wolf."

Cara shifted and dropped her hand from the torc. "A boar means strength and healing, while the wolf means intelligence and cunning."

Lucan's hand cupped her face. She closed her eyes and leaned into his hand.

"Cara."

Her name was a caress on his lips. She shivered, not from the cold but from the passion he awoke within her. When she opened her eyes his face was inches from hers. She saw the gold flecks in his eyes, but more than that, she saw something else, something that made her heart skip a beat.

"Cara," he said again as he drew her toward his mouth.

She parted her lips for his kiss. His taste intoxicated her, making her drunk from his essence. She shifted to her knees and wrapped her arms around his neck. He slanted his mouth over hers, deepening the kiss.

Excitement burned through her. She had hoped and prayed he would come to her tonight. Her body needed him in ways she couldn't begin to understand.

She ended the kiss and rose to her feet. His gaze, intense and dark with desire, followed her. Appreciation showed in his eyes when she took off her shoes and rolled down her stockings. He sucked in a breath when she pulled off her gown and chemise, making her bolder with each heartbeat. The chill of the chamber could not penetrate the heat she felt from his eyes.

Her hands itched to touch him, to kiss him and run her tongue over his body. Most of all, though, she wanted to take his rod in her hand again.

She licked her lips when he yanked off his boots. He jerked off his tunic as he climbed to his feet. Cara's nipples hardened under Lucan's gaze. The delicious throb she had felt the first time he touched her returned stronger and needier. She squeezed her legs together and sucked in a breath at the sensations.

Her mouth went dry when he removed his breeches and his thick, hard arousal sprang free. She reached for him, but Lucan grabbed her wrist and spun her away from him. He pushed her against the wall.

"My God, I hunger for you," he whispered in her ear.

His hot breath sent chills over her skin. He rubbed his cheek against the side of her head, his mouth brushing her neck while his stubble scratched her skin. All the while, he ground his cock into her back.

Cara's breasts swelled and her breathing quickened. She tilted her head to the side and moaned when Lucan's mouth closed over her neck. His teeth scraped her skin and his tongue laved her. She shivered.

And wanted more.

The hand holding her wrist against the wall tightened for just a moment before he caressed down her arm. His message had been clear: *Leave your hand.*

She wasn't surprised when he moved her other hand to the wall. Her fingers gripped the uneven stones as his hands wandered over her body. He lifted her thick hair in one hand and kissed the base of her neck.

"So much hair," he murmured. "I've wanted to run my fingers through it since that first moment I saw you."

His lips kissed first one shoulder, then the other.

He grabbed her hips and rubbed his rod into her buttocks. She moaned and arched back against him. He licked the lobe of her ear while his hands caressed her belly.

She needed him to touch her, to ease the ache that had started when he had walked into the chamber, but Cara knew Lucan was taking his time. He would prolong her pleasure and bring her exquisite ecstasy.

He cupped her breasts, pinching both her nipples. She gasped and leaned her head back against his chest.

"Lucan."

"Aye, beautiful. I feel your desire."

She rotated her hips while he rolled her hard peaks between his fingers. Pleasure spiked through her and centered between her legs. She felt herself grow damp and squeezed her legs together again. The throb was low and deep, the need sharp and greedy as it coiled low in her belly.

"Please, Lucan. I need you," she begged.

He nuzzled her neck. "And you will have me. First, I want to take my time with you. I needed you too desperately the first time. I willna be rushed now."

Cara put her forehead against the cool stones and moaned. He massaged her breasts, teasing her nipples until they ached and the throb between her legs made it nearly impossible to stand. She closed her eyes in rapture when his fingers parted her curls and touched her heated flesh.

Her legs trembled, her heart thudded, and all the while Lucan leisurely traced her sex. He pushed a finger inside her, and Cara cried out from the pleasure.

His free hand threaded through her hair and pulled

her head to the side. "More, Cara?" His voice was husky with his own desire.

"Aye. More."

Instead of moving his finger inside her as she expected, he withdrew it and circled her clitoris. Her knees buckled under the sensations.

Lucan gathered her in his arms and walked to the bed. He laid her down and leaned over her to suck a nipple deep in his mouth.

She clutched his head to her breasts, the yearning swarming her. He bit down gently before moving to her other nipple. Her sex throbbed, eager to have him fill her. She raised her hips and rubbed them against his chest.

When he kissed down her stomach, she watched him. He nipped first one hip, then the other, before he glanced up at her and settled between her legs. Cara sighed as he licked the inside of her thigh. She had no idea her skin was so responsive there.

A heartbeat later she cried out when his tongue licked the sensitive flesh of her sex. His tongue was hot and wet and felt wonderfully sinful. He licked and suckled her clitoris until she was mindless with need, her body shaking with desire.

She clawed at the cover as he wound her tighter and tighter toward her climax. And suddenly the heat of him, his hardness, plunged inside her. Then he began to move with short, quick thrusts and long, hard thrusts. Each time he took her higher, her body floating with pleasure.

With his hands on either side of her head, she gripped his buttocks and felt his muscles clench and shift as he drove inside her. She looked into his eyes and saw his hunger.

"We are bound," he whispered.

She screamed his name as she peaked. Wave after wave of bliss stole over her, drowning her in an abyss of joy. She clung to Lucan and felt him shudder as he plunged inside her and touched her womb. His seed filled her as he whispered her name into her hair.

CHAPTER TWENTY-ONE

It took Lucan a moment to catch his breath. When he opened his eyes he found Cara staring at him, a soft, contented smile on her face. He had given her that look. He had been the one to pleasure her fully. A satisfied smile tilted his lips. He pulled out of her and rolled onto his back. She turned and curled against him, her head on his chest.

He wrapped an arm around her, needing to touch her. It scared him how much she meant to him. The thought of losing her sent him into a panic. He had tried to tell himself it was because he had been without a woman for so long, but he knew that for the lie it was.

"How long do you have before it's your turn to stand guard?" Cara asked.

"A few hours yet."

"Hmm."

He glanced down at her and grinned. "Do you have something in mind?"

"Oh, aye. I do."

He chuckled and kissed her forehead.

"Thank you for the window covering."

"It will help keep out the cold. This way you can light as many candles as you need."

"We need to save the candles."

"Don't worry over the candles. You light as many as you need."

She turned his face to her and ran her thumb over his lips. "You're a good man."

He grabbed her hand and kissed her palm. "You wanted Galen here. Do you really think he can help?"

"You don't trust him." It wasn't a question.

He shook his head. "I find it difficult to trust anyone."

"You trusted me."

"It was your eyes."

"My eyes? What about them?"

"They're stunning. I looked into them and was lost." As soon as he said the words, he knew them for the truth they were.

She kissed his chest and smoothed her hand over his abdomen. "I believe Galen, Lucan. Give him a chance."

"I am or he wouldna be here now."

"What is it you don't trust?"

"I find it hard to believe that so many Warriors escaped Deirdre. She's too cunning for that."

She shrugged against him. "I gather from listening to Galen that things have changed in Deirdre's mountain. If she has imprisoned so many, then it is logical that they could escape. Especially if they're Warriors."

"And not be detected? I don't know."

"I don't think we will know that until we realize how many Warriors there are. If Galen is right and there is a list, we could get an idea of the number."

He wound a strand of her chestnut locks around his finger. "I've been thinking back to the tales of the Warriors I heard as a child. I used to not understand why they were repeated so often, but now I know it was because the storytellers wanted us to know what had happened."

"But were too afraid to write it down in case it fell into the wrong hands."

"Aye, I think so. No matter how hard I try to think, I cannot remember if we were ever told how many Celtic clans there were."

She traced designs on his chest with her nails, lulling him. "Was it clans, as you've been told, or families? There were many clans, but with each clan there were several families, and each could have had a Warrior."

Lucan stilled. "It could be something else to throw off anyone who sought to find the Warriors again. They would think it was one number . . ."

"When there were actually many more."

"God's blood, Cara. If it passed down to brothers like it did with us, we could be looking at any number of Warriors."

She leaned up and kissed him. "You MacLeods are a rare breed. I cannot think of another family who would have three strong Warriors at the same time."

"We were a feared clan," he said as he rolled her onto her back. "Have you not heard the legends about us? There are no other Highlanders like a MacLeod. We're loyal and some of the greatest lovers to ever walk the earth."

Her hands wound around his neck. "Oh, aye, milord. I've seen for myself your skills as a lover."

"I don't know. I think I may need to give you more lessons."

She laughed as he nuzzled her neck. "I think you might be right."

A whistle echoed in the silence of the night. Lucan stilled and lifted his head to listen.

"What is it?" Cara asked.

"Fallon or Quinn saw something."

Her eyes widened. "A Warrior?"

"Nay. It was a short, soft whistle. No danger, just an alert that something is out there. It could be nothing more than a boar or a wolf."

She buried her head in his chest. "I wish we were in another time, Lucan. Some place where we could have a normal life."

A place where he could marry her and watch her stomach swell with his child. He threaded his fingers in her thick, luxuriant hair. "Aye."

Lucan turned onto his back and kept her against him. He opened his mind to memories long buried, memories of his father and mother. They would have liked Cara. Lucan's mother especially would have enjoyed Cara's spirit, while his father would have loved Cara's bravery.

Lucan stared into the darkness, the light from the candle flickering on the wall while the fire gave a soft glow to the chamber. He wanted to stay there forever. No Deirdre, no Warriors, and no Druids. No ancient god inside him.

He allows you to protect Cara in ways you never could.

That was true. In that regard, Lucan liked having the god inside him.

No matter how much he and Cara wanted everything to fall away, it wasn't going to. Deirdre would come. Cara was a Druid and needed to learn of their ways and of her magic. And he, well, he was going to find the spell that would bind his god once again.

He would live a normal life with Cara.

Not likely to happen and you know it.

Lucan squeezed his eyes closed. It frightened him, this unquenchable hunger he had for Cara. Quinn had nearly gone insane when he lost his wife and son. Lucan knew that if Cara was taken from him, he would go daft.

He hadn't realized until Cara was in his life how desolate it had been. She had brought a burst of being, of joy, into his days.

He looked down to find her sleeping, her breathing slow and even. There never seemed to be enough time for the two of them, at least not yet. Lucan was going to make sure Deirdre left Cara alone.

The fire had died down to embers when Lucan slowly moved his arm out from underneath Cara. She sighed in her sleep and rolled to her other side. He didn't want to leave her, but it was his turn to take watch.

He dressed, then built the fire back up and lit a second candle in case the first went out. As he stared down at Cara he wondered at the fierce protectiveness she brought out in him, not to mention the jealousy that had sparked when he had seen her talking to Galen in the forest.

The need to make her his in all ways drummed in his mind. Yet he was a Warrior. How could he take her as his wife? A life with him would be dangerous and hard, not the kind of life he wanted for Cara.

His name was whispered from the other side of the door. When he glanced over his shoulder he found Quinn poking his head inside the chamber.

With one final look at Cara, Lucan turned on his heel and left the chamber. He closed the door behind him, ignoring Quinn's frown.

"You're only going to make yourself hurt worse," Quinn said.

Lucan continued down the corridor to the great hall. Galen sat in one of the chairs, a leg draped over the arm and his eyes closed.

"Did you hear me?"

Lucan stopped and faced Quinn. "I heard you, but I'm not going to answer. This is my affair, Brother."

"Nay, it's not. It's all of ours."

"Enough, Quinn."

"What if you get her with child?" Quinn asked. "Have you thought of that? What will it be? Mortal, or a monster like us? You always think of everything, Lucan, but now you aren't thinking at all. At least not with your head."

"Leave it," Lucan growled, the need to smash Quinn's face overwhelming. "Cara is mine."

Quinn watched his brother stalk from the castle. He hadn't meant to say anything, but when he had seen Lucan staring down at Cara with such desire it had sparked something awful and vengeful inside Quinn.

"Why, Quinn?"

He turned at Fallon's voice to find his eldest brother in the doorway of the kitchen, his hands braced on either side of the entrance. How could Quinn begin to explain what had come over him? No one would understand, least of all Fallon.

Fallon walked into the great hall to stand before him. "Lucan has found some happiness. If Cara gets with child, we will deal with it. Leave him be."

"I'll try."

"What is it exactly that bothers you about Lucan and Cara? Is it the fact Lucan has found some peace?"

Quinn shook his head. "Of course not."

"Then what is it?" Fallon demanded.

Quinn turned away, not ready to confess what had been plaguing him for decades.

"Quinn. Answer me. It's jealousy over Lucan finding a woman, isn't it? Just admit it."

Quinn clenched his hands. He looked down to find his skin black, rage burning in his chest. His claws cut into his palms. He welcomed the pain, for it was a reminder of what he was.

And what he had lost.

"Don't ignore me."

Quinn spun around and lashed out. Fallon jumped backward before Quinn's claws could sink into his flesh.

"You want to know what's wrong?" Quinn bellowed. "I can't remember her, Fallon. I can't recall her face or the taste of her kiss. I no longer recall the shade of my son's eyes or the sound of his laugh."

Quinn let out a breath as shame poured through him. The least he could do was remember his wife and son, but even that had been taken from him.

"You cannot blame yourself for that," Fallon said, and placed a hand on Quinn's shoulder. "Time heals us so we may face the future."

Quinn took a step back. There was so much more going on than the fact that he couldn't remember his wife's face, but he had told Fallon too much already. The rest, well, the rest would stay a secret.

"You're right, of course," Quinn said.

He hoped that was the end of the conversation. He didn't want to talk of it again. His chest ached from his admission. When he turned to leave, Quinn saw Galen had risen and stood by the chair watching them.

How could he have forgotten their guest? Quinn cursed himself. Galen shouldn't have heard any of the exchange with Fallon. Quinn waited for Galen to say something and, when he didn't, walked from the castle. There would be no rest for Quinn this night.

He had already served his watch, but he would take up post on one of the towers anyway. Beneath the stars, hidden in the dark. That was his peace, his salvation.

CHAPTER TWENTY-TWO

Cara rolled onto her back and stretched her arms over her head. She smiled and touched the spot Lucan had slept in. It had been wonderful to fall asleep in his arms. She had never felt so wanted or safe.

She rose from the bed and lifted the edge of the wool tartan to look out the window. Dawn had already broken. She washed and dressed. She had just finished braiding her hair when there was a knock on the door.

"Aye," she called.

The door opened and Lucan stepped into the chamber. "Hungry?"

She laughed. "Famished."

He held out his hand for her, and she took it without hesitation. Even the weight of her magic as a Druid and their uncertain future couldn't dampen her happiness. What she had with Lucan was special, and she intended to enjoy it to the fullest for however long they had together.

"Did you see anything last night?" she asked.

"Nay, though Fallon did catch a glimpse of a wolf."

Lucan smiled, but she saw it didn't quite reach his eyes. Once in the great hall, she noticed they were alone. He escorted her to the table, and when she had taken her seat he slid onto the bench opposite her.

Only after he had handed her an oatcake and a slice of bread did she lean over the table and take his hand. "What is it?"

He sighed and shook his head, his brow furrowed with worry. "It's Quinn."

"What's wrong with him?"

"That's just it: I don't know. He warned me about being with you last night."

Cara wasn't surprised. She would do the same thing if her sibling were in this predicament. "He's looking out for you."

"I think it's more than that. Fallon told me later that Quinn admitted that he couldn't remember what his wife and son looked like."

She winced, her heart aching for Quinn. To blame himself for their deaths, then to lose his memories of them. It was a terrible blow to one such as Quinn. "I can see how that would bother him. He blames himself for their deaths."

"How did you know that?"

"It's in his eyes. He was the male, the one that was supposed to take care of them, but he wasn't there. He will carry the weight of their deaths with him forever unless he can forgive himself."

Lucan shook his head. "He willna ever forgive himself, Cara."

"Then all you can do is be there for him just as you always have been." Cara chewed the food and wondered at the frown marking Lucan's brow. There was something else. "What else did Quinn say?"

Lucan shrugged. "He said I might get you with child."

Cara paused and swallowed. A child. It had never occurred to her, though it should have. She wanted very much to have Lucan's child, but he might not view it that way. "Can you get a woman pregnant?" she asked instead.

"I don't know. I haven't been with a woman since we were changed. None of us have."

"Would Galen know?"

Lucan scratched his neck. "I asked him, and he doesn't have an answer."

"So we could be worrying for nothing."

"It isn't nothing, Cara. The baby could be like me."

"Or it could be like me." She squeezed his hand. "Is it that you don't want a child?"

He shook his head. "Not at all. But getting a woman with child hasn't been something I've thought about in three hundred years."

"Then don't think about it now." She knew she was asking a lot, but in truth, it didn't matter to her. If she became pregnant, she would welcome the child. If she didn't, then it was God's choice. None of them knew whether being a Warrior would allow a man to impregnate a woman or not.

"You wouldn't mind a child by me? Even with the god?"

"Nay, Lucan. I wouldn't."

He smiled and warmth filled her. When she would have pulled her hand away, he laced his fingers with hers and gave her a wink.

The door to the castle opened then and Galen sauntered in. "Good morn."

"Good morn," she replied. "Have you already eaten?"

Lucan snorted. "He's constantly eating. I don't think I've ever seen a person eat as much as he does."

"What can I say? I'm hungry." Galen gave her a lopsided grin. "Fallon told me you were the one that baked the bread."

"Aye."

"Is there more?"

Cara pointed to the bread on the table. "That's the last of it, but I can bake more."

"Later," Lucan said. "She needs to train this morning."

Galen held up his hands. "All right. By the way, Lucan, Quinn went down to the sea to fish."

"I thought he might. Thanks."

Galen bowed his head and left.

Cara tapped her finger on the back of Lucan's hand. "Admit it."

"Admit what?"

"Don't play dense. Admit that you like Galen."

Lucan sighed loudly. "Maybe a little."

But it was enough for now. Cara had the feeling Galen was going to play a big part in the coming battle—and the MacLeod brothers' lives. "So, I'm to have more training?"

"Of course. This time, I won't be using a wooden sword."

"I never thought I would look forward to this kind of instruction."

He nodded knowingly. "You like it, don't you?"

"I do. It's like a chess game, though it moves much quicker. You have to be prepared for your opponent to do any number of things. If your enemy outmaneuvers you, it's over, so you must stay aware at all times."

"It's easy to think it's fun while you're training, but remember, it will be much different when the attack comes."

She swallowed down the thread of fear. "You worry that I will be too afraid to fight."

"I worry that you'll be separated from me somehow and that the Warriors will take you before I'm able to get to you. You have every right to fear what's coming, Cara. If you didn't, I would be worried."

His words helped to soothe her. "I wish we knew how many were coming."

"Sometimes it's better not to know."

"How so?"

He finished the last mouthful of bread, his thumb stroking her hand. "You know there are four Warriors here. If we learned there were twenty Warriors coming and a hundred wyrrans what would you think?"

"That we don't stand a chance."

"Exactly. Once your mind sets on that, there's no turning it back. You will fight, but you won't fight to win."

"I see," she said, as understanding dawned. "By not knowing, your mind is set to win."

"At all costs. Now. Are you ready for your training?"

Cara grabbed the last of her oatcake and rose. "I'm ready."

She wasn't surprised to find Fallon and Galen sitting on the castle steps deep in conversation. She touched Lucan's hand when he glanced at his brother and frowned.

"What is it?"

"Fallon. He's changed."

"I've noticed. He's not drinking as much."

Lucan bent his head near hers. "It's more than that. He's . . ."

"More like he used to be?"

Lucan nodded. "Aye. A wee bit."

Cara waited until they were in the bailey and away from Fallon before she asked, "Has he tried to . . ." She waved her hand, searching for the right word. "Transform?"

"Nay. I don't think there is anything that could make him turn to the god inside him."

Cara wasn't so sure. Fallon's gaze that was once unfocused and distant was now sharp and intent. He had forgotten the man he was, but she had an idea he was gradually remembering.

"I just wish Quinn would get better," Lucan said.

"Maybe he will." And she held out much hope for the youngest MacLeod. Quinn's problems ran deeper than Fallon's. If Quinn wouldn't face his, there was no chance for him.

Cara backed up a few steps from Lucan and looked around for her sword and dagger. She spotted them to her left, but when she grabbed the dagger she realized it was different from the one she had been using.

The blade was curved and the hilt was engraved with the head of a griffin. She jerked her gaze to Lucan. "You?"

"Me," he said with a nod. His eyes held hers and she saw how deep his feelings went. "The hilt should fit your hand better."

It did, but that's not what made her eyes water. Lucan had made something for her, something that bound them. A Highlander did not give his symbol to a woman carelessly. Her thumb caressed the griffin head as her heart thudded in her chest. Nay, a Highlander did not give his symbol to just any woman. When he did, it was for life.

She straightened with the weapons in hand. "It's stunning, Lucan. I shall treasure it always."

"I have a sheath for it as well. You need to keep it on you at all times, Cara."

She widened her stance and gave him a nod. She was ready to begin the day's training. One moment he was Lucan standing before her with his green eyes twinkling, and the next he was a black blur coming toward her.

Cara ducked the arm she saw coming toward her and sidestepped to the left. She barely had time to get her bearings when he came at her again.

Lucan's claws were extended, but she knew he wouldn't harm her. It surprised her how close he got to her, his large hands inches from her face. She dodged one swipe after the other. She was hesitant to use her weapons, because even though she knew Lucan would heal, she didn't want to hurt him.

Yet the quicker he came at her, the more she knew he was waiting for her to use them. Cara spun to the left and slapped the flat of her new dagger on his thigh before repeating it again behind his knee. She was moving away when his hand grabbed her hair.

He yanked her back against him. "Don't worry about the second hit. It gave me time to reach you."

"You're so fast." His arm was under her breasts, reminding her of their lovemaking. Her blood heated and her nipples puckered.

He kissed the side of her cheek and released her. "You kept up."

Cara shook her head to clear her passion and faced him. "I was losing energy fast."

"There will be more than one coming at her," Fallon called from the steps.

She blew out a breath. Fallon was right. There would likely be several wyrran attacking her at the same time. And Warriors.

"We'll keep the Warriors busy," Lucan said.

The crunch of footsteps told her Fallon and Galen had moved from the steps.

"You mean we'll try," Galen amended. He looked over Cara's weapons. "She's good. How long has she been training?"

A satisfied male smile pulled at Lucan's lips. "Just a few days."

Fallon moved in front of Cara. "Forget it's Lucan in front of you. Use your weapons at all times. Get as many hits as you can, but he was right. If your enemy is quicker, don't worry about the second hit. Just make sure you get out of his reach."

"And stay out," Lucan added.

Cara nodded. "Let's go again."

This time when Lucan launched himself at her, she was ready. She used her sword and her dagger to stop several swipes of his hands. Then she used her quickness to stay just out of his reach, coming close only long enough to slap her weapon against him.

"Good," Fallon called when she had caught Lucan three times in a row without him touching her.

She smiled up at Lucan as his eyes shone with pride. "How was that?"

"You're getting better every day."

She beamed. Until she saw Galen watching her with a calculating look.

"That was impressive," Galen said. "But as we told her, there is likely to be more than one attacking her."

Lucan raised a brow. "She's not ready for that."

"I need to be," she said in her defense. "Give me a moment to rest and we can try."

"Tomorrow."

Fallon folded his arms over his chest and stared at Lucan. "They could attack tonight. Don't you want Cara prepared?"

She heard Lucan mumble something beneath his breath that sounded suspiciously like he was going to rip Fallon's head off his body.

Fallon just smiled. "You always did hate when I was right."

"Don't," Lucan said, and pointed a claw at him.

Cara chuckled as the brothers glared at each other. "Lucan, please."

He lowered his arm as the black faded from his body. "All right, but rest first."

It didn't matter how many times she saw him transform; it still intrigued her. She watched him walk to the steps and sit.

"May I see the dagger?"

She jerked, startled to find Fallon had moved closer to her. She held the dagger out, hilt first. "Of course."

"Interesting." He examined the dagger closely before testing the weight. "It's been a long time since Lucan has made any weapons."

"I didn't know that. It will mean even more to me now."

Fallon held the dagger pommel up and regarded the griffin head.

Cara wrapped her fingers around the hilt. "My feelings for your brother run deep."

"Apparently, his do for you as well. He wouldn't have given you the griffin if he didn't care greatly for you."

She took the dagger from Fallon and started to turn away when his words stopped her.

"Love can do wondrous things, Cara, but it canna stop death."

She knew that all too well. "You're referring to me being mortal and Lucan immortal."

"I am," Fallon said.

"I cannot say what tonight will bring, much less next year. No one can. All I know is that when I'm with Lucan, I'm complete. I don't want him hurt any more than you do. I tried to leave."

Fallon held up a hand to stop her. "I know. He went after you. He'll always go after you. You are Lucan's, and he is yours, regardless of what anyone wants."

"You don't approve." She liked Fallon. Being with them had felt like a family, a real family. It hurt deeply to think he might not want her to be a part of Lucan's life.

Fallon shook his head. "I like you, Cara. You're good for Lucan. What I fear is what will become of him when you're gone."

She knew that Fallon meant when she was dead. There were no words she could say to ease his fears, so she turned and walked to the steps. Lucan raised a brow in question, but she shook her head. She would not tell him of her and Fallon's conversation. Lucan was already upset that Quinn had questioned their being together.

The problem was the brothers had a right to question it. She had been Lucan's from the first moment they kissed. Yet no matter what she knew was for the best for everyone, her heart wouldn't allow her to follow it. Her place was with Lucan.

For now, for eternity.

Lucan wasn't a fool. Fallon had said something to Cara that had distressed her. The vivacious smile that had graced her beautiful face moments before was gone, replaced with a thoughtful frown.

Lucan handed Cara the sheath for the dagger. "So you can keep the weapon with you always."

His gaze watched her for a moment as she tied the sheath around her waist and slid the dagger in place. The gold griffin head shone in the sun. It felt right for her to have that part of him.

"It's a clear day," Galen said. "Spring is shaking loose winter's hold."

Lucan glanced at the bright blue sky. There wasn't a cloud in sight. "Just how much do you know of us?"

Galen grinned and shrugged. "I've heard stories of the MacLeods since I was but a wee lad. Tales of how the clan was killed, how three brothers escaped, never to be seen again. You and your brothers are spoken of from the Highlands to England. I doubt there are a few who don't know of you."

"Interesting." Lucan wasn't at all happy to hear that. If he was ever to leave the castle, he would have to change his name. And that's one thing he didn't want to do.

"And you've been here the entire time?" Galen asked.

Lucan looked up at the castle. "For most of it. There was nowhere else for us to go. Our lands were divided, but the castle still stood. People were afraid of it, so we used that to our advantage."

"A brilliant idea."

"And you? You stayed in the forest?"

Galen shrugged. "I venture out every now and again. I like to keep up with the world. It's changed so little, yet so much."

Lucan glanced at Galen's threadbare kilt. "Aye."

"There is no telling how long any of us will live, Lucan. You need to leave the castle and see the world. There's no reason you can't blend in."

Lucan glanced at Cara to find her watching him. "I could, but Quinn cannot. Fallon, either, for that matter. We're a family. We stay together."

Cara's hand slid around his arm. He covered her hand with his. The simplest touch from her was like a piece of heaven. He gazed into her mahogany depths and found serenity.

"Ready?" she asked.

He stood and helped her to her feet. "Ready."

Fallon leaned against the castle, his arms crossed over his chest. Lucan knew that staid look of his brother's. Fallon wouldn't transform.

That left only Galen.

Lucan grimaced.

Galen laughed and jumped to his feet. "Don't look so upset, Lucan. I wouldna hurt Cara. I like her."

Lucan felt his teeth lengthen as anger burned his veins. Galen's knowing grin told Lucan he had known exactly what his comment would do to him.

"Stop it," Cara said. "Both of you. Lucan, Galen won't hurt me. Galen, Lucan needs to trust you. This isn't helping."

"You're right." The smile faded and Galen faced Lucan with sincerity in his blue eyes. "My apolo-

gies, Lucan. It's been a while since I've needled anyone. I couldn't help myself."

Lucan nodded to Galen, then turned to Cara.
"We'll start out slow and pick up speed."

He glanced at Galen, who gave a tilt of his head
as they both turned. Lucan was the first to attack Cara.
He went after her hands, but she was quick and kept
out of his reach. Her blade hit against his chest as
she spun away.

Lucan followed her, and this time Galen attacked
from behind. She arched her back to avoid Galen's
reach and put the tip of her sword at Lucan's neck.

He smiled at her as they stepped back. The next
attack, Galen went first. He reached for her. She
slammed the hilt of her dagger in his face. He
wrapped his arms around her waist and lifted her.
Lucan joined in, and when he would have grabbed
for her legs, she kicked him in the gut.

Lucan staggered back, amazed at the power she
wielded in her legs. When he looked at Galen again,
he was bent over, holding his nose, while Cara stood
a few paces away.

Fallon clapped. "You get better each time, Cara. I
almost feel sorry for the Warriors and wyrran that
try to attack you."

"Aye," Galen said as he straightened. He wiped
his nose, even though the blood had already stopped.
"What have you been teaching her, Lucan?"

Lucan looked at his woman, pride swelling his
heart. "She's a natural."

Galen snorted. "I don't know that she needs much
more practice. It might be good if we could get Quinn
and Fallon to join in, give her an idea of what it will
really be like."

"Maybe." Lucan didn't want her to experience anything. He wanted her kept safe, locked away where Deirdre could never reach her.

But deep down Lucan knew Deirdre would capture Cara. There was nowhere he could take Cara, nowhere he could hide her, that Deirdre wouldn't find.

Whether he wanted Cara prepared or not, she had to be.

She walked to him. "I'll stay by your side in the attack."

He pulled her into his arms and covered her mouth with his. She sank into him, parting her lips so their tongues could meet. His body hardened, hungering for yet another taste of her. His balls tightened as he imagined lifting her in his arms, her legs wrapped around his waist as he buried himself in her wet heat. When he broke the kiss, the pulse at her neck jumped and her eyes dilated.

"That was nice," she whispered.

Behind her, Lucan saw Fallon and Galen turn away. He didn't care that they had seen him kiss her. He wanted them to know Cara was his. He wanted to shout it to the world, that this amazing, courageous woman was his.

He was about to take her into the castle to make love to her when he heard Fallon say something.

"What was that?" Lucan asked.

Galen laughed and walked into the castle.

Fallon turned around and shrugged innocently. "I asked if either of you were ready to work on the traps."

Lucan didn't believe him for a moment. Even with Lucan's advanced hearing, his desire for Cara had prevented him from hearing what Fallon had really said.

"Aye," Cara said, and pulled out of Lucan's arms.

Lucan had no choice but to follow. However, he intended to find some time alone with Cara. Soon.

CHAPTER
TWENTY-THREE

Cara had just finished setting aside some bread to rise when Quinn walked into the kitchen and laid six large fish on the table.

"I don't think that will be enough with Galen's appetite," she said with a smile.

Quinn shrugged. "It's why I'm going hunting."

"The others are setting the traps for the Warriors."

He glanced at her, his green eyes holding no emotion. "Let Lucan and Fallon know I'll be back later."

Quinn left the kitchen on silent feet. It was obvious he wanted, and needed, time alone. She wished she could help him. None of the Warriors were responsible for what was inside them. They deserved happiness, but it appeared some didn't want it.

She reached for the fish and began cleaning them. Once that was done, she found herself in the garden. She was almost afraid to touch the plants, but if Galen was right and she could help them grow, she wanted to try.

Cara knelt by the herb she had nearly killed the

previous day and cupped her hands around it. She stroked the leaves with her thumb, putting all her energy into the plant.

"I'm sorry I hurt you," she whispered. "It wasn't my intent. I'm new to my magic. Grow for me. Please."

One heartbeat, two, three . . . and still nothing happened. She was about to give up when the small leaves that had been brown and wrinkled began to unfurl. Bright green replaced the dead edges.

Her heart pumped faster as she witnessed the alteration. She wished Lucan was with her, but she could show him later. Until then, there were other plants that needed her help.

Cara moved from plant to plant, coaxing them to grow for her. Many that had been overtaken by the weeds needed more magic. She held her hands over the dirt and closed her eyes while she pictured the herbs growing.

She laughed when she removed her hands and saw the first growth of green pushing through the ground. Every time she saw a plant respond, a strange euphoria overtook her. It was so addictive she wanted to touch everything and help it grow.

Yet she made herself stop. She didn't know enough about her magic to know what was happening. How she wished there was another Druid she could talk with. The last thing she wanted to do was something wrong that could jeopardize Lucan and their mission to defeat Deirdre.

Cara spotted Quinn walking through the bailey with some pheasants and hares. She rose and met him at the kitchen doorway.

"You've been busy," she said as she reached for the dead animals.

He glanced at the garden. "You as well."

"I wanted to see if what Galen said was true, that I could help the plants grow."

"He was right."

There was no censure in Quinn's voice, only mild curiosity. She looked down at the ground, suddenly afraid she was making a mistake in using her magic.

"Trust your instincts," Quinn said. "Trust yourself."

Her gaze met his. "I don't want to do anything wrong."

"I cannot see how aiding plants to grow could hurt anyone."

She shifted her gaze to the garden. "I know so little about the Druids and my magic."

He blew out a breath. "Even after three hundred years there is much I don't know about the god inside me. We'll watch out for you, Cara."

Quinn left before she had time to answer, not that she would have known what to say.

Lucan stood back and looked at the trap. "This should hold a wyrran for a considerable amount of time."

"Maybe," Fallon said as he tested the net. "Their claws are as sharp as a Warrior's."

"But not as strong. I agree with Lucan. This should hold them for a bit," Galen said.

Lucan glanced at the opening in the tower. The tower was at the back of the castle, making it a perfect entry point for an attack.

They had set up traps all through the castle, leaving only Cara's chamber, the kitchens, and the great hall alone. Lucan inhaled and got a whiff of bread baking.

"I've missed that." Galen's eyes were closed, his lips turned up in a smile. "Fresh-baked bread. I hope Cara made several loaves."

Fallon chuckled. "I don't know where Quinn is getting the supplies for Cara, and I'm not about to ask. I'm enjoying the bread too much."

Lucan nodded in agreement. "I'm hoping Quinn caught some fish. We're going to need it with Galen here."

"I'm hungry," Galen said. "It's just the way I am."

"We'll be hunting extra now with an added mouth to feed," Fallon said with a teasing grin.

Lucan snorted. "Consider Galen five extra mouths."

Galen laughed and started toward the great hall. "Don't worry. I'll do my share of hunting. I know of a village not far from here where I've bought food before. I can get Cara whatever she needs."

"Good idea," Lucan said. "We'll talk to her today."

"I can leave at first light and be back before supper."

Fallon licked his lips. "It's been a very long time since I've tasted a decent meal. Get whatever Cara wants."

Lucan laughed and shook his head. It was good to see Fallon almost like his old self. They walked single file down several flights of stairs, then through the corridor. Fallon stepped into a chamber with a burnt door.

"What is it?" Lucan hesitated by the doorway. Lucan knew by something in the way Fallon moved, the intensity of his gaze, that something was wrong.

Galen turned and walked back to him. "Fallon?"

"Someone is coming," Fallon said. "Wait. There are two, nay, three of them."

Galen turned and ran to the great hall without another word.

Lucan hurried to Fallon's side. "Warriors?"

"Could be."

"Let's go see, shall we?"

Fallon turned and put his back to the wall. "And if they aren't Galen's friends?"

"Then we fight them if they're from Deirdre. If they're mortals, we make sure they continue on their way."

"Are things so simple for you?"

Lucan took in the lines of worry around his brother's eyes. "I make things as simple as I can. We won't know who they are until we go see if they're coming to the castle."

"They're coming," Fallon said as he walked past Lucan and into the corridor.

Lucan followed. Instead of taking the stairs, he jumped to the floor of the hall. He wanted to find Cara, to tell her to hide, but there wasn't time. Already he could hear Galen's voice. All Lucan could hope for was that Cara had kept her dagger with her.

When Lucan walked into the bailey he found Galen on the battlements near the gatehouse. Lucan hurried to the stairs that led to the battlements. A glance over his shoulder found Fallon following him.

As Lucan approached Galen he could tell by Galen's tone he knew the men.

"I told you they would come," Galen said as he faced Lucan. "I know two of the three. The big blond is Hayden Campbell. The one on his left is Logan Hamilton. The other, I'm told, is Ramsey Mac-Donald."

Hayden stepped forward. "We saw Galen's message. Is it true? Are you really the MacLeods?"

"Aye," Fallon said as he came to stand beside Lucan. "We are the MacLeods. I'm Fallon, and this is Lucan."

"Where is Quinn?" Ramsey asked.

Lucan glanced at Fallon. "He's about."

"May we enter?" Hayden asked.

Lucan turned to Fallon. "What do you think?"

"Do we have a choice?" he asked. "We need them."

Galen crossed his arms over his chest. "You still don't trust me?"

Lucan rubbed his eyes with his thumb and forefinger. "We can take care of ourselves. It's Cara I'm concerned about."

Galen chuckled. "I saw her train. You needn't worry. Anyone that knows how to read the markings I left is a friend."

Fallon waited for Lucan to make a decision. The steady look Fallon gave him reminded Lucan so much of their father. Lucan blew out a breath and turned back to the men.

"Welcome to MacLeod Castle."

Fallon and Galen walked down the stairs to greet their guests. Lucan prayed they were doing the right thing. He would never forgive himself if one of the Warriors he welcomed into the castle went after Cara.

"Come, Lucan," Galen called.

Lucan jumped to the bailey, landing beside Fallon. Hayden with his kilt of bold black, dark blue, and olive green was the first to hold out his arm. Lucan grasped the tall blond by the forearm.

Hayden's dark eyes held Lucan's as the blond gave a small jerk of his head. "It's nice to see Deirdre hasn't been able to hold you."

"Not for lack of trying." Lucan then turned to the next man while Fallon and Hayden spoke.

Logan held out his arm, a friendly smile on his face and his hazel gaze direct. "Lucan." Logan's kilt was of muted dark reds, dark orange, and orange. Vibrant, yet suited together.

Lucan took Logan's arm before turning to the last man, Ramsey. Ramsey was quiet, reserved. His black hair was worn shorn to the collar of his black tunic, and his gray eyes didn't miss anything. Ramsey didn't wear a kilt like the others. Instead, he wore tunic and breeches as Lucan did. They sized each other up for a moment.

"Welcome," Lucan finally said, and held out his arm.

Ramsey accepted it. "Thank you."

"Come inside and we'll fill you in on everything," Fallon said.

Hayden's lips thinned. "Everything? I knew something important must be going on to make Galen leave the forest. What is it?"

"Deirdre," Lucan said as he walked past them. He wanted to warn Cara they had visitors, but another part of him wanted to keep her locked away so no one else could see her.

It was irrational and barbaric, but he wanted Cara all to himself. She would laugh if she knew what he wanted to do, tell him everything would be all right, that they needed the help. She would be right, but it didn't stop the jealousy from taking root.

"Lucan," Fallon whispered when he caught up with him. "What is it?"

"Nothing. I'll be fine."

Fallon shook his head, not believing the lie. "Cara

will be all right. Go and get her so we can introduce her."

"Not yet," Lucan said. He wanted to get to know the men better. "I wish Quinn were here."

Fallon sighed. "Me as well. He needed to be alone today. We've never begrudged him that."

"We've never had to fight Deirdre or prepare for visitors before, either."

"Let's just hope he gathers enough food. If they eat like Galen we'll never have enough food."

Lucan couldn't stop the chuckle. He let the new arrivals and Galen take the benches at the table while he and Fallon stood at either end.

"So," Logan said, and put his elbows on the table, his fingers threaded together. "You mentioned Deirdre. What about her?"

"She's planning an attack," Fallon said. "Actually, she's already sent two Warriors and a dozen wyrrans."

Ramsey's gray eyes narrowed. "What is Deirdre after?"

Hayden chuckled. "The MacLeods, of course."

Lucan felt Fallon's gaze. He was going to let Lucan fill in the Warriors about Cara. "We're an added bonus. She is after . . . something else."

"Something of great value," Galen added.

Fallon crossed his arms over his chest. "We stopped her and killed one Warrior and all her wyrran, but the other Warrior got away."

"He knew us, knew Deirdre had been looking for us," Lucan said. "They'll be coming back. The fact Deirdre has waited several days tells me she's gathering her forces."

Ramsey laid his hands on the table and cocked

his head to the side as he looked at Lucan. "You have a Druid." It wasn't a question.

Lucan paused for a moment before he nodded.

Hayden whistled through his teeth. "There are few Druids left. The ones Deirdre hasn't captured either have left Scotland or have hidden themselves away. It's no wonder Deirdre is after your Druid."

"She's not going to get my Druid," Lucan said.

Logan looked around the great hall and rubbed his hand over his jaw. "What's the plan?"

Lucan let Galen and Fallon fill the others in on the traps they had already set. He kept himself turned toward the kitchen doorway so Cara would see him first. The smell of bread filled the castle, and with the way Galen kept glancing at the kitchen it wouldn't be long before someone asked for a slice.

Lucan walked out of the great hall without a backward glance. Fallon had everything in hand. Lucan stepped into the kitchens and saw the fresh-baked loaves of bread sitting on a table cooling. Fish, hares, and pheasants had been cleaned and readied for cooking.

Quinn, he thought. When he didn't find Cara, he knew she was in the garden. Lucan moved to the door that led outside and leaned a shoulder against stones when he caught sight of her.

She knelt beside the plants, her hands covered in dirt. It had always amazed Lucan that anything could be grown in the rocky soil, but in the small patch of earth his mother had spent years cultivating a garden. She had been proud of her achievement.

Lucan smiled as he imagined his mother beside Cara, their heads together as they discussed a plant. It was too bad Cara would never get to meet his mother.

He watched when Cara cupped her hands around a plant and leaned her face close to it, whispering words he couldn't make out. Before his eyes the plant grew. Not a lot, but enough that he noticed.

Cara's head lifted and her gaze met his. Her mahogany depths sparkled with delight and . . . magic. "Lucan."

At the sound of his name he pushed away from the doorway and walked to her. She rose and stepped into his arms. He leaned down and inhaled heather, a scent he would never again smell without thinking of her.

"Did you see?" she asked.

He pulled back and nodded. "I did. Are you all right?"

"I'm perfect." She smiled and turned to look at the garden. "I've encouraged all the ones here to grow. There were some that still had seeds in the ground that I managed to coax, but there are others that are gone forever."

Lucan put a finger under her chin and turned her face to him. "Are you all right, Cara?"

Her smile was gentle and pure. "Aye, Lucan. I wish you could feel the magic that flows through me when I'm talking to the plants. It's a heady experience."

"I'm sure." He knew firsthand what power felt like, thanks to the god inside him.

Her brow puckered. "You're not happy."

"I'm delighted you've found some good in your magic."

"Then what is it?" She ran a finger over his lips. "I can tell by the hard line of your mouth that something is wrong."

He sighed and tucked a strand of hair the wind

had snatched from her braid behind her ear. "We've company."

"Deirdre?"

"Nay," he hastened to say. "Warriors. Galen's friends, to be specific."

She licked her lips and set her hands on his chest. "How many?"

"Three. Hayden, Logan, and Ramsey. I wanted to tell you before you walked into the hall and found them."

"It's a good thing Quinn has been doing so much hunting. Will more be coming?"

He shrugged. "I don't know."

As he looked into her eyes, he felt his desire stir as it always did when she was near. The mere scent of her made his blood rush through his veins.

She grinned and rose up on tiptoe to wrap her arms around his neck. "I know that look."

"Do you?"

"Oh, aye. I know you quite well, my lord."

He chuckled and rubbed his nose against hers. "You'll have to convince me."

"I can do that," she whispered, and placed her lips against his.

Fire erupted in Lucan. He tightened his arms around Cara as she sank into him. His cock throbbed with need so intense, so pure, it nearly brought him to his knees.

He wanted her. Right then, in the garden with the sunlight shining upon them. She was nature's child, and it only seemed right. His fingers found the end of her braid and loosened the strip of leather that held her thick tresses. Once it was undone, he dropped the strip on the ground and plunged his hands into her thick length. He loved the feel of her hair in his hands and how the locks slid over his fingers like the finest silk.

The sound of someone clearing his throat brought Lucan to his senses. He ended the kiss and looked over his shoulder to find Galen.

"What?" Lucan demanded.

Galen kept his gaze on the ground. "Sorry to interrupt, but Fallon wants you to bring Cara into the hall."

"A pity." Cara rested her cheek on Lucan's chest and fingered one of the braids at his temple.

Lucan was torn. He wanted to tell Galen to go away while he took Cara down to the beach and made love in the sea, but he knew too much was at stake to disregard their visitors.

He tilted her face to his and gave her another kiss. "Later," he promised.

"I'm going to hold you to that, MacLeod," she said with a smile.

He turned toward Galen and took Cara's hand in his own. "The men know we have a Druid. They don't know whether you're *drough* or *mie*."

"You want me to keep it that way?"

"For now."

She shook her head. "Lucan, you're going to have to trust people one day."

"I do. I trust you."

CHAPTER TWENTY-FOUR

Cara's body was so caught up in the desire Lucan so quickly had kindled that she didn't realize her hair was loose until she walked into the great hall.

Lucan's knowing smile brought forth a chuckle from her lips. She leaned close and whispered, "I didn't know you had removed the binding of my braid."

"Then my kisses were doing what they were supposed to."

She reached back to braid her hair, but his hands stopped her.

"Please," Lucan said. "You have such beautiful hair. Let me see it."

How could she refuse such a request? His sea green eyes held hers, a silent plea in their depths. "Aye," she whispered.

One side of his mouth lifted in a grin. The sight made her heart melt and her blood heat. Lucan always managed to bring such delicious emotions swirling inside her. She couldn't imagine a day without him, didn't want to imagine a day without him. He had become her life.

She forgot everything and everyone as she rose up to kiss him. One of his hands cupped her face while the other held her against him.

"You have no idea how much I want you," he whispered against her lips. "But I don't enjoy others looking while I'm kissing you."

Too late, she remembered the visitors. She closed her eyes and groaned in embarrassment.

Lucan's thumb caressed her cheek. "I will protect you, Cara. Never forget that."

She opened her eyes and gave him a nod before she turned and faced the table. Galen, on the one hand, stood off to the side and smiled at her. Fallon, on the other hand, simply stared at them from his position at the foot of the table.

But it was the other three men sitting at the table who drew her attention. Two faced her while the other turned on the bench to look at her.

Lucan placed a comforting hand on her back. "The blond is Hayden Campbell."

Cara's gaze swung to the big man. He looked to be even bigger than Lucan with his huge shoulders and massive arms. He nodded in greeting, his dark eyes regarded her with doubt and worry.

"The one next to him is Logan Hamilton," Lucan said.

Cara looked to Hayden's left and into hazel eyes. Logan's dark hair had strands of gold throughout, and she had no doubt that with Logan's good looks he had women falling all over him.

Lucan shifted his feet and motioned to the man turned on the bench. "This is Ramsey Mac-Donald."

Ramsey's gray eyes missed nothing as he looked her over. She found no censure in his gaze, just curiosity. He was handsome but aloof, with blue-black hair shorn to his collar.

"And I am Cara," she said.

Ramsey rose from the table and walked to her. She felt Lucan stiffen by her side, but she didn't fear anything, not with Lucan near her.

Ramsey stopped in front of her. "You're the Druid."

"Aye," she answered, "though I only recently learned of it."

He gave a small nod and turned his gaze to Lucan. "Do you think Deirdre wants Cara bad enough to come for her herself?"

Lucan shrugged. "It's a possibility."

"Deirdre doesna leave her mountain," Hayden said. "The last time she left was almost two hundred years ago. She sends Warriors and the wyrran in her stead."

Cara wasn't sure she wanted to meet Deirdre, not after everything she had heard of the woman.

Fallon moved to stand on the other side of Cara. "Deirdre wants Cara, and from what the Warriors said, Deirdre will stop at nothing to get her."

"What makes her so special?" Logan asked. "Deirdre wouldn't go to this much trouble for just any Druid."

Cara looked up to find Lucan and Fallon exchanging glances over her head. Lucan didn't want the men to know, but Cara realized the more information they had the better they would understand what they faced.

"My mother was a *drough*," she said. She pulled out the silver vial, the Demon's Kiss, and let it rest between her breasts. "Deirdre killed her and my father when I was just a child. I was hidden and therefore overlooked."

Hayden got to his feet, his gaze narrowed on Cara. "A *drough*?" he spat.

"Cara isn't a *drough*," Fallon said. "She was raised in a nunnery."

"Cara had no idea what she was until we told her," Galen said.

Ramsey drummed his fingers on his leg, his expression calm and patient, so different from Hayden's. "Has she done the blood ritual?"

"Nay," Cara answered. "I'm not a *drough*."

Logan blew out a breath. "*Drough* or not, she needs to be protected from Deirdre. I don't want that evil bitch to get her hands on any more Druids."

Hayden shook his head. "She has *drough* blood in her. She'll turn."

Lucan's nails lengthened into claws, and Cara knew things would erupt into a fight if something wasn't done.

"I'm not a *drough*," she repeated. "I'm just learning of the Druids, but I'm not going to follow in my mother's footsteps."

"You canna know that for sure," Hayden argued.

Cara sighed and opened her mouth to convince him when Hayden's skin shifted and turned a deep, dark red. He snarled at something behind her, his lips peeled back to show his long fangs.

She turned to find Quinn standing in the doorway of the kitchen staring at Hayden. Quinn growled, his arms held out to his sides and his claws extended as the rest of him transformed.

"Cara is under our protection," Quinn said. "You have a problem with that? Leave. Or die."

Hayden took a step toward Quinn. Cara blinked, unsure if she had seen the small red horns that stuck straight up on the top of his head through his blond hair.

"You don't know what evil the *droughs* can do," Hayden said. "If you did, you wouldn't allow her in your castle."

In the next heartbeat Lucan transformed and put himself between her and Hayden.

"You don't understand!" Hayden bellowed.

"Nay, Hayden." Galen's skin had turned green. He walked to stand between Quinn and Lucan. "It's you who don't understand."

Hayden shook his head. "You know, Galen. You know what the *drough* can do."

"I do," Galen admitted. "I also know it is a choice each Druid makes. Cara hasn't been raised as a Druid, much less a *drough*."

Fallon took her arm and tried to move her behind him, but she yanked out of his grasp and walked to stand between Hayden and Lucan.

"Enough!" she shouted. "We have a common enemy, Hayden. Deirdre. You cannot fight her alone, and neither can we. Either side with us or leave, but make your choice."

"Now," Lucan growled.

The hall was tense, everyone waiting for the others to move. Ramsey sighed and walked around Hayden before coming to stand beside Fallon.

"Cara is right. We need to stand together to defeat Deirdre," Ramsey said.

Logan slapped his hands down on the table and rose. "I know your pain, Hayden, but Cara hasn't done the ritual. She isn't a *drough*. We need to protect her."

Cara watched as Logan walked past his friend,

cuffing him on the shoulder. Logan didn't stop until he stood next to Lucan. Hayden shook his head and closed his eyes. She could see his pain, knew he was conflicted. Whatever a *drough* had done to him in the past had left deep scars.

Finally, Hayden changed back into a man and lowered himself on the bench. All but Quinn reverted back. Quinn gave her a nod and stalked out the castle door into the bailey.

"Good choice, Hayden," Galen said.

Lucan's fingers wrapped around her arm before sliding down to her hand. His heat surrounded her, comforted her. She had never expected to see men have to decide whether to defend her or not. She knew without a doubt Lucan and his brothers would have fought along with Galen to protect her. It was a good thing the other three had realized they were better as a team than individuals.

She let out a breath she hadn't known she was holding and leaned against Lucan's calming strength.

"Since there are seven of us, I'd like five men posted on lookouts while two guard Cara," Fallon said.

"I can stay in my chamber," Cara volunteered.

Lucan shook his head. "Nay. A Warrior could get to you too easily. You need to be somewhere safer."

"The hall," Galen said. "Keep her here. It's centralized, and with us standing guard, she'll have added time to prepare herself for when they get through."

"Good idea," Lucan said.

Cara wasn't looking forward to sleeping in the great hall in front of everyone, but she wouldn't argue with them. They were trying to protect her. The least she could do was make things easier on them.

Fallon glanced at Lucan. "You will be with Cara always. The rest of us will take turns being the second guard."

Lucan gave a quick nod of his head. "Agreed."

Cara didn't stop Lucan when he pulled her out of the castle.

He released her and walked down the steps to pace the bailey. She swallowed and lowered herself onto the top step.

"That was close with Hayden," Lucan said.

Fallon sat beside her. "Too damn close."

She hadn't heard Fallon follow them, but she wasn't surprised to find him there.

"I don't trust him around Cara." Lucan shook his head. "I don't want him alone with her. Ever."

Cara clasped her hands together in her lap. "We don't know what happened to Hayden, Lucan."

"It doesn't matter, not when he threatens you."

Her heart swelled. She had just been Cara, alone and unwanted, until Lucan. He wanted her, had safeguarded her since the moment she fell into his arms. When she looked into his eyes, she saw desire, yes, but she saw something else, something deeper.

Fallon sighed. "Until we know what is going on with Hayden and why he reacted so strongly to Cara, we might want to make sure he's watched."

"I'll make sure I'm not alone with him," Cara said.

Lucan winked at her in response. "Thank you."

The castle door opened and Galen stepped out. "Is supper ready? I'm starving."

Cara laughed and looked over her shoulder at him. "Aye, it's ready."

"Galen," Lucan halted him before he could return inside the castle. "We'd like to know why Hayden reacted the way he did to Cara."

Galen leaned back against the door and crossed his arms over his chest. "We all have a story to tell. Hayden is no different."

"Maybe," Fallon said, "but none of the others wanted to harm Cara."

"I don't think he would have hurt her."

"You don't think?" Lucan asked. "I saw his eyes, Galen. The word *drough* made him go daft."

Galen was silent for long moments before he blew out a breath. "Hayden's story is his own, but I will tell you that at one time Deirdre used the *drough* for her own purposes before she began killing them. The *drough* did truly horrific things in their quest to find Warriors."

"Thank you." Cara stood and faced Galen. "I'll gather the food for supper now."

Galen moved and opened the door for her. Something tugged the end of her hair, and she glanced back to see Lucan wrapping a strand of her hair around his finger.

She was saddened for Hayden, for all of them. They couldn't help the anger and hate that fed them. She held the same hatred for Deirdre for her parents' deaths. The difference was Cara didn't have a primeval god inside her giving her added powers.

But you do have magic.

Aye, she did have her magic.

Hayden clenched his hands into fists. It had never entered his mind that the MacLeods had a Druid, much less one with *drough* blood in her—and around her neck.

The need to kill her, to end the existence of any evil, burned him. It was fitting that the god inside him was Ouraneon, the god of massacre, since that's what the *droughs* had done. And it was what Hayden wanted to do to Cara.

Yet when Ramsey, and even Logan, had chosen to stand with the MacLeods and the Druid, Hayden's ire had cooled. For the time being.

The Druid was correct. They did have a common enemy. But once Deirdre was dead . . .

Supper had gone much smoother than Lucan had anticipated after Hayden's outburst. Hayden himself didn't look up from his trencher. Nor did he have much to say. The others, however, spoke freely.

Lucan learned that Ramsey had his god unbound shortly after they did. Ramsey had been taken by the wyrran while traveling. Though Lucan was curious, he didn't ask Ramsey how he had escaped from Deirdre's mountain.

Logan told them even more. "I met Ramsey in the mountain. I was there for a score of years, and he was there before me."

"How long did Deirdre have you?" Quinn asked Ramsey.

Ramsey set down his goblet. "Too damn long."

Logan chuckled. "Ramsey isna much of a talker."

"How did Deirdre find you, Logan?" Lucan asked.

Logan paused in his chewing. "I was returning home from meeting a lass who had caught my fancy. My brother saw the wyrran take me. I feared they might hurt my family, so I went with them willingly."

"A good thing," Fallon said, and pushed his empty trencher away. "The wyrran would have killed them."

Lucan glanced at Hayden but realized the big man wouldn't answer any questions. Yet the more withdrawn he became, the more worried Lucan got.

"I think you should have built a bigger table," Fallon said. "We're squeezed in here."

Lucan had Cara sit on his knee while they ate. She had wanted to eat by the fire since there wasn't room at the table, but Lucan was on the end and had patted his leg.

"I didn't anticipate having guests," Lucan said. "Next time I'll make a bigger table."

Fallon smiled, a true smile that reached his eyes. It had been so long since he had smiled that Lucan was taken aback.

Cara rose from his leg and walked to the kitchen. He quickly followed. His cock had been hard since their kiss in the garden, and with her now bedding in the great hall, time alone would be scarce.

He caught her around the waist and spun her back against the wall. Her chestnut waves teased him as they fell around her shoulders and down her back. She looked up at him with a welcoming smile.

"I had hoped you would follow me."

Lucan inhaled her scent and kissed the spot below her ear that always made her shiver. "You did?"

"Oh, aye." She was breathless, her pulse racing.

"Why is that?"

She threaded her fingers in his hair. "Because I want you."

His balls tightened at the sound of her husky voice whispering in his ear. He slanted his mouth over hers for a kiss, deepening it when she moaned. His need, his *hunger*, for Cara overshadowed everything else. All he wanted was her, in any way he could have her.

He gathered her skirts in his hand until they were

bunched at her waist. Then he lifted her. She wrapped her legs around his waist as he ground his hard rod into her.

"Lucan, I need you."

He shifted her so that he could unfasten his breeches, and as soon as his cock sprang free, he slid inside her. She leaned her head back against the wall and closed her eyes. Lucan buried his face in her neck and held still, loving the feel of her slick heat surrounding him.

When it became too much, he started to move with short, slow thrusts. As their passion built, he plunged deeper and deeper into her, their rhythm increasing each time.

Cara's nails dug into his neck as her body stiffened. He claimed her mouth, drinking in her moans of pleasure as she peaked. He held off his own climax as long as he could to draw hers out, but the feel of her clenching around him was too much. He gave one final thrust that buried him deep.

She held him, stroking his back and shoulders as his body jerked with the force of his orgasm. She whispered his name, of how much she loved his touch.

He lifted his head and looked into her mahogany eyes. He wanted to show her how much she meant to him, but he wasn't sure how.

"Lucan? What is it?"

He shook his head. "Nothing."

She ran her fingers down one of the braids at his temples and smiled. "It is something, but if you don't want to tell me, that's all right, too."

Reluctantly, he pulled out of her. He moved to the doorway as he fastened his breeches to keep anyone out who wanted to come into the kitchens while she fixed her own clothing.

"Are you sure we cannot stay in the chamber?" she asked with a smile. "I don't think I'm done with you."

Lucan walked to her and lifted a strand of her hair to his nose. "When this is over, Cara, I'm going to take you somewhere where we can be alone. Just the two of us."

"That sounds nice, but what of your brothers? They need you."

"And I need you. They can survive without me for a couple of months."

She tilted her head to the side. "You really want to take me somewhere?"

"Aye. I've been alive for over three hundred years and I've seen nothing but Scotland. Maybe I'll take you to London."

Her laugh was beautiful and pure. "I'm not sure I would know what to do in London, but then again I don't care where I am. As long as I'm with you."

"Then maybe I'll lock us in the chamber."

"That would be nice." She wrapped her arms around his waist and laid her head on his chest.

Lucan ran his hands over her head and down the length of her hair. He might be a fool for caring for a mortal, since he knew there could only be heartache, but the feelings filling his chest were enough to last an eternity.

CHAPTER TWENTY-FIVE

Deirdre looked at her nails and regarded the long tips. She kept them filed to sharp points for certain occasions. She sighed and drummed her nails on the arm of her chair as she looked at William.

"Mistress, I don't understand," he said.

"Of course you don't." Sometimes she wanted to scream, she got so frustrated.

William shifted from one foot to the other, his royal blue skin shining in the flickering light of the candelabras that hung from the ceiling of her palace. "You don't want us to bring back the MacLeods?"

"If you can catch one, aye, bring him. However, I want the Druid above all. And I have something special planned for one of the brothers."

"Oh?"

That had gotten William's attention. He hated the MacLeods because they occupied Deirdre's thoughts when he would prefer her mind be full of him. William was a wonderful specimen, but he didn't compare to Quinn MacLeod. No one did.

"Take six wyrrans and dig a trap. A hole big enough

that it will daze Quinn and give you time to get him back to me."

William nodded. "How do you propose we get Quinn to this trap?"

"He'll follow a wyrran, of course," she said with a smile.

William grinned, his lips pulled back over his fangs. "And with Quinn here, the other brothers will follow."

"Exactly." She blew out a breath as anticipation of having Quinn with her once more took hold of her. "Get moving, William. I want Quinn in my mountain within the next two days."

"Aye, mistress."

"And William," she called before he walked out of the chamber. "You better have the Druid with you when you return."

When she was alone once more, Deirdre rose and ran her hands down her sides, then over her stomach. How she had longed to have Quinn touch her, kiss her, stroke her. Soon, he would be hers again. And this time, she would turn him to her side.

Cara sat on the castle steps and leaned her head back to watch the large clouds drift lazily past in the morning sky. She had slept soundly despite being in the great hall with both Lucan and Fallon.

As soon as everyone had broken their morning fast, Lucan had pulled her out into the bailey for more training. Each day the training became intense, more difficult. Because each day brought the threat of Deirdre that much closer.

Cara had battled Lucan and Galen and Quinn all

at once. At first, she had been so focused on keeping away from them that she kept getting caught by Quinn. When she listened to Lucan's advice to use all her senses, she was able to keep out of all their reaches. It limited the number of hits she put on them, but it helped to make her quicker.

Now, as she and Galen lounged on the castle steps, she found she looked at the castle in a much different light than she had when she had first come there. It had been a pile of ruins before, scary and uninhabitable. Now . . . it was home.

Lucan handed her a waterskin and sat on her other side.

She smiled and drank deeply. She was exhausted but eager to go to the garden and help the plants grow. "Galen, you knew I could use my magic to help the plants grow. What else can I do?"

"Cara," Lucan cautioned.

She knew he worried about her taking Galen's advice, especially since he wasn't a Druid, but she needed to know. For more reasons than Lucan could ever know.

Galen leaned an elbow on a step behind him as he stretched his legs out in front of him to cross at the ankles. "Do you know why the Druids were needed in each tribe?"

She shook her head.

"They were used for more than their knowledge of the earth and their magic with growing plants. The chieftain of each clan had to have a Druid for their wisdom and ability to tell the truth from a lie."

"How?" she asked.

"Magic. The Druids were well-respected members of every tribe. No one would dare to go against a Druid. Just as in all things, some Druids became power hungry. They searched their magic and delved into evil. The power they received from black magic surpassed anything they had ever known. Yet it was never enough."

"Wouldn't they have been able to destroy the other Druids?" Cara asked.

Galen shrugged. "You would think they could have, and would have, but they didn't. I think they knew they needed the *mie*. The *mie*, though not as powerful as the *drough* were individually, together could easily conquer a *drough*. Since the *drough* each sought power, they stayed separated from the others."

"So the *mie* would band as one and destroy the *drough*?" Lucan asked.

Galen gave a small nod. "I was told it happened rarely, but it did happen if a *drough* delved too deep in the black magic."

"Yet the *mie* were happy to go to the *drough* to ask for help with the Roman invasion," Cara said. "Why?"

Galen chuckled. "It was a common enemy they shared."

Cara smiled as Galen used her same words she had used on Hayden. "So, are you telling me I have the power to tell if someone speaks the truth or not?"

"I don't see why you couldn't. It might not be as easy to learn as helping the plants, but I think it is something you could do in time."

"With the help of a Druid," Lucan added.

Cara bit her lip and nodded. "Aye. I would like to find a Druid that could help me with this."

"We'll find one," Lucan said, and took her hand in his.

She smiled into his sea green eyes, but Hayden's words about the *drough* blood inside her made the smile slip.

"What is it?" Lucan asked.

"Hayden said I had *drough* blood, that I would turn. Was he speaking the truth?" She looked from Lucan to Galen. "Will I?"

Galen shrugged. "I know some history of the Druids because I was forced to learn it while in Deirdre's capture. She had us search books and scrolls for any information on the Druids. As to Hayden's claims, I don't have an answer for you."

"I don't want to be *drough*."

"Then don't," Lucan said. "Remember, Cara, you have a choice."

But did she? By the weary, sad look in Galen's blue gaze before he turned away from her he didn't think she did. Maybe she didn't. Maybe she would have to become a *drough* to fight Deirdre.

Cara would have to ask Galen about it later, when Lucan couldn't overhear.

With Lucan by her side every moment, it became almost impossible to get Galen alone, but she had the opportunity when she was getting the noon meal ready and she spotted him in the garden.

Cara walked out of the kitchen to his side. He looked out over the sea, his hands by his sides.

"I knew you would come," he said.

"How?"

He glanced at her. "You want to know about becoming *drough*."

"You mentioned something once about me fighting Deirdre, that I would need to be *drough* to do it."

"I spoke hastily," he said. "You are just coming

into your power, Cara. You've also found love with Lucan. Do you really want to ruin it?"

Love? Aye, she did love Lucan. Desperately.

"Do you?" Galen asked again. This time he turned to face her. "Once you are *drough*, there is no turning back. You will wear the mark always."

"Mark?" she asked. "As in the blood vial?"

"That is part of it. The *drough* are also marked by the cuts from the blade when they do the ritual. The wounds heal, but not naturally because of the black magic involved."

She licked her lips and glanced at the plants growing around her. She had done that, brought them back to life. "Do you know what it's like to be a *drough*?"

"Once the evil has you, Cara, it never lets go."

"I don't believe that. A good person could fight it."

Galen sighed. "Just as the gods inside us don't care what we were before, the evil won't care about your life before the ritual."

Cara's mind was in a whirlwind. "My parents were good people, Galen."

"You were a child, Cara. Your perception of them is distorted. Look at what you have here. Think of that."

"I am thinking of it," she said, and blinked back tears. "I'm thinking of all of it. I would do anything to keep Lucan and the rest of you out of Deirdre's grasp."

He blew out a breath and stepped to her side. "You and Lucan are happy. Don't destroy that."

Cara stayed in the garden long after Galen left, and watched the sea. She thought of his words and knew he was right. Despite the impending battle and an uncertain future, Cara had found contentment with Lucan.

She hadn't lied to him the previous day. It didn't matter where she was as long as he was with her.

"Because I love him," she whispered into the wind. "I love Lucan."

If the time came when she had to choose becoming *drough* to save Lucan, she would do it in a moment. She would do anything for Lucan.

Strong arms wrapped around her from behind. "Cara?"

She leaned back against Lucan and closed her eyes. "I'm here."

"Is everything all right?"

"Aye," she lied. She turned in his arms and pulled his head down for a kiss. "I'm sorry to keep everyone waiting."

"They can keep waiting," he said with a grin.

She laughed. "Galen is likely to eat everything in the kitchen before I can get it into the great hall."

"True," Lucan said with a sigh. "Come. I'll help you."

Lucan sat in the great hall before the hearth staring into the flames as night descended. He'd had an uneasy feeling that had grown as the day wore on. Now that night approached, he knew Deirdre would attack. He had told his fears to his brothers.

They hadn't questioned him; they simply made sure everyone was at their posts at all times. There had been no supper in the great hall. Each man had been brought a trencher of food by Fallon.

Cara hadn't understood why Lucan wouldn't let her bring the food. He didn't want her to worry, not yet. He wanted her to relax and enjoy the time they had before Deirdre attacked.

"What is going on, Lucan?" Cara asked.

He turned his head to the chair beside his to find her watching him. "What do you mean?"

"Did you think I wouldn't notice how edgy everyone is? Fallon hasn't touched his wine since the noon meal."

Lucan couldn't hold her gaze. Not even when he had woken to find himself a monster was he as scared as he was at that moment, knowing Deirdre would stop at nothing to obtain Cara. Despite his power, he might not be able to prevent Deirdre from taking her.

"Please, Lucan."

He squeezed his eyes closed and pinched the bridge of his nose with his thumb and forefinger. "Cara, I . . ."

"It's Deirdre, isn't it? You think she's going to attack tonight."

Lucan opened his eyes and looked at her. He couldn't lie to her, not now. "I think so."

Cara rose and moved to kneel in front of him. She took his hands in hers. "You've done everything you could to prepare me. You found me a sword and made me a dagger. You allowed Galen into the castle, even when you didn't want to, and when others came, you welcomed them as well. We will do what we can."

"And if Deirdre captures you?"

Dark eyes with more strength and bravery than he had ever seen met his. "Then I will fight her. I will do whatever it is I must in order to escape."

"And I will find you."

"Nay," she all but yelled. "Nay, Lucan. You and

the others, you must run to safety. Deirdre wants to use all of you to wage war on Scotland. You cannot let her succeed."

He leaned forward and cupped Cara's face in his hands. "I cannot let her have you."

"How long do we have?"

"I doona know."

She rose and climbed into his lap. "Then let us enjoy what little time we have."

Lucan didn't stop her when she leaned down and kissed him. She straddled him, her sex rubbing against his hardening cock. He gripped her hips and pushed her down as he ground into her. Her moan spurred his need.

She clawed at his tunic while he jerked her gown and chemise over her head. He kissed and licked her delectable skin, stopping only long enough for her to yank his tunic off.

He cupped her breasts and moved his mouth over one nipple, suckling the tiny nub in his mouth until it hardened. He circled her other nipple with his thumb, teasing it until it was as hard and straining as the one in his mouth.

Her hips rocked against him as her moans grew louder. He wanted inside her, needed to be inside her to be as close to her as a man could be to a woman.

When he reached to unlace his breeches, she rose up on her knees and helped him. She grasped his cock when he sprang free and ran her hands up and down the length.

"I want to take you in my mouth as you've taken me."

Lucan closed his eyes and groaned. He could imagine Cara leaned over him, her chestnut locks falling on either side of his legs as she took him in her mouth, her full lips sliding over him.

"You want it, too," she whispered.

"Aye." He barely recognized the croak as his own voice, but Cara had the ability to make him hard and wanting with just a touch.

She kissed his chest, her hands still moving over his rod. She cupped his balls and gently rolled them in her hand. "Let me," she urged.

He was ready to climax. One touch of her lips and it would be over. "Nay," he said. "Not this time. I need you too desperately."

He opened his eyes and reached between her legs to caress her swollen flesh. She sighed and rocked against his hand. His thumb circled her clitoris before he dipped a finger into her heat. She was so damned wet.

Her head fell back, her hair cascading over his legs. "Lucan," she moaned.

He thrust a second finger to join the first, pumping in and out of her in quick, short strokes. Her breath quickened and her hands gripped his shoulders. He withdrew his fingers and moved his thumb back and forth over her clitoris while he pinched her nipple. She gasped and reached for his arousal to guide it into her heat.

She lowered herself onto him. Their eyes met as they began to move. Sweat glistened over his body as he held her hips. Her hands were on his shoulders, her lips parted. His climax was nearly upon him. He wouldn't be able to hold it back, and he refused to go without Cara.

He reached between them and took her clitoris between his thumb and forefinger and gave it a gentle tug. She cried out as her body stiffened. The feel of that first contraction of her body around his rod sent him over the edge.

They reached orgasm together, lost in each other's eyes. When they finally came down, Cara placed her lips on his for a gentle kiss.

"I love you."

His breath locked in his lungs.

She leaned back and caressed his cheek. "I know there are too many odds against us, too much that would keep us apart, but I know what I feel."

Lucan knew he felt something for Cara, but was it love? "Cara—"

"Sh," she said and put her finger to his lips. "Let me give you all that I have to give."

Her love had been unexpected, but maybe it shouldn't have been. It shone in her eyes every time she looked at him. He wasn't sure he even had a heart to give her anymore, but there was one thing he could do: protect her.

A tear fell down her cheek. He caught it with his thumb and brought it to his lips. "We will get through this."

"Aye," she whispered, and laid her head on his shoulder.

CHAPTER TWENTY-SIX

Quinn stretched his shoulder. He'd wanted on top of the towers where he usually sat, but Lucan had wanted him closer when the attack came. So he stood on the battlements, his nerves edgy and ready for the fight. He kept his gaze on the east side of the castle and the cliffs, the same cliffs Cara had fallen from.

That day seemed so long ago, as though Cara had always been a part of their family. Their lives before her had been sedate and boring. If they could have known what her presence meant, would Lucan still have saved her?

Quinn knew the answer would be a resounding "aye."

He paused in his musing as Fallon strode toward him. His eldest brother had changed, and for the better. Though Quinn wasn't sure he liked the attitude that had returned with the absence of the wine.

Fallon had always been a good man. He was good at everything, including leading their clan. Their father had been proud of Fallon's accomplishments, and everyone knew in Fallon's hands the clan would only prosper.

It was good to see parts of him return, yet there was no mistaking the thread of fear in Fallon's eyes. He was right to be afraid of the god inside him, for Fallon had used the wine to dull his senses—and the god.

Now, when they needed Fallon the most, he would likely fail them. But Quinn didn't begrudge his brother. There had been many times Quinn had thought to follow Fallon into the flavorful oblivion.

Quinn had his faults—and they were many—but he wouldn't leave Lucan alone to tend to everything. It was Lucan's way, though. He liked to be in control, in charge. He liked to get things done and see to people's needs. It made him the man he was today.

"Quinn," Fallon said, his voice low in the still night. "How is everything?"

"Quiet," Quinn replied. "You making the rounds again?"

"Aye. One last look before I return to the great hall."

Quinn snorted. "You just wanted to give Lucan and Cara some time alone."

"I did. There's nothing wrong with that. If Lucan's senses are right, they may not have any time after tonight."

Quinn blew out a breath and nodded slowly. "Lucan's senses have never failed him before. He's always known where the boar or deer are when we hunt."

"Aye. It's why I didn't question him."

"The others don't understand."

"I don't give a damn," Fallon said. "As long as they stay on guard and alert us if they see anything, they can believe what they will."

Fallon and Quinn stood quietly side by side for

several moments before Quinn spoke again. "You would have married that woman, what's her name, Da asked you to, wouldn't you?"

Fallon chuckled. "I cannot even remember her name, either. And, aye, I would have. Da said it was for the good of the clan."

"Regardless of what you wanted?"

"It didn't matter what I wanted, Quinn. That's the point of being laird. Sacrifices had to be made. The alliance with the MacDonalds would have been a great boon. Two of the largest, strongest clans in Scotland. It was Da's goal for a long time."

Quinn scratched his jaw and shifted his feet wider. "Your life could have been awful with that woman."

"Maybe, but then I could live through you and your good life with Elspeth."

He cringed and turned away, but he must not have been quick enough, for Fallon's hand gripped his shoulder and turned him back around.

"I'm sorry I spoke of Elspeth. I know you don't like to talk about her."

Quinn looked over the moonlit land. "Speak of Elspeth as you will, Fallon. I didn't speak of her because I failed her and our son. To make matters worse, I didn't love her."

"So why did you marry her?" Fallon's voice was filled with concern and shock.

"It seemed the right thing to do. She wanted me, and I wanted a family. I knew Elspeth had always been of a gentle nature, but once we were married, it became worse. Much worse. I couldna get annoyed without her cowering in fear, even though I never laid a hand on her in anger."

"I had no idea."

"No one did. I wanted it that way."

"There is more, isn't there?"

Quinn leaned his hands on the stones and lifted a foot to rest it in the crenel, the opening between the merlons of the battlements. "Do you remember when my son was born?"

"Vaguely. It was a joyous day in our family."

"It was hell," Quinn said. "The labor was long and the baby had to be turned. Elspeth was so weak afterward and had lost so much blood that she nearly died. The midwife cautioned us about having any more children. In Elspeth's mind, that meant I could no longer make love to her."

"Shite," Fallon murmured.

"The midwife had given her some herbs to take every day so she wouldn't conceive again, but Elspeth refused to take them. And I refused to touch her unless she took them. I may have wanted more children, but I wasn't going to risk her life for them. I was happy with my son, my family that I had."

"Quinn."

He shook his head. "Doona say it, Fallon. There's no need. I married Elspeth because I wanted what Mum and Da had. Those special looks and secret smiles they shared with each other. I thought all marriages would be that way."

"Nay. Not all."

"I learned that too late. I see those same looks between Lucan and Cara, and I envy them what they've found. You've always been the eldest, the one in charge. Lucan has always been able to fix anyone's problems, no matter how big or small. I had nothing. I was nothing."

"You had us," Fallon said as he faced Quinn.

"You are a MacLeod. A fine warrior, and a Highlander I'm proud to call brother."

Quinn slammed his hand down on the stones, cracking them. "Look at me, Fallon. I cannot control the creature, and God help me, but I don't really want to. I'm not fit to be near anyone."

"The god chooses the best warrior from each family, Quinn. The god inside us chose all three MacLeod brothers. What does that tell you?"

"That the god is an idiot."

"That all three of us are the best warriors."

Quinn shook his head, desperately wanting to believe his brother. "You and Lucan are all I have now, but the rage inside me burns and grows the longer I watch Lucan and Cara. I've tried to control it. Lucan deserves joy. I don't begrudge him in the least."

"Neither of you left me while I stayed in my wine-induced haze. We won't leave you now. We'll get through this, Quinn, as we've done everything else. We're MacLeods. We only have each other."

Quinn opened his mouth to answer when something on the cliffs caught his eye. He narrowed his gaze and leaned over the battlements.

"God's blood," he murmured, and watched as a Warrior came in sight.

"I'll go to Lucan and Cara. You tell the others," Fallon said before he ran from the battlements.

Quinn's gut clenched with unease while his blood burned for battle. He cupped his hands around his mouth and gave the whistle that sounded more like a bird than a man. Shadows moved on the castle letting him know they had heard and understood.

The attack they had been expecting for days was upon them.

Quinn tilted back his head and let the rage consume him.

Cara sat in Lucan's lap, her head resting on his shoulder. She didn't regret telling him of her love nor had she expected him to reply in kind. But she had hoped.

They had long since dressed, but they had been unable to stop touching each other. She closed her eyes as his fingers combed through her hair, prickling her scalp with delicious pleasure.

She didn't understand his love of her hair, but she enjoyed it. She had a particular fascination with his body in which she could never look enough, feel enough of him.

Her hand moved over his heart. It beat strong and steady, just like him. She glanced up to find his gaze in the flames before them. He was thinking of the coming battle.

Since he was a Warrior, she didn't fear him being wounded. And since Deirdre wanted all the Warriors, especially the Macleods, Cara didn't worry about their heads being chopped off.

But Lucan worried about her.

Her gaze shifted to her sword, which stood next to the hearth, leaned against the stones. Her dagger, the beautiful dagger Lucan had made for her, was strapped to her hip. All they could do was wait.

Suddenly the sound of Quinn's whistle, the alarm for danger, sounded. Cara jerked upright and met Lucan's gaze. The battle was upon them.

The door to the castle burst open and Fallon rushed inside, slamming the door behind him. "Quinn spotted the first Warrior."

Cara started to rise from Lucan's lap when his hands held her down. She looked at him and saw the fear in his eyes.

"Stay with me, Cara."

"I will," she promised.

He slid his hand to the back of her neck and pulled her to his mouth for a kiss that was slow and sensual, full of passion and the love they had confessed. "We'll beat the Warriors again," he murmured.

When he released her, she rushed to get her sword and palmed the dagger in her left hand. She missed Lucan's warmth already. She had dreaded this night, for she knew her life would be forever changed.

Fallon leapt on top of the table, two swords in his hands. She waited for Lucan to ask him to transform, but he didn't. Lucan held her gaze as his skin darkened to black and his beautiful sea green eyes vanished beneath the obsidian. He flexed his fingers and the long claws that gleamed onyx in the firelight.

She walked toward him and rose on her tiptoes to place her lips against his. His arms wrapped around her, holding her tight. His fangs gently scraped her lip, but instead of hurting, she found the sensation thrilling, and dangerous.

He released her and she moved against the wall. Lucan stood in front of her and a little to her left so she could see Fallon.

Her heart pounded in her chest and her stomach dipped and pitched so much she thought she might be sick. She wasn't ready for this no matter what she had told Lucan. But no amount of training could have readied her for the coming attack.

She pulled in a shaky breath and made her fingers

loosen on her weapons. She held them too tight, was too nervous. They would be knocked out of her hands without much force.

With a great amount of effort, she steadied her breathing and tried to calm her racing heart. Lucan and the others had taught her how to stay out of reach of the wyrrans and the Warriors. All she had to do was stay near Lucan. He would protect her.

An eerie scream that wasn't human sounded from one of the towers. Cara's heart lurched.

"It seems one of the wyrran found a trap," Fallon said with a joyful smile.

The castle shook as something broke through the stones in an upper part of the castle. Roars and growls and wails of pain reverberated through the castle. Cara shivered and moved closer to Lucan.

The urge to run and hide was strong, but she was a Druid, a woman who had been gifted with the griffin symbol from her lover. She would not run.

Fallon lifted his swords over his head with a battle cry that would have made any Highlander proud, as the first wyrran entered the hall. He cleaved the beast's head off and rotated his swords as he waited for the next.

They didn't have long to wait.

Wyrran poured through the great hall like ants. They crawled down the walls, their pale eyes focused on her. Their inhuman screams made her tremble and long to cover her ears.

"Cara."

Lucan's voice jerked her out of her fear. He gave her a quick nod over his shoulder before he bent his knees and waited for the next wyrran.

It was a beautiful sight watching Lucan fight. He

moved with such grace and skill and beauty that for a moment she forgot her life was in danger.

A blur out of the corner of her eye was the only warning she got that a wyrran had come after her. She lifted her sword and spun around. There was a shriek as her blade penetrated the creature's chest. She wasted no time in cutting off its head.

But as soon as that one fell, two more took its place.

The hall faded away as she focused on the two wyrran. They moved as quickly as she did, but she managed to use her dagger to slice one's ribs while she severed the tendons in the back of the other's knee.

When it went down, she chopped off its head. She sucked in a breath as claws raked down her back. She was careful not to cry out and cause Lucan to lose concentration while he fought. Instead, she ducked and spun, using her dagger to cut the wyrran's head from its hairless body.

Quinn leapt from the top of the battlements to the bailey below where a blue-skinned Warrior had just come through the gatehouse. He landed atop the Warrior and sank his claws in the man's neck. The Warrior howled and reached back to scour the side of Quinn's face with his claws.

Quinn bit back a curse as pain lanced through him, but the pain became anger, fueling his need to kill. He gripped the man's head and tried to twist it to break his neck, but the Warrior anticipated Quinn's move and bent over.

Quinn lost his hold on the Warrior and fell to the

ground. He ducked his head and rolled. He came to his feet with a twist to face the Warrior.

"You won't win," the Warrior said. "No one wins against Deirdre."

Quinn laughed as he recognized his blue foe as the Warrior he had fought in the first battle. "Then you havena tried hard enough. We've stayed out of her evil clutches for over three hundred years."

"Ah, but the Druid will be your downfall."

Quinn narrowed his gaze as they circled each other. "What do you mean?"

"Exactly what I said." The Warrior bared his teeth and ran his tongue over his fangs. "Deirdre wants all of you alive, but I've a need for blood this night."

"Imagine that. So do I."

They clashed with a bone-jarring crash. Quinn jerked his arm away before the Warrior could sink his sharp fangs into him. He threw back his head and roared as the Warrior wrapped his arms around Quinn's middle and squeezed.

Quinn head-butted the royal blue Warrior, sending him stumbling backward. It was enough for him to loosen his hold and for Quinn to break free. As soon as Quinn's feet hit the ground he threw the Warrior against the castle. He fell to the ground with a resounding thud.

The Warrior rose up on his elbow and shook his head. Quinn had wanted a fight for a long time. It felt good to give in to the rage and bloodlust.

A shout from above drew his attention. He looked up to find Hayden and three wyrran fighting, Hayden's red skin glowing in the moonlight as he threw a ball of fire at the ugly creatures.

When Quinn turned back, the Warrior was gone.

Quinn cursed and hurried into the castle, only to stop in his tracks when he saw the sheer number of wyrran in the great hall.

"Holy hell," he murmured.

CHAPTER
TWENTY-SEVEN

Lucan lost count of the number of wyrran he had killed. Their dead bodies littered the great hall, and he had to watch himself so he didn't trip over them. For every one wyrran he killed, another three took its place. They were everywhere, their wails making his ears ring.

He glanced at Cara as often as he could. She stayed near him, just as he'd asked. She had also managed to kill her share of wyrran, though he noticed one had given her a nasty cut down her back.

She moved with the speed and agility that she had shown in their training, but she was tiring. She wouldn't be able to last much longer. And with the numbers of the wyrran, they could be battling until dawn.

Lucan fought his way closer to her so he could take on more of the wyrran. She gave him a quick smile of thanks before she plunged her dagger into one of the yellow creature's chests, then lopped off its head with her sword.

Movement near the castle door caught his attention. He looked up to see Quinn enter the castle. A moment later he dove into the fray.

Somehow, through it all, Fallon had remained in his human form, using his swords as effectively as Cara. Lucan had known Fallon wouldn't transform, wouldn't give in to the god inside him. Fallon feared the god too much.

Lucan's claws ripped down a wyrran's chest before he severed its head from its body. It fell to the floor the same instant Lucan spotted three Warriors rushing into the hall from the stairs.

The traps had slowed the attack, but not by much. Above all the shrieks and growls, Lucan heard Fallon cry out. Lucan turned to see his brother fall, a purple-skinned Warrior standing over Fallon.

The Warrior smiled at Lucan just before he leaned down and sliced open Fallon's chest.

"Nay!" Lucan bellowed.

He leapt over the diminutive wyrrans to land beside Fallon. His green eyes were crinkled with pain as blood seeped into his tunic. With him in this state, it would be easy for the Warriors or a wyrran to cut off Fallon's head. Fury slammed into Lucan. His claws cutting, piercing, and slashing the purple skin, he attacked the Warrior. Lucan moved with movements so quick, the Warrior could only jerk with each gash of his body.

Cara watched in horror as Fallon fell, the purple-skinned Warrior wasting no time injuring him. She was glad when Lucan rushed to Fallon's side, giving him time to rise and move away. It was just a moment later that Quinn joined Lucan but, instead of fighting, he helped Fallon to his feet.

A sharp pain ran through her leg. Unable to stop the cry from her lips, she turned and sank her dagger into the wyrran's face. It screamed and clawed at the dagger.

Cara jerked it out and sliced off the wyrran's head. When she looked up again, Galen and Ramsey were in the great hall fighting.

She jumped back to miss another wyrran's claws and tripped over a dead wyrran. Cara landed hard on her back, but she rolled over and started to climb to her feet when something grabbed her from behind.

"This was much too easy," said a rough, unfamiliar voice behind her.

Cara looked over her shoulder and saw the royal blue face of a Warrior. His smile was sinister, his fangs much too close to her skin for comfort. She struggled to get free, but he leapt onto the wall with her in his arms without difficulty.

"Lucan!" she yelled, and swung her dagger back toward the Warrior.

He jumped over the battle below and landed on the stairs, where he grabbed the wrist that held her dagger and squeezed. She clenched her teeth and held on as long as she could. Her bones brushed against one another, the pain unbearable. When her numb fingers could not hold on anymore, the dagger clattered to the stairs.

"Drop the sword or I break your arm," the Warrior threatened. "Deirdre wants you alive, but a broken bone willna matter."

Cara knew she had to stay strong to get away from him. If she was wounded it would only make things more difficult. She let the sword drop, feeling bereft without her weapons. She had nothing with which to battle the Warriors, but then again, even her weapons hadn't been enough.

Once more the Warrior grabbed and jerked her against his chest. She clawed at his back with her nails and kicked with her feet in an effort to connect with his balls.

The Warrior turned, banging her head against the stone wall. The edges of her vision darkened as she fought to stay conscious. The Warrior continued up the stairs to the landing, his evil laugh making her skin crawl. Just before he turned, Cara raised her head and saw Lucan staring at her.

—————————————————

"Cara!"

Fallon jerked at the anguished cry of his brother. He turned and saw Lucan looking toward the stairs. Fallon caught a glimpse of Cara being carried away by a Warrior.

Deirdre must have planned it, because three other warriors attacked Lucan, preventing him from going after Cara. Fallon looked to Quinn, but just like Lucan, he was overtaken by Warriors.

Fallon forgot the pain of his healing chest and hurried after Cara before he was attacked as well. He followed Cara's grunts and curses as the Warrior took her to the back tower. By the time Fallon reached it, he saw the Warrior was descending the cliff with Cara on his back.

Fallon paused as he recalled the look of horror and fear in Lucan's eyes. Even when they had been in Deirdre's mountain Lucan had never looked so . . . lost.

Lucan needed Cara. Ever since their clan had been destroyed, Lucan had taken care of his brothers. Lucan, who never asked for anything.

Fallon took in a shaky breath and lifted his arms so he could see his hands. He released the rage he'd kept pent up for centuries. The prickle rushed over his skin seconds before he turned black. He straightened his fingers and saw his nails lengthen into razor-sharp black claws.

Fear had kept him from transforming, but for Lucan he would face it—and the future.

Fallon threw back his head and bellowed as a surge of power warmed his skin. He looked over the castle and saw the Warrior and Cara staring up at him. Fallon's claws scraped the rock as he vaulted over the side and plummeted down the cliff.

He stopped himself by grabbing a rock, the force jerking his arm out of its socket. Fallon ignored the pain and smiled when he saw how close he was to the Warrior.

"Hold on, Cara," he called.

She lifted eyes wet with tears, clinging to the Warrior's neck. Fallon couldn't attack since Cara could lose her hold and fall into the churning sea below. But he also knew he couldn't let the Warrior reach the bottom.

Fallon was going to have to think fast.

———————————

Lucan had never felt so helpless in his life. He fought, all the while screaming for Cara, against the Warriors trying to hold him. She was gone from him, he knew, but he couldn't give up.

"Someone looking for a fight?" Logan yelled as he charged into the great hall, his silver skin bright against the chaos.

Lucan noticed Hayden behind him. Lucan killed

one Warrior while Quinn tore off another's head. The others scrambled out of the castle as if they'd been called away. Lucan didn't care why they had left, only that they had.

No one tried to take him or his brothers. He stopped and looked around the hall. "Where is Fallon?"

Quinn pointed to the stairs. "He followed Cara."

Lucan said a prayer of thanks and hurried after them. He couldn't lose Cara, not now. Fallon had left a trail of overturned boards and doused torches to let his brothers know where he had gone.

When Lucan reached the top of the tower, he looked down to find Cara on the back of a Warrior while Fallon tried to stop him.

"My God," Quinn breathed.

Lucan couldn't believe Fallon had transformed. "I never thought he would turn again."

Galen whistled softly from Lucan's other side. "Fallon surprised us all."

"We need to help," Lucan said.

Quinn nodded. "What do you want us to do?"

Just then Cara screamed as the Warrior lost his hold and fell. Lucan's chest tightened until the Warrior was able to catch hold and stop himself, but the impact made Cara's hold slip.

A heartbeat before she caught the Warrior's leg, halting her fall, Lucan screamed her name. He closed his eyes, his heart in his throat. "I've got to get to her."

"We'll help," Quinn said.

"We cannot let him reach the bottom with Cara."

Ramsey walked up beside him, his skin a dark bronze. He leaned over the tower, his claws scraping the stones. "I'll get down there just in case he does."

"I'll go with him," Hayden said.

Logan stepped forward. "I can stay up here if he decides to come back up."

"And I'll go this way," Galen said, and pointed to the left where the cliffs met the castle. "In case he decides to try running across Scotland."

Lucan gave a quick nod, then turned to Quinn.

Quinn smiled. "You aren't going without me."

Lucan wasted no time in climbing over the tower. He started descending toward Cara, praying with each beat of his heart that she survived. If she didn't, he would storm Deirdre's mountain himself and destroy the evil bitch.

He climbed quickly, and despite Fallon's valiant try, the Warrior was able to still move down the cliff because of Cara. Whenever Fallon reached for Cara, the Warrior would kick his leg, sending Cara careening in the wind.

Lucan crawled to the other side of the Warrior while Quinn stayed above him. "Give me my woman," Lucan demanded.

The Warrior laughed. "She was never yours, MacLeod. She's a Druid and therefore belongs to Deirdre."

"I'll see Deirdre in Hell first."

"No doubt."

Lucan stretched his hand toward Cara. "Grab it."

She reached for him, but the Warrior gave a vicious jerk of his leg, making Cara cling to him instead of taking Lucan's hand.

Fury erupted in Lucan. He wanted to rip the Warrior's heart out and toss it into the sea below. Anything to get him away from Lucan's woman.

Her fingers slipped, but she caught herself on the

Warrior's boot. Her mahogany eyes held Lucan's. They both knew she wouldn't be able to take his hand. The Warrior wouldn't let Lucan or his brothers close enough to get her.

She tried to grab hold of the rocks herself so she could let go of the Warrior, but he growled and moved down the cliff. Lucan glanced at his brothers. Fallon's eyes held such gloom that it made Lucan want to rail at the heavens.

"Lucan!" Cara shouted.

He moved down as close to her as he could. His blood pounded in his ears, his chest tight as if someone squeezed the air from his lungs.

"Remember the day we first met?" she asked.

He nodded, confused. And then he realized what she planned. Lucan looked down at the sea that crashed into the rocks at the bottom of the cliff. He gave her a small nod and jumped to the bottom where he saw Ramsey and Hayden. There was no time to tell Fallon and Quinn, but by Quinn's smile he had heard Cara.

Lucan had just planted his feet on the rocks, the water ebbing and flowing over his boots, when he looked up to see Cara let go of the Warrior's leg.

The Warrior bellowed, and Fallon and Quinn leapt atop him, eager to kill him. Lucan focused his attention on Cara, waiting for her to fall into his arms just as she had the day they first met.

"By the saints," Hayden whispered from behind Lucan.

That's when Lucan heard the flap of wings. "Nay!" he yelled when the flying creature tried to grab Cara as she fell. Cara slapped at its hands, preventing the creature from taking her.

Lucan caught Cara in his arms and hugged her against him. Her hands gripped his tunic, her body trembling as fiercely as his heart.

"Duck," Ramsey warned.

Lucan went down on his haunches with Cara still in his arms. He glanced up to see the creature was a Warrior. A Warrior with wings.

Instead of flying off as they expected, it turned and went after Fallon and Quinn. Lucan shouted a warning a moment before the flying Warrior latched onto Quinn and tossed him away from the cliff.

As Quinn fell into the water Lucan heard a splash behind him, but his gaze was on the flying Warrior who managed to free the other from Fallon's grasp.

The two Warriors flew off into the night, leaving silence behind them. Lucan looked down into Cara's face and gave her a quick, heated kiss.

"I thought I had lost you." He had never known such fear and never wanted to again.

She nodded. "You nearly did."

Water splashed on them as Quinn was helped from the sea by Ramsey and Hayden. "What in holy hell was that thing?" Quinn asked.

Lucan sighed and rose to his feet. "A Warrior."

"With wings," Hayden added. "I've never seen the like."

Quinn snorted. "Well, I'd never seen one with horns before you."

Lucan ignored the talk behind him and watched while Fallon climbed down to them.

"Are they gone?" Cara asked.

Lucan shrugged. "I don't know. We need to get to the castle to find out."

Fallon jumped the last part of the cliff and landed beside Lucan. "Is she hurt?"

"Nay," Lucan answered. "Fallon—"

"Don't. I did what had to be done. I doona regret it."

Cara reached out and touched Fallon's arm. "Thank you."

There was much more Lucan wanted—and needed—to say, but it could wait until he and Fallon were alone. "We need to get back to the castle."

Cara groaned as she looked at the cliff. Lucan kissed her forehead. "It will be easier going up."

Since she had been unconscious the last time she had fallen in his arms, she didn't know just how easy. Lucan navigated the jagged rocks and boulders until they moved to the right side of the castle.

"Hold on," he whispered just before he jumped.

Cara latched onto his neck and gave a shriek as he jumped to the top of the cliff and onto the grass. He smiled down at her as the others joined him.

"Thank the saints I wasn't awake the first time you did that," she whispered.

Lucan lowered her feet to the ground. "Let's go see the castle."

"Did the Warriors leave?" she asked.

"I think so."

"Why did they go?"

He wished he knew.

CHAPTER
TWENTY-EIGHT

Cara stared at the bodies of the wyrran that littered the great hall floor. She gripped the back of a chair since her legs still shook. Her idea of Lucan catching her had been hasty, and the fall . . . She shuddered at the memory. The fall had been horrendous, and the terror had sucked the breath from her body.

She hadn't been able to see below her. She had trusted Lucan to catch her. And he had. Though the flying Warrior had nearly gotten her instead.

When she had felt its hands clasp on her arms, she had fought it with everything she had. She hadn't escaped one Warrior to be taken by another. Not when Lucan was waiting to catch her.

If the darkness had scared her before, it terrified her now that she knew exactly what hid in it. Yet with Lucan by her side, she would face those terrors and vanquish them. After all, he could control the darkness and shadows.

Everyone but Quinn had reverted back to their human forms as they began to clear away the dead. She was still amazed that Fallon had let out his god to help save her. There was nothing she could ever do to repay him, especially when she knew how much it frightened him to let out the god.

Quinn's jerky movements caught her eye. The glances he threw her and Lucan worried her. Quinn was acting stranger than normal, almost as if he couldn't decide on something that weighed heavily in his mind. She started toward him to ask when Lucan stopped her.

"You're wounded. You need to rest," he said. "We'll get rid of the bodies."

She swallowed and looked at Quinn around Lucan's shoulder. "I can help."

"You're bleeding, Cara. Please. For me?"

There was no way she could deny Lucan. He turned the chair so that it faced the great hall and she could watch them. She sank into the chair and let him clean the wounds on her back and leg. When he finished she leaned her head against the back of the chair. It was her intention to keep an eye on Quinn and maybe call him over to her, but he left the castle before she could.

The longer she sat, the more difficult it became to focus her eyes. Now that the ordeal was over and she realized that Deirdre had failed, Cara's body felt drained and lifeless. She closed her eyes intending only to rest.

———————

Quinn dumped the four wyrran he had into the pile started away from the castle. Just as with the first attack, they would burn the bodies. He turned and looked at the castle. His home.

He was glad Deirdre had failed to capture Cara, but if he was honest with himself, he couldn't stand to watch her and Lucan together for another moment.

It brought home the fact that Quinn didn't know what love was and likely never would. It also reminded him of his failure as a husband and father.

Time away was what he needed. Fallon had unleashed his god, something he hadn't done since Deirdre had first awoken the monsters inside them. Fallon had set aside the wine and faced his greatest fears.

Quinn clenched his hands into fists. His rage was out of control and growing by the day. He knew he needed to control it, but he didn't want to. It consumed him, sustained him.

He knew what he had to do. If he told Lucan and Fallon, they would only try to talk him out of it. He was the one who knew what was best for him. It was time the others realized that as well.

With one last look at his home, the only thing that remained of his clan and a life before he became a monster, Quinn turned and ran into the darkness.

CHAPTER TWENTY-NINE

Cara woke to the delicious feel of Lucan's mouth on her breasts. His hand massaged one nub, rolling a nipple between two fingers as his mouth suckled the other.

"About time you woke," he mumbled against her skin.

She smiled and plunged her hands into his hair, not surprised to find herself naked. Lucan's hot, hard body touched her skin to skin, his arousal pressed into her stomach. She opened her eyes to see they were in her chamber on the bed. Desire pulsed through her body, heating her blood and moistening her sex that throbbed with need. As much as she loved his hands and mouth on her, she needed him deep inside her.

"I want you inside me."

He gave her a wicked grin that made her heart skip a beat. His eyes held a promise of pleasure that her body knew all too well.

Her eyes slid closed when he grasped his cock and rubbed the head against the swollen flesh of her sex. When he slid inside her, she sucked in a breath and wrapped her arms around him. Her back pulled, reminding her of her injuries, but the pleasure pouring through her dulled the pain.

"My Cara," he whispered into her ear just before he sucked the lobe into his mouth.

His warm breath fanned her neck. She shivered. Lucan knew just where to touch her, just what to say, to bring her the most pleasure.

She tilted her hips until her legs wrapped around his waist. He groaned deep in his chest and pulled out until just the tip of him was inside her. She arched her back and tried to pull him down atop her. She needed to feel him—all of him.

And then he plunged deep inside her. His buttocks flexed with each thrust, fueling her desire. She ran her hands over the hard planes of his back and shoulders, loving the feel of the immortal Highland Warrior who was hers.

She moaned and cried out when he ground his hips against her, rubbing against her clitoris and sending pleasure like lightning through her.

"Open your eyes, love," he said. "I want to see you when you peak."

Cara's body shook with the desire that wound tighter with each thrust of his hips. She was close, oh so close, to climaxing. She opened her eyes to see him staring at her with love in his sea green gaze for anyone to see.

The orgasm swept over her in a sudden blinding explosion. Lucan continued to rock against her, prolonging her pleasure. She clung to him, needing to hold on to him with the intensity of her climax.

He refused to break eye contact with her as he gave a final thrust that buried him to the root. His body stiffened as his warm seed filled her.

Cara held him tightly as he fell atop her. She loved the weight of him against her, the feel of his body along hers. It was erotic and arousing, even though she had just peaked. But it was always that way with Lucan.

He kissed the side of her neck before shifting and taking her lips in a searing kiss that told her of his deep passion. She touched his torc and the griffin head. She and Lucan were one, their souls melding together something that nothing could ever destroy.

Not even time.

"Good morn," he whispered.

She looked at the window behind her but could see nothing with the tartan hanging over it. "Is it morning already?"

"Aye. I brought you up here once we finished removing the filth in the hall. You didn't stir when I removed your clothes," he added with a grin.

"I didn't realize how tired I was."

"You went through a lot. But it's over now."

She frowned. "I don't know that it is. I think Deirdre will be back."

He grunted and rolled to the side. He leaned up on his elbow to look down at Cara. "Or find some way to get us to do what she wants."

"We need to find the scroll of names. Maybe then we can talk to the Warriors before she finds them."

He traced a finger around one of Cara's nipples, his smile spreading as the peak hardened. She squeezed her legs together as desire spiked from her breasts to her sex.

"Have you spoken with Quinn?" she asked to distract herself.

"Quinn? Nay. Should I have?"

She licked her lips and groaned when Lucan's

finger moved back and forth over her pert nipple. "Aye. He looked like he needed to talk last night."

"I'll find him this morning," Lucan promised, and leaned down to close his mouth over the tiny nub.

A loud banging on the door jerked his head up. Cara rose up on her elbows as Lucan asked who it was.

"It's Fallon. You need to come to the hall. Now."

She exchanged a look with Lucan before they jumped out of bed and began to dress. He was ready before her but waited. Once she had her shoes on, she followed him out of the chamber to the great hall.

Her steps slowed when she saw Hayden, Ramsey, Logan, and Galen at the table, their expressions bleak.

"What is it?" Lucan demanded of Fallon.

Cara found Fallon standing before the hearth staring into the ashes, and she stopped on the last stair. His hands were on his hips, his head bowed with a frown that made her stomach clench.

"Fallon," Lucan said.

Fallon ran a hand down his face and turned to his brother. "Quinn is gone."

"Gone?"

Cara lowered herself to the stairs and wrapped her arms around her middle.

Fallon nodded. "He's gone."

"How do you know?" Lucan asked.

Cara's throat closed when she heard the desolation and fear in Lucan's voice. They had all thought Deirdre had lost, but now Cara wasn't so sure.

Galen held out a rolled-up parchment. "This is how. I found it near the gatehouse."

Lucan stared at the parchment. He didn't want to know what was on it because he knew, somehow, that Deirdre had something to do with Quinn's disappearance. Lucan glanced at Cara to see her dark eyes wide with sorrow.

He took the missive from Galen's hand and unrolled it. Lucan's stomach pitched and rolled as he read the words. He let the parchment drop to the floor. "Deirdre captured Quinn. Apparently, he left while we were cleaning. She set a trap for him. Quinn never saw it coming."

Cara was on her feet and hurrying toward him. He opened his arms as she neared. The feel of her soft curves helped to steady him. He leaned his face against the top of her head.

"This canna be happening."

"We'll get him back, Lucan," she promised.

Hayden stood. "Cara's right. We need to get Quinn back."

"Deirdre isn't stupid," Fallon said as he walked to the table. "She knows Quinn may be strong, but without me and Lucan, he isn't as valuable."

Lucan sighed. "She knows we'll come for him."

"Aye. She will want us trapped with Quinn," Fallon said.

"We need a plan," Logan said. "But first, we need to find Cara a Druid."

Cara pulled out of Lucan's arms and nodded. "Logan is right. I can use my magic to help."

"Against Deirdre?" Lucan shook his head. "She's much too powerful."

"But she won't expect me to use any magic."

"Or maybe she will," Lucan argued. "I don't want you near her."

"Nor do I want you near her, but Quinn needs us."

Ramsey shook his head. "A war is brewing. Deirdre knows we've banded together now. We surprised her, but it won't happen again."

"What do you suggest?" Fallon asked.

"We find the scroll of names. Galen can contact other Warriors he knows and bring them here. Everyone is going to have to take sides."

Lucan glanced at Fallon. "Deirdre has black magic, an infinitesimal amount of wyrran, as well as God only knows how many Warriors. We don't stand a chance."

Fallon tapped a finger on his thigh. "I think Ramsey may be right. We need the scroll, if for nothing else than to keep it out of Deirdre's hands."

Lucan thought he knew where his brother was going. "Galen, didn't you tell us that there are some Druids who know how to bind our gods?"

"Aye," Galen answered. "Deirdre has hunted and killed most of them. I don't know if there are any left."

"But if there are, it would give us an advantage."

Cara's brow furrowed. "How? I don't understand."

"Oh, I understand," Hayden said. "If we can get inside Deirdre's mountain and bind the Warriors she's unleashed, it will give us an advantage."

"Only if it doesn't bind your gods as well," Cara said. "It's very risky."

Lucan threaded his fingers with hers. "It's all we have, love."

Cara nodded, her brow furrowed, and moved to the kitchens to bring out food for their morning meal. Lucan was just about to ask Fallon if he had an idea where the scroll might be found when they heard the rumble of horses. Many horses.

Lucan and Fallon looked at each other before they rushed out of the castle to the battlements.

"It's the MacClures," Fallon said. "I had a feeling they might return."

Lucan glared at the Highlanders who rode closer and closer to his home. He estimated there to be about fifty warriors. "Why?"

"I suspect they want the castle, but they aren't going to get it."

Lucan raised his brow as he looked at Fallon.

"This is ours," Fallon said. "We're MacLeods. Our lands were stolen before we had a chance to return. I'll be damned if they think they can take our home."

"The only way to keep the castle is to let the king know a MacLeod still lives."

Fallon clenched his jaw. "Then I'll see it done."

Once more Lucan was taken by surprise. He hadn't expected Fallon to volunteer to go; Lucan had thought he would be sent.

Before he could comment, Fallon walked around Lucan to the gatehouse. When the MacClures reached the castle, Fallon bellowed for them to halt.

The MacClure laird narrowed his eyes on Fallon. "Who are you to stop me from gaining entrance into my castle?"

"This isn't your castle." Fallon's voice was smooth and even but hard as steel. "This is my castle, the Mac-Leod castle. You stole our lands, but you won't take the castle."

MacClure laughed. "You against fifty of my men? You don't stand a chance, lad."

Lucan walked to stand next to his brother. There was movement behind Lucan, and when he glanced over his shoulder he saw the others spread out on the battlements.

Fallon smirked. "As you can see, *lad*," he said the last with his voice dripping with sarcasm, "I'm not alone."

"I'll have my castle!" MacClure shouted.

To Lucan's surprise, Fallon transformed and bared his fangs to MacClure. "Do you want to try?"

There were shouts and curses as the horses reared and tried to run away. Fallon might not be evil, but the god inside him was.

Lucan let his body change and glared at the laird. "Leave and never return. This castle is ours."

MacClure wheeled his horse around, his men quickly following as they galloped off into the distance. The last one to leave was the woman they had seen in the village. Her black hair was pulled away from her face in a braid, but her pale blue eyes regarded them without fear. After a moment, she turned her horse and rode away.

Lucan blew out a breath as he transformed back. When he glanced at Fallon he, too, was once again a man. "I didn't expect that."

Fallon shrugged. "We've lost too much. I refuse to give up the castle as well. No longer are we going to live in it like ghosts. The first thing I want is a new gate built."

"I'll see it done."

Lucan smiled as his brother jumped from the battlements. He had waited so long for Fallon to control the god, and now that he had, nothing was going to stand in his way. Lucan said a silent prayer of thanks and nodded to the others as they followed Fallon into the castle. Plans and strategies needed to be made, for Deirdre was a formidable foe who wouldn't die easily.

As soon as Lucan entered the castle he found Cara

waiting for him. There was one thing he wanted to do first. He walked to her and pulled her into his arms for a long, deep kiss. When he raised his head, her lips were swollen and her breathing ragged.

"Marry me."

She blinked. "What?"

"When I almost lost you, I've never known such terror. In that instant, everything was clear to me. I love you with everything I have to give, Cara. I want you for my wife."

"You already have me."

He chuckled. "I know, but I want our union to be blessed by the church."

"I know where to find a priest," Logan said. "I can have him here in two days."

Lucan nodded to him before he looked at Cara. "Well? Will you be my wife?"

"Despite the fact that I'm mortal and we may never find a Druid to bind your god?"

"Aye. One year with you is better than forever without you."

"Oh, aye, Lucan MacLeod. I'll marry you."

He smiled just before he lowered his head for another kiss.

EPILOGUE

The sun shone brilliantly down upon the small group gathered in the bailey. Cara smiled up at Lucan, still amazed he had asked her to be his wife.

Logan had been true to his word. He had arrived with the priest just that morning. Fallon had gifted her with a beautiful gown the color of cream and threaded with black. It was a perfect day.

The other Warriors stood around her and Lucan with Fallon next to his brother. The only one missing was Quinn. His absence was hard on Lucan and Fallon, but their determination to get him back was strong.

Lucan had said his vows with a clear voice, but when it came Cara's time, the words lodged in her throat. She blinked past her tears and repeated the words. The smile on Lucan's face was blinding when he pulled her into his arms for the kiss that sealed their vows.

The bailey erupted with cheers only to be silenced by a whistle from Logan.

"A woman approaches," he said as he looked through the gates.

Cara bit back a smile when all six Warriors moved to surround her. She peeked around Lucan's shoulder to see a tall, shapely woman walk into the bailey. The woman paused for just a moment until her eyes landed on Cara.

The woman smiled and continued toward Cara.

"Halt," Lucan said.

The woman lifted an auburn brow. "You must be Lucan MacLeod."

"Who are you?" Lucan demanded.

The woman smiled at Cara. "I've come because of Cara."

Lucan tensed, but Cara put her hand on his arm and moved to stand beside him.

"Who are you?" she repeated Lucan's question.

"Sonya. I was sent here to help you."

Cara stared into the woman's amber eyes, amazed at her beauty and the long, red hair that fell in curls down her back. "I don't understand. Who sent you?"

Sonya grinned and lifted her hand. "The trees of course."

"By the saints," Galen said, awe in his voice. "She's a Druid."

Sonya nodded. "I am. I've come to teach you, Cara." Sonya glanced at Galen. "If your new husband will allow me in the castle."

Cara was speechless. The trees, *the trees*, had told Sonya to find her. It was too amazing to believe. "Thank you," she said. "Please join us."

When Lucan didn't respond, Cara jabbed him in the ribs. He grunted. "Aye, Sonya, we would be happy to have another Druid."

"You're going to need one. Deirdre isn't happy about losing Cara. It's all the trees have been talking about."

Fallon chuckled and welcomed Sonya while the other Warriors introduced themselves. Cara stared at their newest addition, almost too afraid to believe she would now learn all her abilities.

"Are you all right?"

She turned and smiled at Lucan. "Aye. I've married the most perfect Highlander, and a Druid, sent by the trees, came to teach me."

Lucan chuckled. "I shouldn't be surprised by her words, but I admit I am. Trees? Who knew they could talk?"

"Apparently, Sonya."

"You aren't going to start talking to trees, are you?" he asked.

"Hm," Cara said, and wound her arms around his neck. "I might. Would that be so bad?"

"Not at all, love. I think it would be amazing."

He claimed her lips in a searing kiss. They had found a love that stretched the boundaries of time, a love that bound their hearts and their souls.

Cara had never been happier. Lucan's laughter as he lifted her in his arms and swung her around as the others cheered told her he had gotten just what he wanted.

Their future might be questionable, but they had their love. It was enough.

Quinn held his head in his hands and rolled to his side as his skull pounded with a pain that made his stomach churn. He cracked open his eyes to find darkness surrounded him. The coolness around him told him he was belowground. The stench of stale air and unwashed bodies filled his nose.

He remembered leaving his brothers and running

off into the night. It had felt so good to give in to that desire, uncaring if anyone would see him.

He ran for hours until he had spotted a wyrran. He had chased it, intent on spilling more blood as his rage consumed him. Then he recalled falling. The ground must have caved in. He closed his eyes and tried to think. He remembered the sound of his leg breaking in the fall and the unbearable pain as it began to heal.

There had been someone above him; of that he was sure. The man had looked down at Quinn but refused to help when he asked.

Quinn grimaced as a wave of dizziness swept over him. He hadn't felt this bad since before his god was freed. Despite the pain, Quinn thought back to when he fell and to the man standing over him.

The man had laughed and then jumped down beside Quinn. He had rolled onto his back as he held his leg. The man leaned over Quinn and he looked into the man's face.

Quinn's eyes flew open as his memories returned. It wasn't a man but a Warrior.

Quinn forgot the pain as he looked around him. His claws dug into his palms as he heard the wails of people being beaten below. He had heard the same screams before.

When Deirdre had held the brothers prisoner.

Read on for an excerpt from **Donna Grant**'s
next book

FORBIDDEN
HIGHLANDER

"There is something I need as well," Iver said.

Fallon quirked a brow. "What is it I can help you
with, Baron?"

"There is a woman."

It was always a woman, Fallon thought. Just then,
the crowd around him thinned, and he caught a flash
of color. He turned his head and found himself staring across the hall into the face of unbelievable grace
and beauty. She was so stunning that he had pushed
away from the wall and started toward her before he
realized what he was doing. But the need to get closer,
to take in her loveliness goaded him onward, much as
his god pushed at his rage.

"She's incredible, isn't she?" Iver whispered by
his side. "There isn't a man in the castle that doesn't
want her in his bed, and there isn't a man that wouldn't
kill for her if she but said the word."

Fallon kept his feet rooted in place by force of
will alone, but he couldn't tear his gaze from her
lovely oval face. She held herself with elegance and
dignity, a noblewoman by birth. Someone bumped

into her from behind, and there was a subtle shift of awareness around her that only a warrior would understand, only a warrior would see.

He was more intrigued by the moment. Though Highland women were known to be strong and courageous, they weren't warriors.

Just as quickly as she had taken stance, she relaxed, the perfection back in place.

"That is what I want, MacLeod," Iver said. "I want her for my own. Lady Lenora Monroe."

"How am I supposed to help you with that?"

Iver slapped him on the back. "I'm sure you'll figure out a way."

Fallon moved away from Iver before he punched the little weasel. Fallon weaved through the mob around the perimeter of the great hall. He edged closer to Lenora Monroe, admiring the cut of her burgundy gown and the way it clung to the swells of her breasts before hugging her trim waist. She held her hands together at her waist, her long, slim fingers intertwined as she listened to some older woman with a bulbous nose speak.

Fallon peered through the space of two men and watched the beauty with skin the color of cream. Her face was striking with her extraordinary cheekbones and high forehead. She had wide, expressive eyes that captured whoever she looked at, and full lips he knew he would get drunk from kissing.

Then she turned her head and looked straight at him with eyes a dark, smoky blue that seemed to see him for what he really was. She tipped her head in acknowledgment, her golden halo of hair a beacon in the hall.

As soon as she turned her gaze away, he stepped

back through the crowd and into the shadows in a corner. He recognized the lust that flared inside him. He recognized it, and feared it.

Fallon licked his lips as he hungered for a taste of wine, anything to help dull the ache of lust in his loins.